The

Adventures

of

Raven and Rayne

The Journey To Bytar

By:

J. M. Morvel

The Adventures Of Raven and Rayne The Journey To Bytar

Cover design by: James M. Morvel

ISBN-979-8-9899123-1-5

Dedication:

This book is dedicated to my wonderful wife Odalys and our daughter Isabella. Odalys, without you telling me to start writing down my words and keeping track of this story it definitely would have never become a reality. Isabella, you were the true inspiration for this story about our two young adventurers. You are both amazing. I'm so happy and privileged to be a part of your lives and I thank God every day for making it so. Special thanks to my parents who have always believed I could write something great for others to enjoy. To our cat Angel who always kept me company while I wrote.

To my most valued reader, I hope you enjoy the adventure you are about to partake in. I truly appreciate each and every one of you.

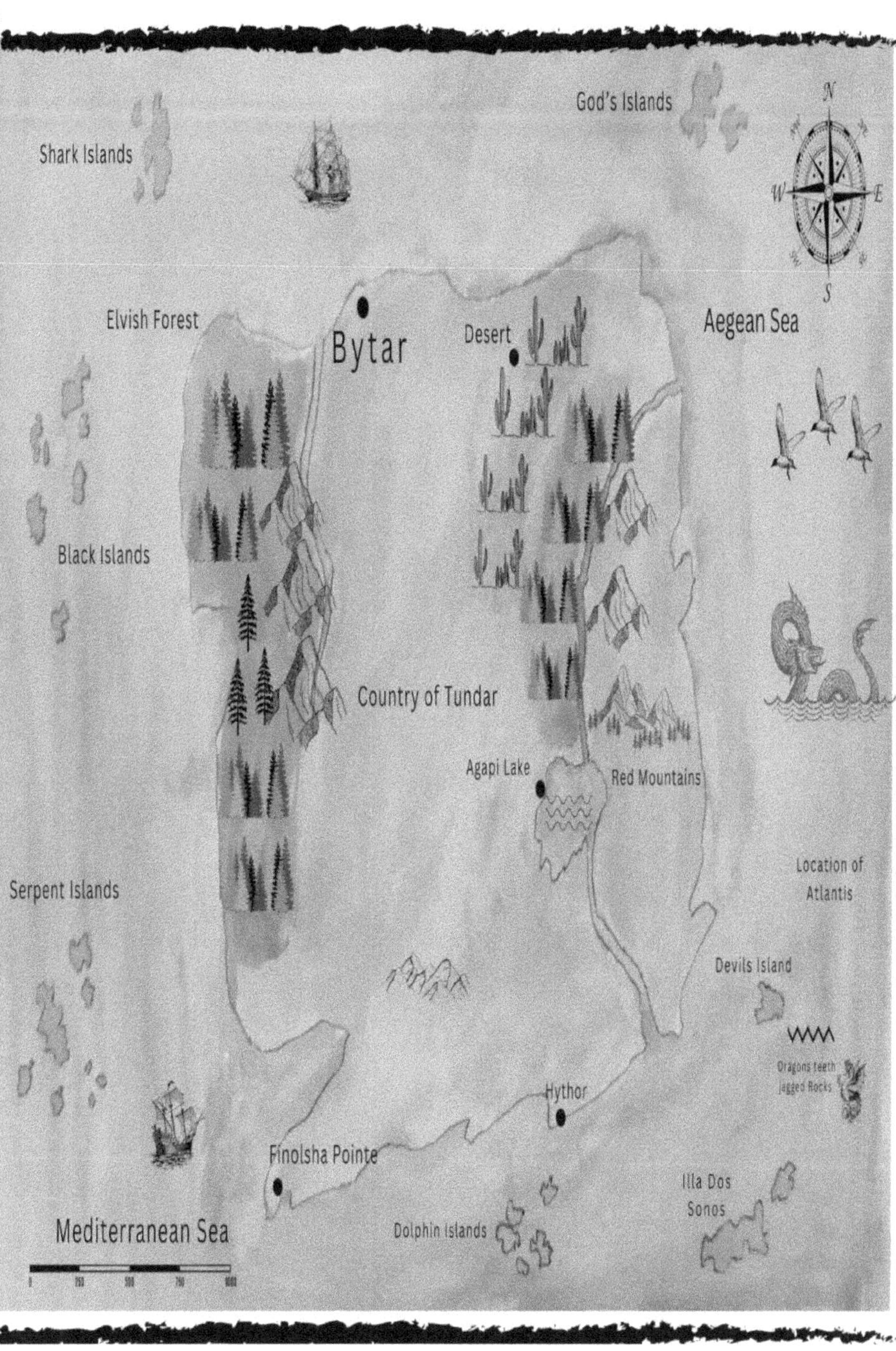

Shark Islands
God's Islands
N
W E
S
Elvish Forest
Bytar
Desert
Aegean Sea
Black Islands
Country of Tundar
Agapi Lake
Red Mountains
Location of Atlantis
Serpent Islands
Devils Island
Dragons Teeth Jagged Rocks
Hythor
Finolsha Pointe
Illa Dos Sonos
Mediterranean Sea
Dolphin Islands

Chapter One

The Siblings: First you must walk then you can fly...

As Nicias approached the small stone buildings near the edge of town, his vision was drawn to what could only be described as an old farmhouse. The large building had been painted red but due to the years of heavy rain and wind it was falling apart; he knew the captain would be inside. For the past two days, Nicias had traveled by horseback, but after arriving at the town last night decided to continue the rest of his journey on foot. It was during this time he had on more than one occasion seen the drunken remnants of some of the captain's army sprawled out like sleeping bears in the dark corners of some of the smaller buildings here and there. The sun was beginning its peaceful transition into the sky and his quiet walk had only been disturbed from an occasional outburst of girls laughter or the sound of a bottle being broken in the distance. The pungent smell of horses manure and smoke in the air did not deter him as he approached the partially opened front door of the farmhouse, Nicias was on a mission. A cursory check of his surroundings confirmed his suspicion that there were no soldiers around so he proceeded to push the door open. He stepped inside and immediately raised his forearm up to his nose to combat the assault his nasal cavity was now under. The odor was intensified inside and with the combination of pigs, horses, urine and manure his eyes almost started to water. Thanks to the numerous cracks in the roof, his vision was filled with stripes of sunlight that penetrated the darkness of the barn effectively and illuminated not only the ground but also his target who was lying motionless a top a bed of hay. He pondered for a moment what would be the best way of waking him up and suddenly a clever answer to that question appeared to his left in the form of a large water barrel. He walked over and picked up a small bucket that was nearby then submerged it into the large barrel of rainwater then turned back to face the large sleeping captain. A bucketful of cold water in his face was the last thing Captain Asal wanted to feel this early in the morning.

"Wake up! You and your men have had enough time to rest."

Sitting up quickly and rubbing the water over his sore eyes Captain Asal slowly surveyed the tall old man standing in front of him. The warm spot he had been lying on was now soaked and the echoing sounds of horses eating hay was all around him. "Who the hell are you," the captain replied to the old man.

"My name is Nicias and I require the use of your army."

"You don't say," the captain smirked.

The old man pulled out a medium sized red-velvet pouch from under his cloak and dropped it at the captain's feet.

"There's fifty times that amount at the end of two months' time so bring a few of your best soldiers and meet me at the waterfall at noon."

Loosening the string that held the pouch closed he peered inside of it then pulled out a beautiful gold coin and stared at its shiny magnificence in the palm of his hand, he immediately sobered up.

"We'll be there!" he replied.

With a sly grin on his face the old man turned and walked out of the barn. More of a conjurer at this point, not yet a true sorcerer he waited at the waterfall patiently watching the soldiers approach on horseback. Without the amulet he wouldn't fully have control of the army so he had prepared a small magic show first. The soldiers dismounted and walked toward the tall thin figure with their captain leading the way.

"What's this all about?" Captain Asal said sharply.

"There's another sorcerer hiding behind this waterfall and he has something of mine that I want back."

"Another sorcerer?" The captain replied with a surprised look on his face.

Nicias surveyed the soldiers with a raised eyebrow, "Yes, didn't I mention that?"

With that said he opened his cloak with both hands and in a flash threw something on the ground which caused a great deal of smoke to rise up. His men started fanning the smoke away from their faces but discovered that he had disappeared from their view then mysteriously reappeared behind them and started to speak again.

"You see my dear captain it is easy to sneak up on regular people but not so easy to do the same to a sorcerer."

A few of the men had instinctively drawn their swords at the first sound of his voice. The sorcerer looked taller, thinner somehow with his long red cape flying in the breeze behind him.

"Put your weapons away," the captain said to his men calmly. "What is this item of yours that you need?"

"It's an amulet he wears around his neck, but I don't believe he will give it up so easily."

Captin Asal replied with a sinister grin, "I'm hoping he doesn't." With that the group, led by Nicias proceeded to walk around a small path that lead to the side of the huge waterfall, the sound of the crashing water into the lagoon was deafening. He certainly wasn't about to tell the soldiers that he had learned of the amulet's location from a dream.

To the captain's surprise there actually was a very large cave behind the waterfall. They paused for a few moments just inside the cave to give his men time to light a few torches, then they cautiously proceeded deeper into the cave. He had only brought five men with him, three of them were carrying torches and the other two were walking, swords at the ready. The stone floor inside the cave although wet, was not slippery. The group noticed the distinct smell of smoke getting stronger as they proceeded deeper into the cave, enveloping them and penetrating their nostrils. The cave came to a fork a short distance from the falls and while they were discussing which way to go, left or right, a ball of fire shot at them from the left side engulfing one of the captain's men. The remaining soldiers either ducked or rolled to their right to avoid another fireball while Nicias had instinctively taken several steps backwards to avoid any fighting, which was his way. Another quick fireball engulfed a second soldier but the captain's quick eye spotted its origin and he threw his dagger hitting its mark with a quiet thud. With his remaining men he ran forward calling for Nicias to follow. Captain Asal approached the old man who was writhing on the ground clutching the dagger that was sticking out of his abdomen and looked down at him with an indifferent stare. Hanging from a chain around his neck was a small flaming amulet. Nicias approached and knelt beside the old sorcerer ripping the amulet from around his neck and leaned to the man's ear, whispered a few quiet words and listened to his responses then stood up. With a self-satisfying grin the soldiers watched Nicias place the amulet around his own neck. He stood there for a few minutes, eyes closed, enjoying some type of euphoria at having his new trinket. When his eyes finally did open they were glowing bright red as if he had an internal fire burning inside of him.

"I hope your army is fully rested captain?"

"Why is that?"

"Because our next destination will be the City of Bytar!"

***

Raven and Rayne are fraternal twins and Raven being the older brother made sure he reminded his little sister of this fact. Our story begins in the ancient town of Hythor. It is a small seaside town which is surrounded by many other inland villages and sea towns that dot the hills and valleys. One of the only exceptions is the northern walled city of Bytar. This is a large city perfectly situated for traders it has the ocean to the front and a large river to the west that flows south through the country of Tundar. The siblings both have long black hair, green eyes, olive colored skin and a very competitive nature between themselves. They had recently finished talking with their father who had explained some new details that he felt would help them in using their new magical gifts. His name was Armolis, he was strong and protective of his two children and even more so when it came to them using these new gifts out in the world. Their mothers name was Zia and like most moms she was also very proud of her children, but maybe a little too protective of them. However, in one respect she was just like her husband in that they had always taught their children to be kind to others and respect the elderly people they meet. They were only fifteen years old and very new to changing into animals, he wanted them both to be safe and secretive.

"Your mom and I wanted to give you both a birthday present so here they are." His father handed a necklace to his sister while his mom presented the exact same one to him. It was a simple leather string necklace with four small iron circles tied at the bottom that were independent of each other. The two on the outside were slightly larger than the two on the inside and their explanation shows why.

"Your father and I came up with this idea, we are the larger circles so no matter where you both are or what you're doing you can always look down and imagine that we have our arms around you to protect you or to give you the feeling of security if you ever become scared."

After hugging each other their father wanted to speak to them about something more serious. He explained to them how their gifts, of being able to change into any living animals and of long life, not immortality, was given to him and their mom then passed down to them, his only two children. This is the story he told them; it was really quite simple and happened completely by accident.

"I was sitting out in the front of the house one night relaxing and drinking some tea when I reached down, grabbed a rock and heaved it at that broken down rock wall that borders the front of our property. To my surprise I heard a faint sound, like a little scream of someone in pain. I ran towards the wall and noticed that two small rocks had fallen on the other side. I looked down and saw this small creature with little clear wings lying on the dusty ground with one of the rocks on top of her. She started talking to me and asked me not to hurt her. I apologized a hundred times for throwing the rock and could immediately see it was a small woman dressed in a white and gold colored gown. I knelt down beside her and picked up the rock that had landed on top of her and was truly amazed at what I was seeing! It was a dream come true.

When I was a child your grandparents told me stories of the fairies, but as I grew older I just figured they were only stories told to children. Are you two paying attention to what I'm saying? This is important!"

They both responded that they were but she punched Raven on his shoulder as if to wake him up from a daydream.

"Sorry," she told him with a smirk on her face, "I thought you were asleep?"

"Ok, you two stop it and let me finish. I reached down, picked her up and held her in the palm of my hand. She was only about three inches tall and on closer inspection noticed that she was very pretty, had long blonde hair, fair skin and a very clear sounding voice. She told me her name was Queen Aanessa and that she was over three thousand years old and didn't speak to humans very often. One of her four little wings had been damaged; she had wings that reminded me of a dragonfly, there were two on each side her back and they were clear in color almost see through. Your mother and I took care of her while her wing mended. She was very grateful for our help, and during this time we talked a great deal and when she was ready to leave used some of her fairy magic to grant all of us long life. She also wanted to give our children a special gift, but we felt that it would be better to wait until you were both a little older and more mature. Now that you are both fifteen we felt that it was time that you knew the whole story because you didn't know the details of how it all began, now you do!"

Raven, remembering this story his father had told them now realized he heard it over one hundred years ago. The siblings are not immortal, they do age, just slower than everyone else. For every one hundred years their bodies would only age one year, that was the shared gift the queen gave to them all, long life. The special gift that she gave to the brother and sister was the ability to change into any living animal that they wanted to.

Chapter Two

Remembering their Past: Fond Memories...

It seems like yesterday that they changed into their first animals, Raven a puppy and his younger sister a small bird. It was such a weird feeling! Looking through the eyes of his new body, seeing his puppy paws and nose for the first time. His sense of smell took quite a bit of getting used to and it was in those early days of their youth that they started to practice changing into different animals and getting accustomed to each animals eyesight, weight and how each one moved. He choose a puppy the first time because their neighbor had one and he thought the puppy needed a friend to play with; it would also give him his first chance at playing around and using his new puppy talents, one being his new sense of smell. He could smell so much better as a puppy, like the apples in the orchards that were far away, he was also surprised at how well he could track people just by tracing the scent of their footprints.

One morning he closed his eyes when his mother left the house and then tried to follow her just by using his sense of smell, he waited until he knew she was long gone then he changed into a puppy and raced outside going over to his new friend's house. The puppy next door was called Asher, and they soon became best friends.

"Asher, can you come with me? I'm trying to follow some footsteps but I'm kind of new at this," he didn't tell him that it was his own mother he was trying to follow.

"Sure Raven, you make me laugh when you say you're new at being a puppy."

He tried to explain things to Asher once before but decided to give up and not complicate things with his new friend. He had told him that he was only there for a little while and sometimes his owners would take him on long trips that would take days or weeks at a time but not to worry about him while he was gone.

It was early in the morning, the sun was up, the weather was nice and cool and his mother had made a right turn just as she exited their front gate. She traveled down a path which was covered with dirt, small stones and weeds. There was a small, old white rock wall that ran along the front of their house and down past several of their neighbors houses, some of the bricks were missing or had just fallen, he never knew who built it but he knew that it was very old.

A short distance down the path he started to lose her scent, "Asher, what am I doing wrong? Stop laughing at me I told you that I'm new at this." Asher trotted over and started to smell over the same path also losing the scent, but he continued moving forward several more feet with his nose to the ground and while moving his head from left to right like he was a true expert. Soon he had picked up the scent again.

"Look Raven, you were going along just fine but you gave up a little too early. The trick is when you think you might be lost to keep on going for several more feet, don't be surprised at how quickly you pick up the scent again, you see?"

"Yes, thanks, you truly have a great nose Asher!" He answered with a grin.

The friends continued to follow the scent for several more houses down, it now went to the right again, through an opening in the rock wall and between two of the houses all the way to the back of one of them where they found her by the stream getting ready to do laundry. With both feet in the water she turned around and saw both of these little puppies staring at her and instantly a smile appeared as she placed her hands on her hips. Recognizing the one puppy was her neighbors and the other was either her son or daughter she said to them both, "Did you two little trouble makers follow me all the way over here?"

He wouldn't forget that day so easily, his mom figured that if he wanted to be so mischievous and far from his home she'd give them both something to remember this day by giving them both a bath in the stream.

Rayne wasn't having much more success. A short time after her brother had been given his bath in the stream she changed into a small red bird for the first time.

"Raven, come over here and watch this! I can fly! It's so easy."

He pranced over, still getting used to his own little puppy feet saying, "Ok, sure let me see, this should be worth watching."

I'm not sure what she was thinking about when she called him over because she had barely spread her wings a few minutes earlier, even then all she did was flap around she hadn't even lifted off of the ground yet.

"Here I go," she started flapping her little wings so fast she actually lifted up a few inches off the ground. She proudly turned to him saying, "See I told you I could fly!"

Just then she actually tried flying and flew right into the side of their house falling down into the dirt with a little pile of dust about her. She turned to him again and started shouting, "Don't you start laughing at me! I just started trying to fly today and anyways, I'm sure you're not an expert either at running as that puppy."

He had fallen on his back and was rolling around laughing at his sister when their father walked around the corner and saw them both on the ground. He couldn't make out what they were saying at all he just saw a puppy laying on his back barking and a bird flapping her little wings around and chirping like crazy but he had a good idea the siblings were probably fighting about something. It seemed like a long time ago that he changed into that puppy for the first time and his sister the little red bird, but by now they were quite the experts on changing into most animals and fish and were physically only sixteen years old. Occasionally, after dinners they would sit back under the open skies and laugh about some of the animals they had changed into over the years and stupid situations they had gotten themselves into.

This latest visit by Queen Aaneesa came only a few short days ago, but it intrigued them so much that they had to accept her offer. She presented herself to them tall this time, almost the size of a human woman not like the description their father had previously mentioned for a fairy. She was about five feet tall and her body was surrounded by a beautiful glow of light which left the brother and sister with a feeling of ease. They were both very comfortable while speaking with her. She was very beautiful and had long blonde hair with piercing sharp blue eyes and wore a magnificent long white dress with a thin gold chain around her waist and little golden colored sandals, she looked very regal. Rayne felt the queen could see right into her heart.

She told them that a great darkness was coming to their land by the hands of an evil sorcerer who was called Nicias. He would take control of Bytar, the northern city in their lands and imprison the king whose name was Thais. Nicias was ruthless! A ruler who knew how to force people to do things they did not want to and with his soldiers would kill and beat people almost daily just to keep them in line. He would force some of the Bytarian's into his army and others to help make weapons for him. More importantly, she was convinced that he was looking for information from an old book that King Thais had in a hidden chamber below his palace.

This is what she thought Nicias was trying to decipher, but he didn't know the secret to this book and she did. The one page in the book that she was most interested in protecting concerned the city of Atlantis, but it could only be read during an eclipse because the moon appeared to be red at that time, that's why it had been called the Red moon, but this strange occurrence only happened once every hundred years. That time is soon approaching! In less than a month it would be here and she needed to have the brother and sister destroy that page, it was the only thing that described the secret location to the underwater city and along with it some other unique treasures it held. Not to mention the book contained untold secrets of the past one thousand years including dangerous magical spells, secret places and artifacts that have the potential to destroy all that is good in their world. It is going to be a very dangerous journey!

There are two items that they would find of great use, but first they would have to travel to the fabled lost underwater city of Atlantis. The first item needed was the famous lost sword of Atlas. He was the first King of Atlantis and his sword was no ordinary one, it was made entirely of fine gold and mixed with a metal called Luxore. This metal was only found on the island of Atlantis, deep inside their largest mountain, it was white in color and was surprisingly very light. Miners chipped small amounts of it out of the rocks while looking for gold. Gold was an item that the Atlanteans had used for hundreds of years so this Luxore, which they ended up calling it was found by accident. None the less, the Atlanteans were an ingenious people and marvelous metalworkers so after some time they were able to perfect the mixture just right so that when it was combined with gold it formed a metal so strong it surpassed all of their expectations. This new combination of metals was very dangerous therefore the Atlanteans made a special sword with it and presented it to King Atlas.

So impressed was the king not only by the strength of the blade, but of the immaculate details on the hilt of the sword he offered it up to the sea God Poseidon himself on the shores of the beach. Poseidon, an eternal God, took the magnificent weapon and not only placed a spell unto it but etched some magical words onto the hilt in gold that allowed only a true and virtuous person to be able to wield the sword properly. Being made of gold you would believe this sword so heavy that nobody could lift it, but since it had magical properties it was light as a feather and for the right person could cut through a marble statue with the greatest of ease! Mounted on the end of the hilt was a beautiful blue stone the like nobody had ever seen before. Part of the magic of this weapon was that no sheath was necessary the owner of it simply would place the sword on either hip or over his back to use it and the sword would stay in that spot as if there was a sheath to hold it. The other item is Atlas' bow and arrow which was made by using a combination of ivory and Luxore powder. The arrows were as white as snow except for the ends which looked like small blue Peacock feathers with little black eyes in them. The bow was presented to King Poseidon the same time the sword was and once that was done the string on the bow was no longer visible and it was not necessary to carry arrows by hand. By simply grasping the bow and pulling back on the invisible string an arrow would always appear magically. To shoot an arrow all you needed to do was whisper to it and it would find its target without fail. Because of the magical properties you could place the bow over your shoulder like the sword and it would stay there without falling until it was needed. Only the worthy and pure of heart could use these items, anyone else would find Atlas' sword too heavy to lift properly and the bow would produce no arrow. Queen Aaneesa gave them instructions on how to find the location of where they would need to go, once there they would have to find the underwater statue of the fallen soldier called "Pelaius," he would point them in the right direction for the rest of their journey to the city of Atlantis.

"Listen to me you two," she said in a soft voice, "after you get these items from the Atlanteans you will at some point return to land to continue your journey, you must not change and fly to the city of Bytar! Do you understand me? You will have to find other means of getting there because there will be a few people during your travels to Bytar that will either give you information or materials to help you along on your way. Be safe!"

"When will we see you again?" Rayne asked, but the Fairy queen had already disappeared before their eyes.

One of Raven and Rayne's favorite things was changing into an eagle and soaring high above the Mediterranean seacoast, they loved gliding with the winds currents high above the beaches and over the clear blue water where Raven knew no other person had been before. With their eagle eyes they could see many things on the beach and in the water, like schools of fish, turtles and all sorts of sea life that made the ocean their homes. Of all the different kinds of creatures they had changed into the great eagle was their favorite. They were big and strong birds with beautiful brown feathers a twelve foot wingspan, long sharp talons and a curved beak. The world looked so small from these heights and they would soar for many miles without getting tired. While in the forms of other creatures the brother and sister never had any problems communicating with each other, that is one thing that they were both still getting used to even after all of these years.

"Do you think you can keep up with me this time?"

She loved taunting him by flying too close because she knew it annoyed him, this time she only offered a verbal challenge. As fraternal twins she knew Raven was only born a few minutes before her, but he never seemed to let her forget who the older one was. They loved bugging each other, but he would often give in and start chasing her just because he knew more times than not he would end up winning. There were however a few times in the past that she did get the best of him. He remembered one time she dared him to change into a pig like her and race around an abandoned cottage many miles away from their home, just to see who was a faster runner while being the same animal. He didn't realize that she had already scouted out the area and found a huge mud hole on one side of the cottage. Now, this was not a race so much as she just wanted to just get back at her brother because she knew he usually beat her in races, but this time would be different. He provided her with a small lead which she had asked for because for her joke to work it was absolutely necessary for her to get to her marker first, which was the third corner of the building. They had already changed into small pigs when suddenly they were both headed full speed around the first corner of the old cottage. She was actually a little surprised at how well she was doing so far in the "race" and was grinning inside because she knew what was coming up. The plan was to make sure she had a decent lead before they got to the third corner because just after that was the mud surprise she wanted him to go crashing into headfirst. She could hear him behind her yelling at how he was catching up to her as she passed the second corner, now she approached the third and as soon as she passed it she immediately changed into a bluebird and flew to a fencepost that was just a few feet away. She turned just in time to see him come running around the corner, stumble on the loose dirt and go sliding into the huge mud hole. Water and mud went flying everywhere as he flipped over his right side and landed flat on his back in the middle of the mud hole. She changed back into regular self and immediately started rolling on the ground laughing, she laughed so much that she had tears in her eyes and a pain in the side of her stomach. He changed back into his human form while lying there on his back fully covered in mud and realized that he had been beaten again after seeing her laughing hysterically at him. The sound of it was contagious and it made him start laughing too. Here they were laughing hysterically at one another, one covered from head to toe in mud and the other a few feet away laying on the ground laughing with tears in her eyes. He grabbed a handful of mud and threw it, hitting the ground next to her getting just enough mud on her to satisfy him.

"Well, you really got me today sis! Good job, I think if we had continued the race I would have beaten you," he chuckled, "but don't worry this is not over."

Today was a little different, there were no mud holes, fences or anything nearby because they were flying hundreds of feet up in the air, the only thing that she could see was the occasional cloud. It was a beautiful day with the sun almost directly over them, the skies were blue and a nice breeze was pushing them along. Rayne kept bothering her brother until he turned his head around, looked over at her and shouted, "Stop bothering me! I am concentrating on finding the area that queen Aaneesa spoke of, you really pick some of the worst times to start goofing around."

That was fine with her because honestly she didn't have any kind of plans in mind anyways. They were approaching the landmarks that the queen had told them about, a bunch of big rocks in the ocean that look like the teeth of a dragon from up close. In the past these rocks had been the misfortune of many a ship that thought they could maneuver through them instead of taking a wide turn and going around them. The second landmark was the protruding tip of the islands Easterly formation which looked like the letter V sticking out of the right side of the island, in reality the ocean waves would just slam into this huge rock wall day and night. This certainly was not an island that anyone would want to be stranded on because it was hot, full of large rocks and had very few trees and even these were small, ending up here could be the death of you that's why it's called Devils Island. They would soon be making their slow decent towards the water. They had to fly lower and get close enough to the waves to almost feel the splashes of water hitting their feathers before making their most memorable change ever.

Chapter Three

Splash Landing: The underwater journey to find Pelaius...

They had already started their descent and were headed towards some of the huge rocks in the ocean that had been described earlier to them as looking like the teeth of a dragon. The sun was almost directly above them and made the visibility into the clear blue waters perfect. From the air they could see the waves hitting the sides of many of these rocks causing huge splashes of white water to lift up over some of them. There were many different rows of underwater rocks, some were just barely protruding out of the water while the peaks of others were high above the waves. They were jagged and sharp like underwater knives waiting to pierce the hulls of unsuspecting ships as they were forced into this part of the sea due to the high winds that are common along this coast.

Queen Aaneesa was correct in saying that no ship would be able to come even close to anchoring around here because there was too much wind and many rows of unseen rocks all around the area that prevented anyone from accessing the beach.

With their huge wings flapping they slowed down and hovered over the ocean waves by twenty or so feet. It gave them some control and stability so they could change before entering the water and making their next change into Merpeople. Neither of them had ever actually seen any of the Merpeople before, they had only heard stories of them, their descriptions had come from Queen Aanessa herself, and she was able to give a detailed account of how they look and even presented them with drawings to help explain some details of the Merpeople.

At three thousand years old the queen was one of the oldest fairies in existence but did not show any signs of slowing down at all.

She said good luck to her brother and immediately transformed in midair into her desired form and following him dropped effortlessly under the waves. They had traveled underwater before but only as fish, now for the first time they were underwater as a merman and mermaid. Once she changed into a squid because a small boat had capsized in their harbor and it was the easiest and fastest way to help in gathering the lost cargo. This was totally different! They both had the most incredible underwater vision and nearly looked like their regular selves with some major exceptions. Their hands were bigger and fingers were longer, they felt much stronger than before, and they both noticed the strange webbing of skin between all of their fingers, they knew it was meant to help push themselves along while swimming. They were both bare chested, but it definitely was not the same as being above on land. Also their skin did not feel as soft as human flesh, it felt tougher somehow, just a bit gritty in a way and had a different hue to it, a slight silvery bluish tinge he thought. They did not have scales like fish, Queen Aaneesa made that point clear to them. She also said that the men do not wear any article of clothing only that the women looked like they wore some type of shirt on top.

She swam over and looked into his eyes and could see that it appeared he had several layers of eyelids, she couldn't really tell if it was two or three but her own eyes felt like there was a clear smoothness to them, the saltwater was not negatively affecting them at all. The most fantastic difference to her was that she no longer had regular legs, from the waist down her legs were replaced with the bottom half of a fish. Not a fish like a shark whose tail fin was positioned vertically, but it reminded her more of a dolphins tail. She could feel the strength inside of this tail, like a solid single muscle just waiting to be commanded to swim. Just by thinking like she would on land to walk she did now underwater to swim, these huge powerful legs moved seamlessly now as one, which propelled her through the water faster than she thought was ever possible. They were not cold or hot just very comfortable, their breathing was just as easy as it had been above on land, not labored at all. Raven was the first to speak.

"This is the most incredible thing we have ever done! I never thought this was possible."

He started to swim around her in circles to test himself and immediately swam quickly towards the ocean's surface and leaped clearly out of the water and back down without hardly making a splash. They were floating in front of each other now, checking themselves out and admiring all of the differences between their regular human forms and these new ones as Merpeople.

"We must look for the watcher the Queen spoke of," she said.

"Yes, of course," he replied.

"We entered the water in the area she mentioned to us, we are just east of the large cliff. She said the watchers name was "Pelaius" a broken magical underwater statue that lies on the oceans floor in about one hundred feet of water."

They swam around for many hours looking for this statue but also used this new freedom to explore the underwater world. The water was incredibly clear and blue, and moving through it was as easy as a thought to them. She called to her brother, "Come over here and look at this big beautiful turtle I found." He approached and they began to swim with the turtle for a short distance, each of them on either side with their hands placed softly on his back as they silently drifted through the water. The turtle slowly turned his head to look at her and then without warning gave a few heavy flaps of his arms and legs and just kept on his slow forward course without a worry in the world. They swam to the bottom and Raven grabbed a handful of sand, it felt very smooth and was almost completely white. He noticed on the ocean floor what looked like ripples in the sand as though even at this depth the sea was still alive and moving. To the right was a gradual sloping drop off where they witnessed thousands of colorful starfish making their slow march over and around different sized rocks and what looked like a huge bed of green seaweed sticking right out of the sandy bottom heading upwards trying to reach the surface. The seaweed moved ever so slowly to the left and right in tune with the flow of the current.

The ocean was a huge place even for their great vision, it seemed like it would take weeks to find what they were looking for. There were what seemed like thousands of colorful fish around a coral reef which they found themselves following for a little while when Rayne looked up towards the surface and could tell the light was fading. She knew it would be dark soon but didn't know if they would be able to see well in the water at night or even where to take shelter. She was starting to get a little concerned and called Raven over so they could discuss what to do next because they hadn't realized that they had already been in their new watery atmosphere for several hours. Suddenly, to their left they both saw a partially buried huge steel anchor right in the middle of an empty white area of sand. They both swam over with a sense of happiness and pride at discovering something at least. They figured this anchor was about twice as tall as the both of them put together, it was huge! It must have been made for a ship of grand proportions even though they didn't see one nor any evidence of one, not even any wood from a ship could be found. However, while turning their heads left and right to scan the surrounding areas they noticed about one hundred feet away a lot of brownish colored clay jars on the seafloor. As they approached they saw some were broken, but many of them were still intact and right next to these was a beautiful, partially buried statue lying not quite straight upright but just slightly angled on his left side. They swam over and there it was! This was what they were looking for, the statue of Pelaius! It had to be him.

Even under water it still drew the breath from their lungs, he was a spectacular looking statue. Standing about seven feet above the sand and of a creamy colored white marble with some grey lines throughout the body he looked like a great general with a commanding and strong face even here in this underwater grave. They could tell he wore some type of military uniform even though the bottom half of the statue was indeed broken, which probably happened when his ship sank and the bonds that were holding him became loose causing this huge statue to hit the ocean floor violently and at an odd sideways angle destroying the lower portion.

It was near dark now but surprisingly their vision had not diminished that much. The moon was nowhere near to being full yet but there was enough of a moon that the light from it was penetrating the depths and giving them enough light to take advantage of. They were about one hundred feet under the surface of the water and it seemed like as if they were able to use whatever small amount of light in the water to help them see in the ocean depths. She raised both of her hands to her face and waved them back and forth rapidly and saw that although she could see very well and still had great vision for distance and depth, objects seemed to have a slight glow to them. The slightest bit of light particles were miraculously stuck to each stationary object she looked at, even if it was just a little it made swimming and moving around in this night environment much easier.

While admiring their nighttime surroundings they had not noticed that bubbles had slowly started to form at the bottom of their statue, moving upwards quickly until the whole chest and face area was brilliantly covered with them. The bubbles were moving upwardly much more rapidly now and they could barely make out the outline of the statues face which moments earlier was as clear as day to them. All of a sudden there was a quick and explosive burst of bubbles from the bottom of the statue, but then a moment later as quickly as it started it stopped. They looked at each other in bewilderment not knowing what on earth to expect next, the statues eyes and mouth opened slowly and a resounding deep voice spoke to them.

"Hello, my name is Pelaius, who do we have here?"

The siblings, nearly frightened out of their skins, without realizing it had shifted their bodies and drifted away from the statue about fifteen feet. They were both in upright positions only a few feet off of the bottom of the seafloor needing only to barely move their hands back and forth to propel themselves forward within a few feet of our statue. Raven somewhat recovered and took control of the situation saying, "Hello," back to the statue and introduced themselves as brother and sister called Raven and Rayne.

Raven said, "We must apologize to you sir, we have never spoken to an actual statue before."

Pelaius then shouted out a single word, "What? A statue you say?" Then with a hearty laugh said, "Well, of course I am. I do not speak with many people as you might imagine down here so please excuse my loud and possibly alarming introduction. I can sense when the Merpeople are close by and sometimes they stop and speak with me, they are a wonderful old people, yes, very old indeed. I never knew they existed until I spent some time here in my underwater world. Sometimes I am not even sure if this is all real," as he again laughed. "So what do you two think?"

"There are quite a lot of things that do seem strange to us Mr. Pelaius," she answered.

"Let me stop you there, please just call me by my name, Pelaius, that will suit me just fine, besides I have a feeling we are all going to be great friends for a very long time."

She shot a quick glance over to her brother then returned her answer, "Of course Mr. Pelaius, Oh, I'm sorry, Pelaius. We have seen so many wonderful things in these many years that strange is now becoming a distant word to us." She explained that they were from a village called Hythor on land, and they had been sent to find him by the fairy Queen Aaneesa.

"I have heard of her, although my time underwater has been somewhat short her name has reached even me in these watery depths."

They were so curious to know the story of how he ended up as a statue at the bottom of the sea, and he was eager to relate as much of the story to them as possible.

"I remember being a soldier once and enjoying many military victories but it seems like it was ages ago now. We had recently finished defeating a terrible enemy far to the south on a large island and were sailing back to our homeland. We could see in the distance the island which now sits just to the north of where we are now, we used to call it, "Silver Island," because during certain times of the year it looked as if the tops of the hills shone like silver. I vaguely remember getting caught in a terrible storm that night, it just came up on us all of a sudden, the wind was fierce and the rain and waves were pushing us towards those terrible rocks, we knew they were out there but we could not see them. Our visibility was almost zero and we no longer had any control of our ship; there was a total of fifteen ships all together with about one thousand soldiers on board.

I was in the lead ship, this statue, which I am now speaking to you from was secured and tied up with ropes near the front. It had been made by some of the stone masons before we launched to sea as a gift to our soldiers for courage and bravery. That is about the last thing I remember. It seemed for a while like I was in a dream, then one day I opened my eyes and found myself here, underwater and looking out at this beautiful white sand and blue seas. I tried to speak to someone, but a lot of good that did as you can imagine, who is going to listen to me here. Then one day I felt the water all around my face whirling faster and faster until, there in front of me was a face, an old man. He had a long white beard and hair, bushy white eyebrows and sparkling blue eyes, eyes like I have never seen on anyone before, they were so blue and sparkled with a kind of electric energy inside of them, just the most dazzling and mesmerizing things to behold. What I initially thought was an old man, didn't really look so old now, as I focused on his face I perceived a youthful vigor and sharpness, but also an elegant wisdom and maturity. It was like looking into the face of a well-traveled man, who was still young. His long white beard confused me at first. Now, I could only make out half of his body, from his waste up, below his waste it kind of just shimmered, like millions of bubbles or maybe little silver and white fast moving fish. I couldn't tell. He wore no shirt but, was very muscular and in his right hand he carried a magnificent golden spear, it appeared to be about eight foot long. The end of it is what made it spectacular looking to me. It went from a single bar where he was holding onto it up to three razor sharp points, the middle being longer than the two on either side. At the bottom of it was a brilliant blue stone encircled by fine gold strands.

He would soon tell me that it was not a spear at all, it was a magical weapon that he called a trident. Even with this most imposing person in front of me I was not scared at all. Admittedly, I was a little surprised by that I must tell you two but as he spoke to me I felt no fear at all, I was completely confident that he was someone who was honest in his words and actions. He told me that his name was Poseidon! Of course, I had heard of that name before, but I thought he was just an ancient legend. He preceded to tell me that people have called him by many different names over the centuries like: King of the Sea or God of the Sea, but he preferred the name Poseidon. He said that I had been here on the ocean floor some fifty years, since that terrible storm wrecked our ship. Unfortunately, I drowned that fateful night and my body sank to the ocean floor not far from this statue. He asked me if I wanted to become a watcher and guardian of the fabled underwater City of Atlantis. Then he used some of his magic to put my restless spirit into this statue you see before you now to assist the Merpeople in protecting the city. He continued to tell me he could bestow some more of his magical powers into this statue that would allow me to wake up at any time I choose and summon the Merpeople if I needed to speak or warn them. I said of course, that it would be a great honor to help and also thanked him for everything that he had done for me in not leaving me alone on the ocean floor any longer. Well, that is about the extent of my story and it brings us to where we are right now."

After hearing his explanation they turned and looked at each other not realizing that their mouths were open in amazement, they quickly recovered their composures and both focused their attentions back to the statue.

"There are so many great things in this world that I did not take the time to notice while I was alive. So caught up in war and fighting that I missed a lot of the simple, beautiful things that make up our daily lives and we seemingly all take for granted. For example, like watching the sun rise or set, it seems simple enough but when you can't see something like that any longer you start to think and realize how many of the simple things did I not notice. Take advantage of everyday you have! Take it from me and enjoy your lives, sit back sometimes and just notice the simple things as you go on from day to day."

"That is truly an incredible story Mr. Pelaius," Raven said.

The statue now giving the brother a quick frown, "Sorry sir," he said in a hastened reply, "I meant Pelaius. Thank you for telling us your story. You're right, I do not honestly remember that last sunrise I looked upon, but then again I am usually always the one who sleeps in late according to my sister, she's the early bird."

Now it was at about this point that they had a similar thought, "Pelaius, we really do not know what to do now, we were told to find you and that you would be able to help us but, we're not sure exactly how you were going to do that?"

With a gleam in his eye he responded to her by saying, "I have already called you some help young lady."

"Help!" Raven said with a surprised look on his face, "what help?"

"The kind that I believe you two will require for the rest of your underwater journey, the kind that Queen Aaneesa knew only I would be able to give you," replied the statue in a kind of grandfatherly tone of voice. "Turn around and look behind you, they have been here for some time now listening to us."

They moved their arms immediately and spun around so that their backs were facing the statue now. They weren't quite used to maneuvering themselves in the water yet with these new forms and I'm sure they looked quite an awkward site in doing so.

"This is definitely going to take some time getting used to," Rayne thought.

Once turned around they were shocked to see three of the Merpeople several feet away from them, floating there, looking directly at the two of them!

Chapter Four

Meeting the Merpeople: The start of a great friendship…

She could tell immediately that two out of the three were mermen, the third was a mermaid but sadly none of them were smiling! Several minutes went by without a single word being exchanged even though it felt like hours. By the looks on their faces he could only guess that they were being sized up, "Great, these Merpeople probable think we look like two ducks floating underwater."

Finally, the mermaid who was situated in the middle of the three spoke to them, "Hello, my name is Alexina," she then motioned to her right, "this is Aegeus," and with a similar motion to the left said, "this is Medios. Who are you two and how have you come here?"

Raven, not wanting to seem too hesitant responded before his sister could, "Hello, my name is Raven and this is my younger sister Rayne, we were directed to come here and seek out the watcher Pelaius as he would be able to help find two items of great importance to us."

Alexina responded by saying, "Who told you that information? Especially, where to locate Pelaius?"

"Queen Aaneesa of the fairies gave us the information on whom to look for and also our directions on where to begin our search by using a few landmarks before we entered the ocean. We are humans and live in a village on land called Hythor," motioning upwards towards the surface of the water to indicate to them what he meant. "Our magical abilities enable us to change into other forms and with a detailed physical description of what the Merpeople look like along with some drawings she provided to us we were able to change into what you see before you now."

The three Merpeople looked at each other and quickly gathered themselves together and started speaking in hushed voices. It was too low for either of them to make out what was being said and they certainly were not about to interrupt them. While they waited for them to finish their discussion Rayne turned her head and looked back at the statue of Pelaius, raising her eyebrows as if to ask the statue how he thought things were going. He figured what was going through the mind of his new young friend and gave her a wink to show her everything would be fine. She responded by showing him a slight smile back and thought, "Maybe things will be alright," it certainly made her feel a little more confident.

Rayne turned back around to face everyone, as if somehow she had forgotten she was underwater and surveyed her immediate surroundings. She heard sounds that were around her like splashing water coming from what she figured was near the water's surface, she also heard some type of clicking sounds in the distance but at that moment could not figure out what could be making them.

Suddenly, the three Merpeople turned around and Alexina again addressed them both, "Please excuse us for ignoring the both of you like that but we wanted to discuss a few things in private. We certainly know Queen Aanessa, she has been a friend to the Merpeople for nearly one thousand years and if she sent you to seek out Pelaius it must be very important so we have all agreed to help you in any way that we can."

At this time one of the mermen spoke, the one on her right side, his name was Aegeus. He had a very clear and nice sounding voice, it was not too deep nor too high, it seemed to fit his appearance very well.

"I must admit to you both when we first arrived here we did not really know what to make of the two of you, this is the first time that we have met creatures such as yourselves. The three of us lingered behind you both and were very surprised that neither one of you turned around to greet or address us in any way. It was like you both were deaf! We watched you both for several minutes and your movements just did not seem right to us, you both seemed a little uncomfortable, even trying to swim in place looked a little difficult for you. But, I think we know why, you're both so new to these forms, as you say, that you have no real idea what to listen for or how to really swim or behave like mermen because you have only been one for such a short time. Do not worry though, we will teach you what we can in the short amount of time that you're with us."

The three Merpeople each cordially said their greetings to Pelaius and expressed their gratitude for calling them there; this meeting was truly a unique experience for all of them. Of course, having the great personality and voice that he had he was all too happy to be of service to them.

Although these three Merpeople looked somewhat similar there were differences between them, of course the mermaid Alexina, being a woman was the easiest to tell apart. Rayne thought she was very pretty, she had long black hair much longer than the men and wore what looked like a top, that covered herself like a small shirt, but it was also of a bluish color like her skin. In the middle of her shirt near the top was attached what looked like a small piece of jewelry, a small upside down triangle that looked like it was made of gold. There was nothing else that she could see for now, she definitely had a feminine appeal about her and her voice was certainly that of a woman, very soft and pleasing to hear. All three of them had very large dark eyes like them, it was a little difficult to tell now but they looked almost totally black.

Aegeus of course was the one speaking now, he had short black hair, no obvious jewelry or markings of any sort, and was beginning to be a little more talkative now, maybe because they were starting to get to know us she thought.

The last was Medios, so far he hadn't said a word to anyone and he looked a little shorter than Aegeus, had short brownish looking hair and had a big scar on his left cheek almost to his eye. He was the only one it appeared to be wearing any type of jewelry. He wore a small blackish looking ring on his right index finger and a small black pouch was worn with a strap over his shoulder crossing his body so the pouch was positioned at his lower right abdominal area. He was not mean at all she thought, right now he certainly was the more standoffish of the three of them.

"We have somewhat of a small journey in front of us but before we get to our destination there is something you will need first," Aegeus said. Just then the quiet merman swam forward.

"Hello, my name as you both know by now is Medios. I am charged with giving you both something that has only been worn by the Merpeople up until now, it is called an Irnshell. These are as old as the Merpeople themselves and will allow you to speak to most underwater sea creatures. There are some however you will not be able to speak with and you will know why soon enough. The first are sharks, they are as old as the oceans and as far as we can tell have never had the ability to communicate verbally with other fish, we believe them to be too primitive and never really evolved past the basic hunters that they are. They do not respect anything! We the Merpeople, do not have any favor with them as you can see from the scar I have on my cheek. Someday, perhaps I will relate that story to you both but for now you need to be very careful and watchful while underwater especially now at night because that is when they feed. I tell you this because our beliefs are to be respectful of all living creatures under the sea and even though we do not agree with some of their actions we continue to live in harmony with them but we remain watchful of all of our surroundings."

Medios reached into the little black pouch he had fastened at his side and pulled out one little white shell, "This is an Irnshell, we have had these since the beginning of time, this is how you will be able to speak to the sea creatures," he then swam up to Rayne. Still holding the small shell in the palm of his right hand, he then placed his left hand behind her neck and the hand with the shell in it he placed on the front of her throat.

"Please close your eyes and do not move," he asked her, then he started mumbling a few quiet words in a language that neither one of them could understand. A bright greenish light started emanating from the hand with the shell in it and Rayne could feel a slight tingling feeling at the base of her neck where the shell was. Almost immediately after it started the light was gone and as Medios moved backwards the shell remained stuck to the base of her neck, it didn't fall, she reached up to touch it and found it was in place very securely. He soon performed the exact same ritual with her brother and when he was finished turned around to face the other two Merpeople.

Without a word Aegeus turned his head to the right, made some quick screeching sounds then seemingly from nowhere there appeared two beautiful dolphins. Medios turned around and gave the other two Merpeople a quick nod the mermaid then glanced at Aegeus and back to the siblings with a big smile.

"Ok, it is done! We were not sure if it was going to work? That is, giving you both an Irnshell, but by the looks of them so far and the fact that they both melded correctly to your throats tells us that they should work fine. We will test them in the morning." Rayne's right hand shot up immediately like she was asking a question in a classroom.

"Excuse me? What is melded? Can you please explain what that is, it sounds very close to melted and that sounds painful."

Her brothers mouth opened wide and by the looks on the faces of the three Merpeople you would have thought that his jaw had fallen off and hit the white sandy ocean floor beneath them.

"That's a bit rude don't you think sis?" With a stern look on his face, Raven, like usual was trying to be the diplomat and not hurt anyone's feelings.

The mermaid approached them both, lifted her arms and touching both of their shoulders said with a warm smile, "That is quite alright I am sorry," she was almost face to face with his sister.

"I forgot that you both are very new to these forms and do not know any of our words yet, melding is simply what we call it when the, Irnshell is introduced successfully to one of us. The tingling feeling I am sure you both felt at the front of your throats in combination with the bright greenish light are all good signs that the melding worked the way it was supposed to. This is always done to our young children or as we call them sometimes, "chapes" (pronounced chaps,) when they are old enough and start speaking they are ready for the melding and their own Irnshell. That was the second reason we thought perhaps the melding might not work on the both of you because clearly you are not children. So you see my friends, there is no pain involved!"

"Now, you mentioned needing two items, what are they?" Aegeus asked.

"Oh, yes of course," her brother answered, "the first is the lost sword of Atlas and the second is his bow."

Medios shrugged his shoulders and said in a hushed tone, " Here I thought you two came all this way just to sightsee."

Rayne gave a chuckle but thought to herself, "Wow, he actually has a sense of humor, I would not have figured that."

Ignoring his remark Alexina said, "We know where to find these items but it's dark now and we should be going."

The brother and sister didn't realize it but they were thinking the same thing which was that the mermaid seemed to be in charge of that party of three. Rayne had a small grin of satisfaction on her lips thinking, "Here we are in a beautiful underwater world and the woman was in charge, it's not always like that in the world above."

Everyone turned to face Pelaius who for this whole affair had not said a single word, the three Merpeople all said a farewell to him and thanked him again for calling them. Just as Raven and Rayne were going to speak he cut them off and said, "I know, I know, it was a great pleasure for me to meet you both too but listen to me, this is not a goodbye! Do you hear me it is only a farewell, I will see you both very soon I'm sure, the Merpeople like I have already told you are a great people and will take very good care of you both. Get out of here and get some rest, tomorrow is going to be a busy day for you both."

"Follow us," the mermaid said as she turned and swam off into the darkness closely followed by the two mermen and a small group of dolphins.

A moment later they were swimming through the water at a quick pace but before the question was asked the answer came to them.

"We travel quickly now because the sharks feed at night and we do not want to run into any problems before we get to safety so that's why our dolphin friends will accompany us to our destination."

Medios stretched out his left arm and placed his hand softly on the side of one of the dolphins saying to him, "Thank you for accompanying us my friend."

"It is our pleasure," he heard the dolphin respond!

They continued for about an hour swimming just above the smooth oceans floor passing an occasional coral rock formation. Suddenly, the ground dropped off and their party headed down into deeper water, he had no idea how deep they had actually gone. Finally, they were on the oceans floor again and heading in the same direction as before. She looked ahead and could swear she saw a dim light, it was growing brighter and brighter as they approached it.

"What is that light ahead?" She asked.

"That is our destination my friends," Medios answered, "we will be there soon."

Not only was the object getting brighter it was also looking bigger, much bigger than what she thought. Their party was still traveling at a decent speed and maintained a distance above the sandy oceans floor by about ten feet or so. All of their faces now had a whitish glow reflected onto them from this object which clearly now she could see wasn't a small object at all, it was a massive underwater dome! They stopped several feet short of the dome. While the brother and sister could hear the Merpeople speaking softly to the two dolphins, the both of them were completely awe struck at this immense underwater structure. The two dolphins sped off into the darkness and Alexina approached them both asking, "So what do you think?"

"What do we think?"

His response was mumbled slowly barely audible by their party.

"It's absolutely stunning, beyond belief, we have never seen anything as beautiful or large as this." He didn't turn his head to look at the mermaid, the words just came out.

"What is this place?" He asked in awe.

With a proud and steady reply she answered, "Welcome, my friends...to the City of Atlantis."

Chapter Five

Atlantis: The Lost City No Longer...

"What! That's impossible. We thought the city was destroyed a thousand years ago by a flood or something?" uttered Rayne.

"Not quite, but almost, we were spared or shall I say actually saved by Poseidon himself. After we enter the city we'll tell you the whole story. The only creatures who can enter through this magical barrier and into our city are the Merpeople. We are the Atlanteans!"

The brother and sister were left speechless after hearing the news that the Merpeople were also the Atlanteans.

"Now, as you approach the outer dome stretch out your hand and touch the barrier it will take a moment but you will be harmlessly pulled through to the other side, hopefully, with a look of uncertainty. On the other side we are transformed back into humans but for you two it might not happen the same way we're not quite sure. You might have to transform yourselves the way you normally do, we will see no one has ever entered into the city who was not an Atlantean. We have a magical spell upon us so our physical bodies change automatically when we pass through the barrier."

At this point Alexina turned and swam up to the barrier and with both hands, palm forward, touched it. Almost immediately her hands began to glow a bright bluish-yellow color then were drawn into this thick jellylike barrier which the siblings were awestruck while watching.

"Oh my, are you watching this?" Rayne asked.

The question seemed to bounce off of her brothers head and return back to her, like a small ball on a rubber string.

"Raven, Raven, are you alright?"

"Huh, oh yes, sorry sis it's just so unbelievable isn't it!"

What seemed like several minutes in fact was less than fifteen seconds or so, Alexina's hands, arms and whole body passed through the barrier and was now seen somewhat blurry on the inside of the dome. They couldn't tell from their vantage point but she had already been transformed back into her human body. Aegeus, who they would soon learn was Alexina's mate now turned to them and said with a wave of his hand, "Ok, my friends it is your turn now, don't worry it is quite safe. You do not need to say any special words or phrases just swim up and touch the barrier and it should do the rest for you."

"I'll go first!" and with that Rayne eagerly swam up to the dome did exactly what she saw the other mermaid do and experienced a similar result.

Once her hands were placed onto the barrier they were drawn into this thick jellylike material and momentarily glowed the same bluish-yellow colors. She closed her eyes and felt as if she was being pulled into the barrier by an invisible force; at this point a warm sensation passed over her entire body, the next thing she knew it was over. Now through the barrier she opened her eyes slowly and looked forward, even though she knew it was nighttime what filled her immediate view was the presence of many white columned buildings in front of her. Once all five members of their party was through the barrier they were immediately greeted by one of the Atlantean guard members, his name was Orien. He was not a soldier by any means, although he did carry a sword on his left side, the Atlanteans had no use of an army anymore, they did have however sentinels posted around the city at different points of their barrier to greet their people as they returned, usually from gathering food or materials.

"This guard is quite handsome," she thought.

He was young, she figured early twenties and wore a white loose fitted shirt without sleeves and a type of loose fitting shorts that stretched to his knees.

Raven approached his sister, "Are you Ok?"

"Yes, I'm fine, I couldn't be better and what an experience."

He looked around at his party and noticed they were all humans now. Neither one of them had to use the fairies gift to mentally return themselves to human form, the barrier did it for them. His eyes turned to Alexina the once mermaid, she was very beautiful! In fact she did have long black hair and was about the same height as Aegeus who was standing right next to her. The bluish white top she wore was now a long white dress just below the knees with a white belt of sorts. The two of them had their backs to him and were speaking to a young man who was facing him and nodding his head in approval of something. He recognized Medios by the large scar on the left side of his face which now on dry land was more visible.

"Come here my friends let us introduce you to Orien," Aegeus said.

"It is my great honor to meet you both," although, our young guard turned his attention and eyes a little more towards his sister.

"It is quiet now as you can tell, most of our citizens are still asleep and will not awaken for several more hours."

"Thank you it is our great privilege to be here." His eyes now fixed at the immense buildings behind Orien. They were standing at the outer part of the city, he couldn't really tell how immense the city actually was, yet...

The sand where they stood was soft and dry with only small pebbles strewn about. Oddly no one was wearing any shoes except for him and his sister which was normal because they were wearing the same clothes they had on before they changed into the great eagles the day before. He turned back around to look at the dome barrier then tilted his head back to look straight up.

"Wow," he mumbled.

He could not tell how high the barrier went but it looked like from here that it stretched many hundreds of feet high. Instinctively, he reached out to try to feel the barrier again but his hand was snatched back before he could make contact with it. Medios smiled at him, "Be careful my friend, remember you can touch the barrier, but if you push your hands too hard into it you will automatically be pulled back through and into the ocean again."

"Oh, of course, I'll remember from now on it's just that it has the most remarkable properties," as his eyes now focused on a section of the barrier in front of him. "It's kind of clear, but not completely see through and it feels soft and squishy but doesn't stick to my hands, I could not tell exactly but it felt like it was two or three feet thick, if I were to guess," turning his head to the side now to see if there was any reaction from Medios. "Possibly," was the only word uttered by his new friend.

"Let's go and try to get some sleep," Aegeus said.

"I thought we could tell them the story of how we," but before she could finish her sentence he softly grabbed her left hand and squeezed it.

"I think our new friends have had enough excitement for one day, besides we are all tired and could use the rest. You are both welcome to stay with us while you're here if you would like?"

The brother and sister looked at each other agreeing with his proposal, "That's fine with us," he said soundly, "if it's not a problem?"

"No, it's not a problem at all, we would both be honored," as he looked to his mate with a smile. "Alexina and I are husband and wife you see, and have been now for what?" he paused.

"Almost ten years," she finished his sentence with an elbow to his ribs.

"Yes, yes my love," wrapping her up in his arms. "Medios, we will see you in the morning," as each of the two men as a sign of friendship clapped each other's right shoulder with an open hand.

"Good night Alexina, and what an unexpected day we had." Medios remarked. Looking at the brother and sister, "Good night to you too my friends," he said walking away and into the distance towards an unknown part of the city.

Aegeus said, "Orien is going to stay here but I'm sure you will see him again," he exchanged the same farewell with Orien then turned to his wife, "come my love," and with a nod of his head they started walking together. "Let's go my friends, we will show you to your sleeping quarters for the night."

The guard shuffled his feet quickly making a sound in the sand and rocks causing them to look at him before starting off. "It was nice to meet you both," he said with a smile.

"Orien seems like a nice guy," she said with a wry smile.

"Yes, they're all very courteous here," Raven responded a little sarcastically, "can we get going now?" Motioning to her with both hands.

The four of them started walking straight towards the city, even though it was dark out he observed quite a few fires that were lit on top of pedestals sporadically placed around and inside of the city. Rayne wasn't talking that much anymore, she was tired, exhausted really, she had not slept in what felt like days and just wanted to lay her head down on a pillow.

"How far is it to your home?" Raven asked, all the while his eyes were darting to the left and right trying to absorb everything he saw.

"Not far, about ten minutes or so, are you both hungry?" She asked.

His sister interjected at this point, "I just want to find my bed," she laughed, "I am so tired, if it's ok with you I'll eat in the morning.

They were approaching two large pillars that were positioned at the entrance to the city one on either side of the wide dirt road they were walking on. There was more beach sand closer to the barrier, the ground here was more of an even leveled dirt road with small stones about, but very little dust was produced as Raven kicked a small stone forward. When he got close enough he saw that the stone pillars were circular in design and about twelve feet in height. At about the eight foot mark mounted on the inside of the pillars closest to the road there was placed one conch shell, open side facing up. A brilliant yellow-orange light was emanating out and upwards for two feet making a beautiful display on the pillar itself, but there were no flames to be seen.

"Aegeus, one last question," Raven said.

"Of course my friend what is it?"

"How is there light on the sides of those pillars; I don't see any flames or smoke?"

With a surprised look on his face he answered the question, "Because the light does not come from fire my friend, inside of each shell is a single blue pearl called a Poseidon's eye, they produce light when in the darkness. They come from oyster beds much deeper in the ocean, but we've been using them for light as far as I can remember, many hundreds of years."

Soon they arrived at a modest single story stone building, noticeably there was an arched entryway without a door, no lights were on and it looked very cozy.

"Welcome to our home." Aegeus casually walked inside and within moments there were two separate light sources seen turning on. By now they had all entered the house and learned that the Atlanteans do not use doors because they didn't have crime. Raven saw the first light source was another one of those pearls laying on a small V shaped bowl suspended in the middle of the room from the ceiling by a string, the other was coming from a room to the right side where Aegeus had just come from.

"There are two small adjoining rooms through there," he indicated with a pointed finger to the doorway he just exited. "Everything you need should be in there, but if you have questions please ask us, we will be over here," pointing to a room on the other side of the main room they had just entered.

"Thank you, we should be fine," Raven replied with a smile.

After settling in Rayne walked to the doorway of his room and asked, "Are you asleep yet?" She was dying to ask him a question that had been building inside of her since the moment they entered the city.

"No, not yet," he replied tiredly, "what is it?"

"I just can't believe that we are actually inside the City of Atlantis. I mean, At-Lan-Tis," she mouthed slowly to him.

"You know I remember mom and dad telling us the story of this place when we were kids. I would lay in my bed afterwards for hours thinking about this cool magical island where the people were so smart and knew about the stars, mathematics and languages. I would think of these incredible stone buildings and statues molded out of pure marble, water fountains bigger than our house shooting water into the air fifty feet!"

"Bigger than our house? Really, and you talk about me being a dreamer," raising her hand over her head to signify the size of their house.

"Yes! Bigger than our house, it was just a mental picture I had is all and to answer your question no, I really can't believe I'm here either" now turning in for the night to get the sleep they so desperately needed.

The aroma of freshly cooked eggs was a pleasant and welcomed surprise to awaken to Rayne thought. She washed up and walked into her brothers room, of course seeing him still sleeping like usual, she then walked back into the main part of the house that they had entered into last night. The sun was shining brightly outside and partially into this room due to the fact there was no door. She could hear plenty of sounds now coming from the outside, the one in particular that stood out were the sounds of children laughing and playing. Unconsciously, this brought a big smile to her face but before she got to the front door her host called out to her from behind.

"Good morning Rayne, how did you sleep? We made some eggs and have bread, water and fruit if you're hungry now?"

"Yes, I am thank you. I was so tired last night, but I slept great. What time
is it anyways?"

" I believe it's close to ten now, we have a central time piece near the center of the city but you can't see it from here."

"A what?"

"Many years ago our engineers developed a device to keep time, way before I was born, it sits on top of the great library for everyone to see."

About an hour later her brother stumbled out of his room, joined them at the small four person wooden table and enjoyed his own breakfast.

"After speaking with your sister this morning we decided to show you both around the city if that's ok with you? The city is very large and it would take several days to show you everything, but we can look at some of the main buildings."

"Great! I can't wait," Raven replied with a renewed energy for life.

A sound sleep and hearty breakfast had done wonders for them both.

"Before we leave, my brother and I would love to hear the story of how the city ended up at the bottom of the ocean."

Alexina paused for a moment to study the brother and sister more carefully. They were both young and attractive and had similar length long dark hair and brown eyes, the boy was several inches taller than his sister but they had the same tanned complexion and youthful innocence about their faces. She liked them both!

She took a sip of water and started speaking, "Ten centuries ago we were a flourishing people, similar to the way we are today. Our King Titus was the greatest and last king of Atlantis and had developed a bond with the sea God Poseidon. No one knew how or when it started but he was given a warning by Poseidon of an upcoming massive flood and told that a volcano might be erupting on a neighboring island. This volcanic eruption could destroy the entire city. After one day of heavy winds and waves battering the island, toppling buildings where several people were killed, it is said that King Titus asked Poseidon to spare his people and kingdom. The story goes on to say that the decision was made instantaneously. A massive wall of water shot up into the air one thousand feet high and surrounded the entire island of Atlantis. The ground shook and the wall of water started to cover the entire sky; people were screaming and running for shelter, columns fell, but in less than one day it went from total chaos to almost complete silence. We are told that the first few days were the scariest.

King Titus had mysteriously disappeared after that first day, then he suddenly showed up and called a large meeting in the center of the city to share with everyone some exciting news. Atlantis is now, and has been since that first day located near the volcano that erupted all those years ago. He showed our people about the barrier and how to go through it, our transformations into Merpeople and how to do some things differently than we had been accustomed to in the past. One year to the day later he just completely disappeared! A massive search was conducted for him, but he was never found. The only two items that we did find were his sword and bow which were laying atop his throne, but centuries later his disappearance is still a mystery to us."

"That's an unbelievable story Alexina! Earlier this morning I heard children laughing outside, so I see you have been able to adapt and thrive with your new environment."

Alexina continued to speak, "Yes, we have been very fortunate here, it helps that Atlantis is a huge city many miles wide. In many ways we have everything we need here, including fresh water, trees, many of which are fruit bearing and our farmers grow beautiful vegetable gardens and fields with grain for our bread. We have skilled engineers and mathematicians and we continue to promote education and knowledge to our children. Every Atlantean can speak at least two languages. The reason for this is that we are taught at a young age that every person can do more with their mind rather than by using a sword. We are a peaceful people and have always been so. We have avoided a lot of conflicts and bloodshed because our city has been on the oceans floor so maybe it was also destiny that also helped us. Take today for example, what do you see?" She waited a moment and could tell by the looks on the faces of her young guests and by their silence that they had no idea what point she was trying to make. "I'll give you both another hint, maybe a better one, let's all go outside and we'll start to show you both around, how does that sound?"

They pushed their chairs back, stood up and agreed with their hosts that that was a great idea. Her brother was really looking forward to exploring the streets of Atlantis. Ever since they were children their parents had filled their heads with stories about ancient mythical creatures, hero's overcoming seemingly impossible tasks and of course the fabled lost City of Atlantis. One by one they all exited the house passing through the arched entranceway and walked down the few stone steps leading to the smooth dirt road in front of the house.

"Now, we came from that direction last night didn't we?" Her brother asked, indicating to the right with an outstretched arm.

"Yes, that's right, the barrier is about a half mile that way," Aegeus answered.

Once in the middle of the road and with her eyes clearly fixed upon Rayne she continued to press her earlier point to them.

"A few minutes ago I said I would give the both of you a better example of how I feel we are fortunate, "look up, what do you see?"

She cleared her throat and hesitantly said, "Well, I see blue skies, the sun and." "Exactly!" She exclaimed cutting her off mid-sentence. "The sun, that was the answer I was looking for. We are hundreds of feet beneath the ocean and yet magically every day for a thousand years we have had weather. The same weather you have above. We see blue skies, feel the heat from the sun and when it rains above it rains here which helps us grow our crops. So, yes we have all been most fortunate."

"Now, my friends," her husband said, "we have a lot to see today and I have a feeling the day is going to pass by quickly."

They started walking and quickly made a left turn then headed up another street towards the center of town. There was a mild breeze and with it came the pleasant scent of lavender. On the sides of some of the homes were rows of lavender bushes that decorated the normal white and blue colors of them. They passed many homes similar in size to their hosts home and during their entire walk they were greeted by many people in the streets that had heard the news of visitors from the land above. They walked down side streets and back up others where Raven noticed several groups of children or as the Atlanteans call them, chapes, playing and having fun. Every three to four blocks, and always in the middle of an intersection was a decorative fresh water fountain. The water in them wasn't going fifty feet in the air like he had imagined, more like five, but that didn't deter him one little bit from asking question after question during their walk.

"Aegeus, how do all of these fountains work?" He cupped his hands and reached over the small stone wall of one of them and into the cool water for a refreshing drink.

Aegeus was always happy to indulge his new young friend with an answer, "As you can imagine our engineers with the use of small pulleys, pumps and the practical knowledge of hydraulics have been able to provide us with flowing water for centuries. You see we have several large water towers placed amidst the island and using its own weight pushes the water along from a larger pipe continually through to smaller ones which keeps the water at a constant speed."

"Really, pipes you say?"

"Yes, actually in some areas we have used the tubes of the bamboo plant which are great for running water through. Later when we arrive at the library complex you will really see a fountain my friend."

They continued their tour throughout parts of the city making mental notes of statues that were placed in the center of intersections where fountains were not present, these statues were always of a different subject and pose. There were two different types of plinths for the statues, one was squared while the other circular. The tops of the squared version was decoratively curved in a downwards curl at the end of each of the four corners. As for the statues themselves, some were of men or women holding a sword or spear. One was of a woman holding a shield up with her left arm and a sword in the right hand, but the point of the sword was towards the ground at rest. Yet another one was of a horse with the two back legs on the ground and the two front legs up in the air, without question they were all beautifully made!

"We are going to stop at this corner up ahead for lunch," Alexina said.

"Medios came by this morning before you both woke up and we all agreed that word would have to be sent ahead to our elders to inform them of your arrival. All of them have to agree to allow you to take the sword and bow out of the city, so even though we know where they are it is not our decision! We are not allowed to give these items away by ourselves so a meeting will be arranged for the afternoon after we have eaten."

Chapter Six

The Elders: Answering Questions…

"Here we are my friends," Aegeus said, "Medios is waiting over by that table."

He stood up and greeted them all, "Good afternoon to you both and how was your first night's sleep in our city?"

They all walked over to the large wooden table he was standing in front of and Rayne answered him.

"Oh, it was wonderful, I can't remember the last time I slept so soundly. By the way if I may ask, has there been any word yet concerning the meeting we are supposed to be having today with your elders?"

"As a matter of fact, yes. I'm glad you asked about that." He looked over at Aegeus and Alexina and started speaking to them in a different language. She appeared a little bothered by what was said so after a moment she raised her hand to stop him from speaking further.

Rayne, was a little concerned and asked," Is everything all right Alexina?"

"Apparently, our elders weren't very happy with our decision to show you both into the city without first consulting with them. But, Medios did a great job and explained to them who it was who sent you, so they have agreed to see us this afternoon at five o'clock."

"What language was that you two were speaking? It wasn't Greek or Latin but it sounded a little similar to them."

"I was going to say the same thing sis, I didn't understand it at all."

"That is Atlantean," she replied, "it is a very old language, it's a type of cross between them both I'm afraid. Now, let's sit down and eat," as they all sat down per her insistence.

"The food smells great as usual Domaas!" Alexina exclaimed.

At this very moment a tall wiry man with darker tanned skin and balding approached their table. What was most noticeable about this fellow was his huge smile and bright teeth and the fact that he had just come from the kitchen area which was situated in front of their table.

"Hello, hello, my friends," he said surveying the guests around the table especially his two new visitors. "I am Damaas!" He said emphatically, and with an extended hand he shook both mine and my sisters hand while at the same time telling us what type of fish he had for us to choose from. He was very cheerful! He seemed to be talking with everyone and always wore a smile on his face. He certainly moved with a purpose Raven thought. I looked over at my sister and she was all smiles, his friendliness was catching. I turned back to look at our table and saw Domaas had already placed a bowl in the center of our table containing several types of fruits like: red and green grapes, red apples and some figs. I reached out and plucked a few red grapes and ate them while smelling the plates of cooked fish and onions we were now being served. My nose was happier now than it had been in a week.

After eating and saying their goodbyes the small party, which now included Medios, continued the tour of the city for several more hours. Always with the destination in mind being the great Atlantean library, that was basically in the center of the town itself. It was not the center of the island because that was much, much larger. Finally, they exited the city and into a massive clearing, where in front of them were four huge buildings. One columned building to their left, one stone two story building in front of them, and two smaller buildings to their right, the one closest to them on their right was also columned. The buildings were taking up a large space consisting of about six square blocks but had another interesting feature as well. The entrances off all four of them faced the center courtyard which was directly in front Ravens face now, and located in the center of the courtyard was a massive circular based fountain.

His sister commented as he started walking towards the huge fountain, "You can close your mouth now you look a little weird walking like that."

Picking up on her tone, and pointing his finger at the fountain he yelled at her, "See! I told you, fifty feet high, I had always dreamed of a huge fountain in Atlantis with water shooting into the air really high."

Still wasn't quite fifty feet high she thought, but who's measuring it anyways. The closer they got to it the louder the sound of the crashing water was heard. The two-tiered fountain was beautifully decorated and there in the center of it was a huge marble statue of Poseidon sitting on a golden chariot with carved waves hitting his body. He also notated after counting them, twenty marble fish in a circle around the inner base of the fountain just below the waves with water coming out of their mouths and into the clear pool of water at the lower base. Carved into the entire outside of the lower base were scenes of horses, men with shields and swords, some of the scenes were the same ones they had already seen inside of the city at intersections while walking earlier in the day.

"We need to go," Aegeus remarked, "now look, that large columned building to your left is the library, it is also the school and where most meetings are held within the city."

In the courtyard where the fountain stood were men and women walking around in groups of two's or three's, some talking and some just walking silently with bundles of books or papers under their arms. They began walking up the stone steps of the library noting that each step stretched the entire length of the building from left to right. Twenty steps later they were on the main floor and were able to admire the enormous marble columns that made up the perimeter of the library. They were much bigger up close than he originally thought. If he held hands with his sister and two more people they would probably just be able to reach around one column.

The breeze running through the columns here on the main level felt great believing they would make for a great get-a-way on hot sunny days. They continued walking straight again half of the length into the building, made a right turn and proceeded through a doorway and down a few sets of smaller stone stairs through another doorway where Raven thought, "They really don't have any doors on any entrances here in Atlantis."

Exiting the doorway they entered into a large, sunshine lit room with seven people sitting in chairs in a semi-circle in front of them. Raven looked over at his sister but she was looking up towards the ceiling admiring the many beams of sunlight entering into this chamber. He counted twelve individual holes in total cut into the sides of the entire angled marble roof. Three holes perfectly spaced stretched the length of each wall. Each hole was precisely made and identical to the next allowing for a perfect combination of light into the chamber. He also noticed the presence of the same types of shells randomly mounted on the inside walls, but no light was coming out of these. He figured they were for the use of those clever pearl light sources he had seen around the city and inside of Aegeus' home used when it was dark outside. In an elderly woman's voice the woman seated in the center chair said to them, "Please join us, we are all very pleased to meet you both," motioning to them with open arms to sit. They were a mixed bunch, all older, three of which were men the other women. Five wooden chairs had been assembled in front of the elders, so they all sat down. All seven of them were dressed in different colored robes: blue, green, white and purple. Of course Raven again taking note to look the their feet thought, "They are not wearing shoes either, that's funny. I would not have guessed that they didn't have doors or wore shoes in Atlantis." At least he hadn't see anyone so far wearing shoes.

One by one, the elders introduced themselves and after more than two hours of asking them questions from every possible angle the meeting finally felt like it was coming to an end. They knew that they couldn't stay in the city for very long and even though they both loved being there they still had to get into the City of Bytar and somehow destroy the one page inside of a magical book that Queen Aaneesa had told them about. All of these things they told to the Atlantean elders.

Finally, after a few moments of silence the elder seated to their far left spoke, "We have all agreed to allow you both to use our two magical items on the one condition that when your task is completed you bring them back to us."

He was definitely younger than the others and had a neatly trimmed brown beard and long brown hair just past his shoulders.

The brother and sister without looking at each other both replied saying, "Of course," hearing that they had replied at the same time she let her brother finish speaking.

"We will! As soon as we complete our task we promise we will return your items."

"Very well," the same elder said. He raised his right hand in the air and immediately there came sounds and movements from the far right side of the chamber. Two men approached carrying a large wooden table and placed it between the elders and themselves. Those men left only to be replaced by two other men each carrying an object under a large white cloth.

The elderly woman spoke to them again. Her name was Xenos and her dignified voice carried throughout the chamber, "Here are Atlantis' two prized magical items! Come forward Raven and marvel at King Titan's sword."

Nervously he stood up and approached the table, lifted off the cloth and was mesmerized by the silver and gold colored sword lying on the table in front of him. The workmanship and intricate details on it were beyond anything he had ever seen in a sword.

She continued, "If you can lift the sword up from the table then you will be able to wield it in battle."

There was a fantastically brilliant blue stone mounted at the base that was intricately held in place with thin strips of gold. Tensing the muscles in his arm and body he grabbed the sword with one hand and believing it was going to be heavy lifted it up off of the table and into the air with a mighty heave. Shockingly, it was light as a feather and he had to control his arm quickly so as not to drop it on the floor behind him. He assumed a fighting stance and was amazed by its lack of weight, he then started swishing the sword in front of him at imaginary enemies enjoying the intricate swishing sound it made cutting through the air.

Xenos spoke to his sister now, "My dear, stand up and remove the cloth that's covering the bow on the table. If this is meant to be, not only will you be able to lift the bow up but when you pull back as if to shoot an arrow one will appear."

She walked up and removed the cloth, her eyes opened wide at the pure beauty of such an object. She lifted the bow up with her left hand without a problem, held it straight out and somewhat shakily with her right, reached out to pull back on a string for an arrow. Raven had paused what he was doing and watched her intently. She was perplexed at first at not seeing a string in the first place, but did as she was asked to. Pulling on an imaginary string with her right hand, she immediately felt the tensioning of a bowstring, from out of nowhere a light silver glow appeared for a string and a brilliant white colored arrow appeared before her ready to fly. She panicked, she didn't know what to do, her right hand was pulled all the way back and was holding an arrow close to her right cheek. She asked in a panicked voice, "What do I do now?"

Xenos replied, "Just open your fingers to release the arrow."

She turned to her left and pointed the bow at the wall, then let loose the arrow, and as soon as she did that the string and arrow disappeared.

"Now, do the same thing but this time when you have the arrow all the way back whisper to it, tell the arrow where you want it to go, say "the wall," and release it and see what happens."

She did exactly what Xenos had told her and whispered the words then opened her fingers to let the arrow go. It left her hand in a flash, and with a sharp cracking sound went right through the marble wall leaving only a small hole and just the end of the arrow visible. A second later the arrow had all but disappeared.

"You have an unlimited supply of arrows my dear, as you release one, you can pull back for another, but always remember to tell the arrow where to go or what the target is."

At this point all seven of the elders stood up and the woman to Xenos' left now began to speak to them.

"We wish you both the best in your travels, take care of our weapons because they will certainly take care of you."

After some more pointers and practice on using their new weapons the party of five left the chamber and were quickly standing back on the main floor outside of the library. He and his sister walked to the other end of the building just to look out at the large expanse of land that was behind the library. Since they were on elevated land they were able to see huge amount of trees and open fields with small rolling hills behind them. It would be dark soon and they still had a long walk back to Aegeus' home. Just before arriving at their hosts home they had all agreed that it would be best to leave Atlantis in the morning. If they left early enough their hosts would be able to take them to the southern shores of Tundar which was to the west of where they were now instead of the way they came from by the statue of Pelaius which was further south and away from the mainland. It would take several hours to get there but Alexina wanted to make sure they were back before nightfall.

After a hardy breakfast and some more talking they left the only home they had known for the past few nights. Medios, caught them as they again approached the barrier at the same spot they had entered the city two nights prior. There was a solid game plan! It really just entailed the brother and sister simply following behind their hosts wherever they took them. Simple right...

The same young sentinel was at his post when they all walked up. Orien stood up and walked over to Aegeus and Medios giving them the same customary greeting as before, he then turned his attention to Alexina, Raven and Rayne, but probably not in that order and with a big smile said to Rayne, "Hello again and good morning."

Rayne took a moment to survey the area where he had been sitting and saw that it consisted of only three wooden tables and some chairs. He had still been eating his breakfast when they arrived due to the food and drink still on the table. There was evidence of the recent fire he must have used to cook his food over because a few feet away the blackened rocks were still smoldering. There was a pleasant smell of cooked fish and potatoes in the air which judging by his bowl must have been some type of stew he had made. They were in a bit of a rush now to leave so there was no time for asking a bunch of questions about his breakfast.

"I really love your city Orien," she told him, "I'm going to miss being here but I hope when we return we are able to stay longer.

"I would really like that too," he replied.

Aegeus cut in and said, "Alright my friends we must be on our way, I'm sure you remember how to go through the barrier but I will start, when we have all gone through and are back in the ocean on the other side we'll make sure you two are ok! Then I want you both to just follow us."

At that, he turned around, placed both of his outstretched hands onto the barrier and a moment later he was being pulled back through it and into the open ocean.

Chapter Seven

The Fall of Bytar: A City With A New ruler...

The sorcerer Nicias had sent three of his fastest ships ahead of the main army so they would land on the beach just North of Bytar. These soldiers were to march only at night to avoid being seen and when they arrived near the southern gates of the city they knew to stay hidden and wait until the audible signal was given to attack. The sound made by the mystic tree horn was unmistakable! Now the main army was anchored just off the coast of Bytar as hundreds of smaller boats were now headed to shore powered by sweaty, grunting men with their oars splashing through the water in near unison. Soon the quiet City of Bytar was going to be forcibly awakened by war.

***

Inside the peaceful walls of the city, on the second floor of the kings palace sat King Thais. He was a fair but aging king of medium height, silver short hair, a kind disposition and a slightly too visible belly in recent years due to his fondness for eating good food.

"For the second day in a row Simo you have cooked goose! You know it is my favorite," the king laughed out loud. "You must want something in return for this."

"No, no sir, not at all!" Simo replied humbly with a smile and bowing several times, "I have all that I could possible want in my poor life. It is my pleasure as always sir to make sure your belly is full and you have wine when you need it."

Simo, was also a middle-aged man, and had been a cook most of his life, but he was always bowing to the king and very thankful to be cooking indoors rather than in the hot desert because he had cooked outdoors for many years before coming into the service of the king five years ago.

He still wore the long white cloth wrapped around his head just out of habit.

"Thank you Simo, I do value good food as you know," he said with a big smile, "but, you're more than just my cook you see, I like having someone around me that I can wholly trust. That...right there is worth twenty cooked geese, even if it is with your tasty mashed beans and carrots."

"Ah, you are too kind, too kind. Are you going outside on the balcony to rest a bit before going to bed like usual sir?"

"You know me too well, I do enjoy taking a few minutes every night to look over the quiet city from out there."

He walked out onto the balcony and admired his city. Peering into the great distance he could just see over the wall to the west to where the river flowed south to the rest of Tundar. Looking to his right towards where the main gate and ocean was located he felt the familiar cool breeze blowing through his hair which also carried the smell of salt water on it. There were four entrances into the city. The palace was built closer to the smallest east entrance, this led to the mountains behind him, it was really just a solitary wooden door he had placed years later after the city walls had been built. While closing his eyes he took a last deep breath enjoying the smells of the city, lowered his head and turned around to go back inside and go to sleep.

***

The soldiers were starting to land on the beach now, most of them were jumping out of their boats early in about three to four feet of water to quickly help pull the boats to shore. The sounds of their boots splashing through water and the rustling and clanking of swords getting ready to be drawn was heard a little louder. Three lone fisherman were on the beach fixing their nets for the mornings hunt when they noticed all of these soldiers coming ashore. They immediately turned and started running up the sand dune to escape surprising a few of the soldiers who hadn't seen them. Without a chance all three of the fisherman dropped face first into the sand as black arrows silently struck their backs with a profound thud.

The soldiers were there to take control of the city not to kill everyone inside of it. They needed the people alive to replenish some of their ranks and to help feed the army. Nicias gathered his men together including captain Asal. He nodded to the captain who then gave the command for the horn to be sounded; the tree horns crisp piercing sound was now being heard for miles around.

***

Suddenly, the king heard the sound of a horn blaring from his left side coming from the area of the main gates. He spun around and went back to the ledge with his eyes intently focused in that area. The city had defenses! A small group of maybe one thousand men were scattered throughout the perimeter of the walled city. They were by no means a professional army, half of them were good soldiers, but the other half spent too much of their time drinking, gambling or just plain sleeping the day away.

The king suddenly heard yelling coming from behind him, back towards the southern gates. He couldn't see those gates either because they were too far away but the sounds were definitely getting louder. The night sky lit up with yellowish white arrival of hundreds of fire tipped arrows dropping into the city from the direction of the main gates. The metal against metal sounds of sword fighting soon rang out from both sides of the city as the once quiet city of Bytar was now in a panic. The king looked down and saw men running in the streets towards the palace yelling that the main gates had been opened from the inside and that the enemy was already entering the city. King Thais loudly summoned for his trusty cook, "Simo! Simo!" But no response was heard. He ran back into his chamber and saw no cook, nor any of his servants around. He entered the hallway and saw two serving maids running towards him so he said to them, "The city is under attack go and try to hide yourselves now! Wait a minute, have either of you two seen Simo?"

"No, your highness I have not seen him," replied the first maid.

"Nor have I your highness," replied the second.

"Ok, go then," the king told them both.

He headed down the hallway towards the staircase that led to the first floor when he spotted Simo running up them sweating and in a panic.

"Where have you been Simo! I have been calling for you for the past few minutes."

"I'm sorry sir, I was downstairs doing a few errands, I thought once you were finished on the balcony you would just have gone to bed. Sir, we are under attack."

The king cut him off with a raised hand, "I know that, why do you think I've been calling for you!"

"Simo, do what you can downstairs, I don't know who is attacking us or what they want but I'm sure we're going to find out soon enough. Tell the servants to try to make it out of the palace, maybe they'll make it out of the city utilizing the east gate. I'm going to make sure the door leading to the tunnels is secured!"

"I will do that right now, where shall I find you after that sir?"

"Once I check the door, you'll find me back in my chambers." At that the King turned and ran back down the stairs yelling at people to get out of the palace.

After pushing by a crying servant Simo stopped at the heavy wooden double doors of the palaces front entrance and began helping the few guards there lift and place the heavy wooden beams down across the doors steel latches to secure them.

Like clockwork the sound of the horn triggered Nicias' spies on the inside of the city to open the north and south gates like they were supposed to. The west gate facing the river and the smaller mountain gate were both still shut. Nicias' forces numbered close to five thousand men, more than enough to secure the city by nightfall he figured. Although, the gate by the ocean had been breached, the kings soldiers were holding their own, for the moment. They sent several volleys of arrows from the wall down killing quite a few of the invading soldiers. There was heavy fighting now in two distinct areas of the city! Despite the occasional barrage of flaming arrows from the invaders still raining down into the city the fighting had progressed from the gates and had moved several blocks into the city. Many fires, mostly smaller had broken out on top of the small wooden rooftops of some of the homes. By now a lot of the Bytarian people had been awaken due to the commotion growing by the minute. Some of the men within the city, hearing the clashing of swords grabbed their own weapons and ran out into the streets to try and help defend their friends and families. Then again, there were others gathering their wives, crying children and trying to grab what food and clothes they could to make it out of the city before it fell to an unseen enemy.

The surrounding stone walls of Bytar were only twenty feet high as they were originally built to protect the city from the high winds that come off of the ocean. It was only in the past five years or so that the king had placed soldiers on top of the wall to keep watch for enemies. There were two-story wooden staircases sporadically placed around the inside perimeter of the wall that led to wooden walkways so the soldiers could patrol sections of the wall. It was five o'clock in the morning and still dark outside as most of the residents within the city were awake by now and just trying to make sense of the chaos that was around them.

More and more of the enemies soldiers had entered the city by now. There were bodies littering the streets as the kings soldiers were getting pushed back further and further to where they would soon be at the palace.

Nicias was easily identifiable by his tall, lanky looks and red flowing cape tossing in the breeze behind him. He had stayed on the beach with his elite guard in safety during much of this time not wanting to get his hands dirty from blood. He walked through the gates with his small band of protective guards around him, like a blanket keeping him safe and secure. The assorted fires burning feely, confusion and people running around in terror put a sly smile on his face.

***

After watching his cook run down the stairs King Thais quickly followed him. He ran as best as his body would allow down the wide first floor hallway making the first left and then down another shorter hallway to the end. In front of him stood the heavy steel door that led down to the partially paved tunnels under the palace. There were quite a few mazes of tunnels and hidden rooms down there but the only room the king had in mind right now had a valuable treasure locked inside of it. He had to lock this door right now! The heavy lock was present but, it wasn't pushed closed so with both hands he made sure it was secured and he relished the latching sound it made as soon as the lock was pushed together.

"Good," the king thought, "now, I've got to get upstairs to my chamber to await whatever evil person is responsible for this nightmare."

Several hours passed and the sun was now cresting over the mountains and hitting the city for the first time. From inside his chambers he could still hear the occasional sound of clashing swords and men yelling orders at one another to check this or that.

"Who is responsible for all of this destruction and killing and where is Simo? I have not seen that cook in hours, he should have been here by now!?"

He had changed his clothes and put something on a little more, kingly, instead of the nightgown he was wearing previously. He was not the type of king to wear a flashy crown or showy jewelry around his neck but he did wear a simple gold band around his forehead and of course the gold crested ring of Bytar on his right hand. There was a small window in the back room of his chambers that faced the east, peering out of it he marveled at the beautiful snow-capped mountain range. Seeing this peaceful scene in front of him almost, even if it was just for a moment, let him temporarily forgot about the terror that was happening down in his city streets. For the first time since the sun came out the king walked back through his chambers and out onto the same balcony where he had stood peacefully several hours earlier.

He looked out upon a city in which he barely recognized, most noticeably was the number of small fires burning and plumes of black smoke rising into the sky. The streets below his balcony contained broken carts with random animals and people roaming aimlessly about and several motionless bodies. Following the street with his eyes to the right he witnessed a cluster of soldiers talking together, but now a few of them were beginning to point in *his* direction and starting to laugh out loud. He knew that the palace doors and walls had not been breached yet because it was still too quiet. Suddenly, there was a crashing sound behind him in his chambers as if a table had fallen over.

"Sir, are you here? Sir, it's Simo! Where are you?"

He went back inside and saw that his cook had also changed his clothes but he still wore the white cloth wrapped around his head. He had also put on a long white baggy short sleeve shirt that almost reached to his feet, a black belt and sandals, he looked more like an Egyptian now than ever.

"What is this all about Simo? Where the hell have you been?"

"Sir, I'm so happy to see you are alive and safe," still panting and out of breath, "sir, since last we spoke I have been doing as you asked of me. The palace doors were secured and most of the servants and guests were able to get out before the fighting got too bad. There is still a small number of guards in the palace including the two that I brought up here for you."

He looked over towards the main door to his chambers and saw the familiar faces of two of his loyal guards staring back at him.

One of the guards spoke, "Your Highness," with a quick bow, "from all of the reports we have heard the city has fallen. Many of our soldiers are dead and some have been captured but there has been no attempts to attack the palace. We will do all in our power to protect you."

"Thank you, I think at this point enough people have died. Do you know who is responsible for attacking us?"

He looked down at the floor, "Yes, they say the sorcerer Nicias is behind the attack Your Highness."

He turned away from the guard, placed both hands behind his back and started pacing back and forth in quiet thought, "I knew it was this devil, I knew it! There can only be one reason why...He found out about the books location and wants to try to use it for some evil purpose." He turned back around and squarely faced the group.

"Listen to me the three of you, if you try to defend me you will all be killed. I believe your lives will be spared if you listen to me, when his soldiers approach place your weapons down at your feet and do not put up a fight. However, I know that you are both soldiers, and my only wish is to keep all of you alive."

He headed for the balcony, "Simo come with me."

Once the two of them were alone outside the king approached the cook and looked him straight in the eye, "Have you betrayed me my friend?"

"No, no, no Sir, I would never do that! You are my greatest friend sir."

The king felt that he was a good judge of character and seeing the sincerity in the eyes of his friend and cook placed his hand on his shoulder and said, "I believe you. The king raised his hand, pointed to his right at some soldiers in the street and asked, "What do you make of that over there?"

Simo focused his attention on the growing group of soldiers that were down the street. Walking into view from around a corner was a group of twenty or so soldiers with red and black striped capes, but in the middle of them was a noticeably taller man with a solid red cape that flapped in the wind behind him. This new group of men stopped at the first group and apparently some words were exchanged because they all turned and started heading towards them. The king and his cook watched as this band of sword slashing ruffians approached the palace. The palaces main front doors were located just under and to the right side of the kings balcony. The soldiers reached the palace and out from amidst the protecting arms of his men came the tall boney man with the red cape.

The thin sorcerer looked directly up at them standing on the balcony and said, "King Thais I presume and I'm guessing the person next to you must be your trusty cook, Simeon I believe?"

There were a few muffled words spoken behind Nicias and what appeared to be a moment of confusion the king thought.

"Pardon me, I believe I misspoke, your cooks name is Simo I'm told, is that correct?"

His facial expression didn't give away the feeling of surprise he felt inside, instead he stood there stoically not even looking at his cook.

"My name is Nicias, I'm sure you have heard of me?"

"Yes, I have heard of you," yelled the king.

Nicias, now made a small show of things began walking in small circles on the front steps of the palace as they bandied words.

"You have a charming city here Thais," he said in a sarcastic tone and crooked smile, "I'm afraid it's in need of a few minor repairs," meanwhile, his soldiers began to laugh and chuckle. "Come now Thais, open these doors so we can begin talking like civilized men I think it would be most unpleasant for you otherwise."

"I'm told you are a sorcerer of some kind," the king shot back, "well then, open the doors yourself like you opened the main gates."

With a overstated flamboyant wave of his hands, "Oh, you liked my little trick there Thais, well that didn't require much use of magic at all, just gold."

Nicias was a sorcerer, but not the kind that could produce fire from his fingertips or bring down a mountain yet, but with the use of his amulet he could easily destroy a door!

"Very well Thais, as you wish," with a flourished bow and both of his arms outstretched, he then approached the palaces heavy wooden double doors.

On the inside of the doors, with swords drawn several of the kings guards stood ready for battle but they couldn't foresee the calamity that what was heading their way. Nicias stood in front of the ten foot tall doors for a few minutes mumbling to himself with one hand clasping the small flaming amulet around his neck and the other lightly touching both of the doors. His soldiers stood at the ready behind him waiting for any command that was given to them. The heavy log that had been placed on the inside of the doorway to bolt it shut suddenly appeared to have smoke emanating from within it. The four heavy steel clasps that were cradling the log started to get very hot and glow red. Nicias' eyes were closed and there was a serious look of concentration on his face as he continued mumbling to himself. After a few minutes there was a tremendous crack and boom sound and then suddenly the doors opened up but only a few inches. He stepped back nodded to his soldiers led by Captain Asal. He was a large burly bearded man with a neck thick like a bull and equally thick muscled arms. He pushed the heavy doors open and was surprised to encounter no resistance from within. With both doors now completely open they witnessed firsthand the explosive force of what had happened on the inside after the explosion. All ten of the kings guards were dead! Each soldier had been blown backwards and had died from different sizes of broken wood and metal that were clearly sticking out of their now motionless bodies. They had no chance. From the balcony the king could hear Captain Asal yelling furiously at his men to get the mess cleared up immediately.

Nicias turned to his men, "Do not destroy this palace is that clear! Anyone who does not follow my orders will pay with their lives. Captain Asal, bring some of your men and let's see to this king."

They had already walked back into his chambers and were waiting for the inevitable meeting. He sat in his chair simultaneously looking at the backs of both of his two guards and past them down the hallway towards the stairs where he knew that the soldiers were going to be approaching.

The soldiers with the black and red capes bounded up the stairs and then down the hallway with rage filled eyes towards the kings two waiting guards. Instantly, their weapons were drawn, they had already made up their minds that giving up was not going to happen. In a furious clash of steel they fought together bravely and were able to kill two of the caped soldiers only to both fall at the hands of the captain and the greater number of soldiers behind him. The bearded Captain entered the kings chambers and pointed his uplifted sword at the cook as several of his soldiers followed him in.

"We're not armed so there is no need to lift your weapon towards us," said the king.

The cook slowly raised both of his arms in the air indicating that he didn't have a weapon and didn't intend to fight. Just then the sound of footfalls and a pathetic attempt at whistling was heard, with lips puckered and both hands clasped behind his back Nicias casually strolled through the doorway and approached the king, "It is a shame that the bravery in the palace is exemplified more by your guards rather than by you, Thais," snapping his fingers as he looked back at the dead guards on the floor.

"I am a king not a soldier, instead of laying down their arms they choose to fight, now what do you want here Nicias?"

"Oh, come now Thais, do you honestly believe that I traveled all this way for nothing, I want the book! But, first I'm hungry, let's sit and have your cook here prepare us something to eat. I understand he cooks very well! We can talk about what I want after I have a full stomach." He walked over and sat down at the wooden table and with his boney pointed finger said, "Simo is it? Go down and cook us something worthy of a king and don't try something stupid like poisoning me because you don't know which meal will go to your king here."

Without hesitation Simo glanced over at his king "What would you like me to prepare for you sir?"

With a worried look he managed, "Anything besides goose, you choose."

At that Simo walked out of the room with two of the caped guards shadowing him.

Captain Asal sheathed his sword and started to slowly walk around and visually inspect the room, he was not looking for anything in particular just being nosey more than anything.

"Come sit down and join me, I'm sure it will take even your cook a little while to prepare our food," simultaneously, he kicked a chair back from the table that was opposite him for the King.

Without even flinching at the sound of the chair being moved the captain continued looking through things that were scattered about on top of a dresser.

The king sat down across from the boney sorcerer who was now looking over to see what his captain was up to. He noticed the amulet hanging from his neck, it was small and rectangular and looked like it was on fire! The king thought, "How could there be a small fire burning at this man's neck and it not burn him?"

Not impressed at watching his captain any longer he turned his attention back to the table and caught the king eyeing his amulet.

"I see my little trinket fascinates you Thais."

"Why does it burn like that?"

"Burn? It doesn't burn! I would describe it to you as having more of an internal power than anything, like a small flame without heat, but I won't bore you with these small details. Nicias closed his eyes and exhaling slowly and methodically, " Thais, what are we going to do about fetching me that book I require?"

"I don't know where it is? Really," King Thais replied.

The sorcerer burst out laughing and slapped both of his boney hands on top of the dinner table which surprised the king.

"Did you hear that Captain! He says he doesn't know where the book is, should I believe him?" But, without even letting the captain answer the question he continued. "I'm going to give you a perfect opportunity to prove yourself to me Thais."

At this point, the cook had been away for nearly an hour. The sound of people approaching the kings chamber caught everyone's attention and then a few of Captain Asal's soldiers entered the room.

"Excellency," the guard said looking at Nicias, "we encountered another small pocket of resistance near the southern gates, some more of the people were trying to sneak out of the city."

"So what!" Captain Asal responded with a harsh voice.

"We killed all of them except for this one," as one of the other soldiers pushed an unarmed man onto the floor in front of him.

The man looked to be in his forties or fifties, his hands were tied up in front of his body and his face showed signs of a fresh beating.

So he could look into his eyes the captain bent down in front of him and snarled, "Where were you trying to run to fool?"

Nicias interrupted with a calm and soothing voice, "My dear Captain Asal is that any way to treat our hosts? Now Thais, onto the issue of trust and honesty, you can trust me to not kill this fellow Bytarian citizen of yours if you can simply answer my next question honestly. Is that a fair exchange? I'll give you an easy question to start with, the tunnels that run under this palace must have a door or entranceway, where is it?"

Captain Asal at this time had unsheathed his knife and placed it near the prisoners throat.

Glancing over and into the scared eyes of this poor, dirty man lying on the floor in front of him King Thais took only a few precious moments to consider his options. He pondered his options, "Telling him where the door is, is a long way from telling him how to find the book." Finally, he said, "The entrance is located on the first floor hallway, it is a large steel door with bars and a lock on it."

"Excellent Thais! I do believe you're telling me the truth, and as a man of my word, captain, have this man's bonds cut and I want him released back into the city without being harmed."

Reluctantly, captain Asal cut the rope freeing the man's hands and issued instructions to the soldier that was standing there, "You heard Your

Excellency, take him outside and let him go!" He then sheathed his knife in disgust and continued snooping around the room.

"There you see Thais, now that wasn't so bad now was it?"

From the doorway the clanking sounds of pots and pans was heard as Simo returned and entered the room pushing a cart filled with hot food followed by the same two guards.

"Ah, perfect...The food smells delicious Nicias commented. I see now why you value this Simo person as your cook because I'm starving! You know Thais, despite what you might think of me I really hate war and bloodshed, it's hot, dirty and very tiresome, but unfortunately I have questions that needed answering and an army cannot just sit around and do nothing."

Captain Asal grabbed a chair from the dinner table where the king sat and pushing some items aside on a dresser made a makeshift dinner table for himself. With the tray of food next to the dinner table Simo started placing the silverware, he filled three cups half way with wine and left the bottle in the middle of their table. Three small bowls were filled with a carrot, potato and onion stew and given to each person with a piece of bread. The aroma of the onions with pepper and salt filled the nose of the sorcerer and his mouth started to water in anticipation. The first of three silver, dome shaped food covers was lifted up exposing their main course as he placed the first plate in front of the King, the second went to Nicias and the last to the captain. A perfectly cooked fish filet with a slice of lemon on top adorned the silver trays of each man.

"Thank you, it all looks very tasty as usual," the king said solemnly.

His appetite was not the same as the previous nights but he knew he had to eat something, he had to, because he didn't know what tomorrow was going to bring.

"If you need anything sir, I'll be sitting right over there against the wall," pointing to the wall opposite from where Captain Asal was sitting. He had an immediate distaste for the sorcerers top man since he first entered the doorway. No one spoke during dinner. After they had all finished their food Simo casually went about his business like every night clearing the table.

"I don't remember eating that well for a long, long time," the sorcerer finally said leaning back in his chair with a full stretch of his limbs and the cracking sounds that came with it. I have several other questions that require honest answers though so we will be back up here in the morning to discuss your future and my book; tonight though the captain and I have a few matters to discuss then I'll be retiring to bed."

He stood up, yawned and started walking away, "Come captain we need to discuss this steel door of ours."

Unfortunately, The morning came sooner than the king would have liked. The boney silhouette of Nicias strolled into the kings chamber again closely followed by his captain.

"If you wouldn't mind accompanying us downstairs Thais, I would appreciate it."

The sarcastic undertone and fake niceties that Nicias was always saying to the king bothered him, especially how he was never addressing him as King Thais and just calling him Thais.

"Sure, where are we going?"

"We are going to inspect this steel door that guards the underground tunnels so make sure to bring your trusty cook," he said with a grim smile.

All four of them went downstairs where they were met by several of the red and black caped elite guards who escorted them down the hallway until they stood in front of the heavy door with its large lock still intact.

"Where is the key for that huge lock?" The sorcerer asked.

"It's locked? Replied the king, "well that's strange, it's normally unlocked now the key where is it," pretending to check his jacket pockets.

Watching this obvious delay pissed Captain Asal off so he backhanded the cook knocking him to the ground in a flash which caused him to bleed from his lower lip.

King Thais stepped forward quickly and yelled at the captain, "Stop that right now, there is no need for more violence."

Nicias raised his hand ever so slightly to the captain and said, "I'm so sorry for that, I'm afraid Captain Asal doesn't have the gift of patience as I do, now, as I was saying, where is the key?"

"I do not know where the key is, it's usually hanging there on that hook," dismissively waiving to a curved hook on the wall five feet away from the door.

"No matter!"

The sorcerer turned and faced the iron door and like before grasped his amulet in one hand and held onto the large padlock with the other. After a few minutes of mumbling to himself the lock and his hand started to glow red, it got brighter and brighter until the lock started to melt away like drops of water falling from a bucket. He opened his hand and the remaining small pieces of the lock crumpled to the ground.

Nicias backed away from the door and said, "Captain if you would be so kind."

With his big, meaty hands he grabbed the heavy iron door handle and slowly opened the creaking door allowing the accumulated dust around the frame to fill the air around them. Nicias walked up alongside his captain and peered down through the doorway, but was only able to see a handful of stone stairs leading downward into a dark void.

Chapter Eight

Poseidon: The Sea God...

Rayne had been swimming in place with the others after transforming back into her mermaid body waiting for her brother to come through, he opened his eyes and started breathing normally and realized that everything had gone just fine going back through the barrier. His sister was just in front of him with the typical expression on her face which he thought translated to, what took you so long.

Alexina swam up and asked him, "Are you alright?"

"Yes I'm fine," but just double-checking he started turning his head to the left and right, "my vision is great and I'm ready to go."

"I see the sword is hanging there on your right side perfectly fine just like the elder Xenos said it would be."

He didn't need rope or anything to secure the sword to his body, by placing it by his side it would stay there like there was in an invisible sheath holding it up. The same went for his sisters bow, it was lying flat on her back like as if it was naturally meant to be there.

"Since we have a little further to travel this time we'll need to pace ourselves. I know the route that Aegeus will travel and it will take us through some beautiful caves."

Medios let out a quick high pitch screeching sound similar to the one Aegeus had made prior then faced them, "So my friends all is well I see!"

"Yes, it looks like we're in business," Raven said.

"Good, at that moment she heard those same clicking sounds as before. Suddenly, three beautiful dolphins appeared out of the darkness and swam right up to their group. They were still in very deep water but had no problem seeing their way around.

"What are you doing Medios?" Aegeus asked.

"I want to check if their Irnshells work properly and if they can hear and talk to fish, don't you remember?"

"Oh yes, you're right I did forget about that." He turned to face the three dolphins and then starting talking to them, "So my good friends how are all of you today?"

The funny part was that all three of the dolphins responded at the same time.

"I'm fine," one said.

"I'm fine," another answered.

"I feel great, we were getting ready to eat but."

Laughing, Alexina cut them off, "Wait, wait, one of you at a time my friends, we can't listen to all three of you at once."

Miraculously, the siblings were able to listen to the whole conversation taking place.

"Can you hear them talking my friends?" Medios asked curiously.

"Yes, very clearly," Rayne responded happily.

"I can understand them too," she answered.

He turned to one of the dolphins and repeated the same question to them.

The dolphin responded, "Why would I not be able to hear them? Of course I heard them, have these two fish next to me been telling lies about me?" Bobbing his head up and down and making a type of laughing sound.

Clearly satisfied that everyone could understand each other and that the Irnshells were doing their job he finished, "No, my friend they have not, now we can leave."

"Oh boy," the mermaid whispered to them.

"We have to travel to the shores of Tundar today my friends," Aegeus said to the three dolphins, "will you be able to go with us there and back?"

"That is not a problem, we can look for food when we get to the shallower waters," replied one of the dolphins.

"Thank you," he answered, "are you two ready?" looking at their two young faces.

A quick nod by the both of them confirmed their readiness.

"Make sure you do not stray away from our group and if you run into any problems just yell at one of us then he turned and swiftly swam away, but was closely followed by his mate and their dolphin protectors.

It was early in the morning and Raven could feel that they were swimming in an upward direction, but after about an hour of slowly making their way up and not seeing anything except blue water he noticed ahead of them some huge underground rocks. Their three dolphin escorts were always close to them. There was always one dolphin on each side of them and the third usually slightly behind them all picking up the rear. Aegeus led them through a large opening in the rocks which turned out to be the entrance to a massive cave system. He halted their group for a minute saying, "We're still in deep water, but I wanted to show you both these caves because I know of a shortcut through here that will take us a little closer in the end to where we need to go. Be wary, it's easy to get turned around in caves like this! You can swim for hours until you manage to find your way back to your starting point."

They swam for over an hour making their way in and out of different sized caves until finally seeing the clear blue waters near the exit of the last cave.

Aegeus, followed by two of the dolphins made it out of the cave opening first, but no sooner did that happen when one of the dolphins yelled back at them, "Sharks!"

There was a school of Hammerhead sharks that had been hanging around just above the entrance of the cave waiting for a meal to come swimming out of the opening. Aegeus spun around to face the others that were still in the cave while at the same time pulling out a small knife he had attached at his forearm. "Stay there and protect them!" He yelled at his mate. Medios who hadn't exited the cave yet out of instinct had also unsheathed his knife and had it at the ready. The dolphin that had been bringing up the rear swam up next to the four of them, but knew his place, he would not swim out into the fight and leave them alone and unprotected in the cave, he had to stay strong and resist the urge to do that.

The sharks saw their prey as soon as they exited the protection of the cave and three of them started their descent onto what they must have thought was a free meal. They would soon discover there was no free meal here today. The first shark descended, mouth open towards Aegeus but was pounded on the side of his body by the nose of one of the dolphins. Aegeus moved out of the way and sliced at the huge sharks face putting a small gash along the side of it then positioned himself to watch for more sharks. The siblings didn't have knives and Alexina only had a similar small knife with her. After sensing the little bit of blood that was trailing behind the shark that Aegeus had cut several of the other sharks started to drift down to get into the fight. The two dolphins were starting to get tired of swimming around crashing into the sides of several more of these huge beasts.

Alexina was in a near panic and yelled at her mate in desperation, "Swim over here, you can make it!"

"No!" He yelled, "I will not lead them back to you."

They felt helpless being in the safety of the cave and the last dolphin with them was not budging to abandon them, all seemed like a lost cause. Then the brilliant idea of using her bow underwater popped into her head.

"You're going to do what!" Her brother exclaimed.

"I'm going to try it," she replied.

While floating there full of confidence that her idea was going to work, she reached over her shoulder and grabbed the bow; she held it in her left hand, knuckles white from the strength of her grip and pulled back on an invisible string, immediately she felt the tensioning and then a glowing white arrow appeared out of nowhere. She aimed at the nearest shark and whispered to the arrow to hit the shark and then released the arrow. In a flash of white the arrow was gone and easily went through the body of the shark. Alexina and Raven were utterly shocked into silence at seeing what had just happened. The sharks lifeless body started sinking into the deeper water as a very noticeable blood trial followed it down. She was getting ready to pull for another arrow when a loud and commanding voice said to them, "Stop!"

An explosion of lightning flashed horizontally across everyone's field of vision scattering all of the sharks in different directions. Out of the flash and near to where the action had been taking place appeared the upper half of a man's muscular body with an older man's face. He was several times larger than a regular person, donned a long white beard and hair that moved concurrently with the waters movement and despite his size his lower body wasn't defined at all, it was shimmering, similar to a heatwave over the desert sand. In his right hand he was holding onto a three pointed golden staff which Rayne could only guess was the trident that Pelaius had mentioned. This had to be the Sea God Poseidon.

"Are you all alright?" The man asked.

His clear and soothing voice was heard by all, but to her ears it sounded personal, as if he was only asking her.

Alexina immediately swam out and hugged her mate asking him with a concerned tone, "Are you alright? Are you hurt?"

"No, I'm fine my love."

Everyone swam out of the cave including the sole dolphin that had stayed behind with them, he soon approached the other two but was overheard, "I'm glad you stayed and watched over them," said one of the dolphins.

"I did as I was taught even though I was worried for the both of you."

As quickly as the disruption started it stopped and the sea went back to being calm again.

"My lord Poseidon," Alexina started, "I'm so happy you showed up when you did!"

In a deep and relaxed voice he replied, "I'm sorry I couldn't have helped you a few moments earlier but I was tending to someone a thousand miles away. From the deepest depths to the shallowest waters the Merpeople can always find me. What called me to you was the immense power I felt the instant King Titans bow released the arrow killing that shark."

"I'm sorry, I was so frightened for my friends."

"You must be Raven and Rayne, the brother and sister Pelaius told me so much of, do not worry yourselves there is no penalty for protecting your friends or loved ones, the sharks will get their meal elsewhere."

She could see and feel the majesty of the oceans protector and understood the description that the statue Pelaius had given them.

"Where are you all heading today?" Poseidon asked.

"We are taking our two friends here to the shores of Tundar then returning to Atlantis," Medios answered.

"I see, why do they carry King Titan's weapons with them?"

A bit embarrassed, "That is a longer story my Lord Poseidon," he stammered, "the fairy Queen Aaneesa dispatched them on an important journey, but they needed some special weapons to help them along their way. Our elder council spoke with them and approved this on the promise that they would return the weapons when they are finished with them."

The sea God with his piercing blue eyes gazed upon them and probably through them and asked, "Is that true young ones?"

"Every word is true," Rayne replied a bit shakily. "When we finish the quest we're on we promised the elders we would return these beautiful weapons back to Atlantis."

"So be it then, I will make sure that you reach the shore without any further problems and my Merpeople," he paused, "I will also see that you and my dolphins return safely back to Atlantis."

Looking over at the three dolphins Rayne could have sworn she saw what appeared to be a huge water hand caressing the backs of each one of them.

"Poseidon sir," her brother asked humbly, "can you actually do all of that?"

In a loud and commanding voice, one that suited his presence he said, "Of course I can, I'm Poseidon! King and Lord of these oceans," and with that he lifted his right arm up pointing the trident towards the surface, it created a massive bright bolt of yellow lightning which flashed upwards forcing everyone to shield their eyes. Everyone could feel the immense power unleashed in that one blast but when they opened their eyes the sea God had vanished.

The rest of their journey went by quickly as they swam over beautiful coral formations with every imaginable color of fish she thought possible but not a single shark was seen. Before they knew it they were in the shallow waters just off of the coast of Tundar so they headed to the surface for a quick look. It must have looked a funny scene, five heads sticking above the water looking to find their bearings. Now that his head was above water Raven noticed an immediate change in his breathing, it had started to become a bit labored instead of the smoothness he felt below the surface, he couldn't breathe the air right now.

While Aegeus focused on a distant point, the rest looked at other things, then they all submerged and Aegeus said to them, "Did you guys see the tree line I was pointing at?"

"Yes," I saw some palm trees close to the beach," Raven answered.

"That is where we're going to take you, you will be on the Southeastern coast of Tundar and will have to find your way to wherever you are going from there."

They swam for another five minutes and then their group stopped because they were in less than ten feet of water.

"Ok, my friends, please take care of yourselves," Medios said placing his hand on the shoulder of her brother in the Atlantean customary way, Aegeus did the same, but the mermaid gave him a quick hug.

"Be safe and take care of yourself," she said while hugging his sister, "also take care of your brother because we look forward to seeing you both very soon. You know where to find us now!"

"Yes, we do. Thank you very much, the three of you have been so nice to us, I hope in the future we can repay you all."

"Oh, and thank you too my friends," swimming over and hugging the three dolphins, "I think you are all very brave."

Raven said farewell to everyone and they turned and swam closer to the shore, "Listen sis, I'm not sure if we can carry these weapons as eagles so we'll just have to figure it out after we change back into our regular selves."

He was the first to surface and immediately thought to himself what form he wanted to become then casually walked out of the surf and onto the beach, but now he had a beautiful golden sword hanging at his side. Rayne exited the water with her Atlantean bow slung behind her back and from the beach they both looked out and waved at the three heads that were sticking out above the water that were their friends.

Chapter Nine

The Return To Land: A Broken Blade...

It was a little laborious walking through the deep sand, but eventually they made it up and over the dune to the other side where they found themselves standing in an immense field of low green grass with soft rolling hills in the distance. Off to the right was a huge tree where Raven suggested they head towards all the while though he was fiddling with his new sword and amazed on how it stayed in position on his right hip without falling.

"That was a great idea you had back there using the bow underwater, I didn't actually think it was going to work at first."

"Thanks, I don't why but the idea just came to me, can you believe we actually met Poseidon? I'm still stunned! Oh, and by the way, nice job of questioning his abilities," she snickered.

He picked up on her sarcasm and immediately shifted the conversation to another subject. "That lightning blast at the end nearly burned my eyebrows off." He glanced over at her and pretended to check that all of his little hairs were still intact. "I know that we still have a ways to go sis, but we need supplies so I think we should concentrate on finding a village so we can get cleaned up and maybe buy a couple of horses. Traveling by horseback will also help us to go through the mountains quicker and hopefully arrive at Bytar that much faster.

"Do you know of any towns around here?" She asked.

"No, what about you?"

"No, but I could change into an eagle again and search the area by air I think it will be much quicker like that don't you?"

"Definitely!"

"Raven, we haven't been back to Bytar in close to fifty years now and I'm pretty sure no one there remembers us."

"I know, I've been thinking about that too."

She continued, "I wonder how many things have changed since then? Hey, do you remember Findle? What a nice man he was, I didn't realize that we haven't been back there in so long."

"How much money do you have?"

"What, I don't know?" She snapped.

"Well, check and let me know."

She reached into the little pouch on her waste side and produced three copper and two silver coins. Rayne wore a long white, loose fitted shirt with long sleeves and a brown sash around her waist with loose pants, he wore a similar shirt but light brown in color with the sleeves pushed up past his elbows. They also had similar leather sandals with small leather straps that wrapped around their ankles. Their clothing was very typical for ancient times.

"I have one copper and seven silvers coins, that's more than enough to buy two horses, get some food, supplies for the road and clean up a bit."

"Buy horses?" She said dumbfounded, why don't we just change ourselves into centaurs or something and head for the red mountains now?"

"I've already thought about that. Do you remember the last time we were centaurs? We were almost killed! I think it's going to be safer for us to avoid them for now, and anyways, they usually stay hidden in the forests and mountains and we need to travel out in the open."

"Yes, well you might have a point there."

"I think it's going to take us a few days to reach the mountains and besides, we can travel by day and without any worries a lot less suspiciously if we're riding horses. Listen sis, if you want, once we get to there we can release the horses and pass through the mountains a different way or I can also change into a horse and you can sit on top of me. Personally, I like having them because they can carry the supplies we have and I'm not that crazy about you sitting on my back for several days complaining," he joked, but she didn't smile.

"Very funny, we'll decide when we get there then."

"Once we cross over the mountains we still have a few days through the desert and then we'll arrive at the Southern gates of Bytar. That might be another good reason to hold on to the horses because they can carry extra water for that stupid desert we have to trek through."

Rayne handed him her bow, looked up at the blue skies and prepared to leave, "Stay here and I'll change into an eagle and search for a village where we can get some horses." After transforming into her eagle form she gracefully lifted off of the ground and into the air, she turned her head to look back at her brother whose body was getting smaller and smaller as she flew farther away. "*Now to find a town,*" she thought, "I'll be able to glide over a great distance of land once I find a decent wind current."

She headed in a northerly direction along the coast, periodically making huge circles in the sky so her eyes could fixate on smaller sections of land. Some areas were huge green grassy fields while others looked to be tended wheat fields because they had symmetry and rows that a farmer would walk in and out of.

"There has got to be a village close by look at all of those people down there."

Finally she saw a small village, she could clearly see a few fishing boats off shore and the wind carried with it the aroma of smoke and cooked food so she circled back to where she left Raven standing by the trees. She had only been gone for about twenty minutes or so as she swooped down flapping her large wings casually landing under the shade tree and changed back into her human form. She was excited to give her brother the news of what she had found.

"I found a small village a few miles north of here just off of the beach."

"Great, that didn't take you long?"

"Nothing takes that long when you can fly over everything."

They wanted to walk to the village but instead of using the beach where they would have been spotted for a half mile in advance, they decided to walk on the grass past the dunes where they would have some cover by the trees. Small towns and villages were dangerous at times because of superstitious people stuck in places like these who are used to seeing the regulars and strangers are sometimes considered bad omens. After a half an hour of walking they started to see a few more people so Raven approached one of them to have a quick word.

"Is there a village up ahead sir?" He asked politely.

The man was holding a small basket with fish in it and barely stopped to answer the question, "Yes, keep walking in the direction you're going and you'll see it in a few minutes."

"Wow, that guy is lost in his own thoughts," he thought, "thank you sir."

When they arrived at the village he counted ten small buildings built out of logs with brown roofs made out of dried palm leaves. They walked up to the first hut noticing several horses that were tied up to a tree to their left side behind this home. A few huts to their right, sitting in the shade of some palm trees were several men with their shirts off watching them as they neared the front door. She had her bow lying across her back and King Titans' sword was hanging securely on the right hip of her brother. In the distance there were a few children playing in the ocean running in and out of the waves and just yelling and screaming having fun. The smell of cooked fish was heavy in the air as small pockets of wispy smoke floated into the air out of several of the huts.

A small boy of ten or so opened the door at the sound of them knocking, "Yes," the boy asked in a curt tone.

"Hello, can we speak to your mom or dad?" She asked.

"What do you want?"

"We would like to buy two of those horses behind your house. Are they yours?"

"No, they belong to our neighbor so try next door," then the boy shut the flimsy bamboo door in their faces.

"Ok," she said slowly, looking at her brother.

They walked around the house to the main road in the front to knock at this neighbor's house. There were several people sitting on logs in the front of some of the adjoining huts along with a woman who was beating some clothes with a stick that were hanging from a piece of rope that she had tied to two palm trees. Rayne casually looked to her right and saw that several of the men who were sitting at the tables were eyeing her brothers sword now because the sun was hitting it and making the gold and silver on it shine brightly.

"Raven," she whispered.

"What."

"Don't look, but those guys sitting over there are looking over here, I think they want your sword. The last thing we need now is trouble."

He glanced over to his right to see what she was talking about but she grabbed his left hand saying sternly, "I told you not to look and what do you do? You look."

"I'm sorry, it's just habit," he answered. "You say don't look and I look what can I tell you I'm an idiot! I saw them though and you might be right, I don't want any trouble either so let's try to get these horses and the few things we need for the road and we'll leave."

They arrived at the neighbor's house and knocked, a short, older man with a thick accent and bushy little eyebrows answered the door.

"Good afternoon," she continued, the boy next door said the horses behind his house were yours, is that right?"

"Yes, they belong me."

Slowly she asked, "We would like to buy two of them from you," holding up two fingers on her hand.

"How much you have?" The old man asked her loudly, rubbing two of his fingers together in her face.

"We can give you one silver coin for each horse but we also need a little food and we'd like to clean our clothes if possible."

"Those horses very good," the old man stressed to her loudly again for some reason. A small older lady from inside the house walked up behind the man and speaking in Greek started asking him what was going on. He told her he was trying to get a good price for selling two of the horses. Fortunately, the siblings both spoke Greek! There were many languages spoken in these times, but Greek is the most popular. Since they could speak his language they were now better able to settle on a reasonable price because the old man trusted them a little more. They settled on two silver coins for each horse. The old man said that he'd give them food for a week and they could get themselves cleaned up as part of the deal. A few hours later they felt as good as new, they had both eaten, clothes were clean and both horses were waiting for them out back.

"That is a marvelous looking sword."

"Thank you," Raven answered a little nervously, "I need to cover it with something it seems like it's attracting some unwanted attention."

"I might have something just for you, I don't know why but many years ago I made a leather sheath with a cover for a sword but I never used it because I don't even have a sword."

He yelled behind him to his wife, who moments later proudly brought out the soft brown leather sheath.

"I'm sorry it's a little dirty but try it out, I think it will be a perfect fit for that sword of yours and it has an adjustable strap you can tie around your waist or over your shoulder."

Raven held it up and discerned that it was about the same length as his sword was so he pulled the sword from his side and slide it into the sheath flipping the small leather cover over the top of the hilt.

"That's amazing it's perfect! How much do you want for it?"

"Take it," the old man exclaimed dismissively, "it has been laying around here for many years it's yours for free besides it seems that it was destined to be with that sword of yours."

"Thank you so much," his sister said, giving the old man a big hug.

Continuing to speak to them in Greek he showed them around back where the horses were tied up and instructed them to leave as soon as they could that there were a few trouble makers around and to avoid problems it would be best not to hang around any longer.

"It's going to be dark in a few hours, you need to ride for about an hour north and there will be a lake, you can rest for the night anywhere near it."

He bid them good luck and walked towards his home at the doorway he turned around, waved goodbye and then closed the door leaving them on their own again. Grateful for his help they stood in silence eyeing two stunning horses, one was white and the other brown.

"Which one do you want?" He asked.

"Definitely, the white one."

"Do you need me to help you up?" He started to say but she had already grabbed the reins and was hopping up on her horse.

"What did you say?"

He adjusted his new leather sheath to his waist and mounted his own horse then grabbed the reins while his horse walked left in a complete circle for no reason, "Never mind."

"Yah," he said with a small kick to the horses side. Both horses took off at a slow gallop through the grass behind the houses and once they were a little ways past the village he started talking again to his sister.

"How do you think that went?" She asked.

"I think it went great! We didn't run into any problems and we'll make great time traveling with these wonderful horses."

Keeping the red mountains in front of them as a reference they continued at this same pace for over an hour, there wasn't any actual road here so they rode through grass, wheat and even slowly through a field of tall sunflowers.

"Hey look sis, that must be the small lake the old guy was talking about."

"Really, the old guy?"

"Sorry, I can't believe we didn't even get his name."

Approaching a small clearing they slowed their horses to a walk and decided to tie them to a nearby tree, they dismounted and Raven went looking around for some fire wood while Rayne used stones to make a circle on the ground where their fire would be. They had stopped just in time because it was almost dark. Raven started a fire and with the aid of a small pan immediately started frying two small fish filets for dinner. With the exception of their small fire it was pitch black out, there were tons of stars in the sky so after eating they laid on their blankets and talked for a while.

"You're going to have to cover that shiny sword of yours with a cloth or something it's going to continue to attract unwanted attention."

"I already did that sis, once I got on my horse back there I put the leather cover over the hilt, by the way where is your bow?

"I have it right here next to me, believe me I'm not going to let it out of my site."

"Where's your sword?"

"Right here," sliding the hilt of the sword out from under his blanket, "go to sleep, I'll stay up for a while and keep watch. We probably have a good day and a half more of traveling before we reach the base of the mountains and then we can figure out how you want to proceed from there." He looked over at her but she was already asleep! The only sounds that he noticed were that of crickets and the occasional far off cries of wolves so the night passed very smoothly. She woke up early and it was already starting out to be a beautiful day, the sun had already started to rise and there were blue skies with no clouds in site.

"I'm going to take a quick swim but I'll take my bow with me so you can close your eyes for a little while longer and don't worry, I'll cook breakfast when I get back."

"Thanks sis."

He fell back asleep in an instant, in the meantime she made her way to the small beach to find a little quite spot to jump in. It seemed like only a few minutes had gone by when from the water she heard raised voices back by their camp so she swam back to shore quickly and started getting dressed.

"Where's that fancy sword of yours boy?" The first man who was standing in front of him demanded. He was being held from behind by a second man who forced him to stand. This man had his left arm tightly around his neck and in his right hand he held a dagger pressed against Raven's side.

"This guy's underarm smell is going to kill me!"

"It's not here by their horses," a third man yelled.

The first man responded angrily, "He's got to have it somewhere, now find it!"

He reiterated his question, "Where's that sword I saw you with yesterday boy?" Then punched Raven in the stomach doubling the teenager over and watched him gasp for air.

The second man, who was still holding onto him firmly started to laugh adding, "Where's that pretty girl you were with boy, I'd really like to talk with her a while?"

He was still coughing and trying to catch his breath from the punch to his stomach when he finally was able to stand up, just in time to witness the first man kick the blanket away and expose the beautiful silver blade and golden hilt of his sword. In the meantime, his sister had already gotten dressed and had crept up along the shore line of the beach. From her vantage point she could see that one guy was holding onto her brother from behind and two others were standing in front of him.

"There it is!" The first man exclaimed with happiness, "that beautiful piece of steel is going to bring me a lot of money."

He reached down, grabbed the hilt of the sword and tried to pick it up, but even after repeated attempts it only budged a few inches. Raven was scrutinizing the landscape trying to locate his sister, finally he saw her hiding behind a tree slightly off to his right. The same man kneeled down and with both hands grasped the sword and lifted with all of his might, his face turned red and knuckles were white, but the sword still only budged an inch.

"What's wrong with you? Just pick it up!" The second man yelled in disgust.

He haphazardly flung Raven to his left tossing him to the ground.

"Move away and let me try," he yelled.

Admitting defeat the red faced man finally released the hilt of the sword and stood up, but as the second man went to attempt to lift the sword for himself the third man unsheathed his own sword and pointed it at the him.

"What makes you think you get to go second?"

At that precise moment Rayne charged out from behind the tree and with an authoritative tone yelled at all three of the men.

"Get away from there Now!"

The three thieves spun around in surprise, they were not expecting to see the pretty teenage girl standing there, even Raven was surprised at hearing the commanding voice coming from her.

"Get away from that sword I said!"

He looked at her face and could tell that she meant business, but he used this opportunity to sneak back over the few feet to his sword, all he had to do was just grab it.

"Look here little girl," the first man said sarcastically, "we're just trying to have a little fun. Hey, we don't want no trouble little girl, we just wanted to look at that fancy sword of his, that's all."

All the while he spoke she saw that his hand was inching closer and closer to his belt where he had a small throwing knife hidden. All of a sudden Raven grabbed his sword and stood up. The third man, who already had his sword out, turned it to face him, but King Titans sword would not be defeated by a cheap piece of steel. He easily and smoothly swung the sword around cutting the man's sword at the hilt causing the useless blade to fall at his feet. At the same instant Rayne pulled her string back and produced another brilliant white arrow. Yelling the word "dagger" at the arrow she released the string as the man grasped his dagger and while raising his hand to throw it at her the arrow hit the dagger before it left his hand causing him to yell in pain and the dagger to fly backwards.

Her brother took control of this mess saying, " Get out of here! All of you, and don't come back here or the next time we will kill you!"

The men ran to their horses and jumped on them fleeing as fast as they could into the distance without even looking back at the brother and sister.

She ran up to him yelling, "Are you alright? Did they hurt you?"

"No, I'm fine, I'll live. Wow, you were amazing! I never knew you had that in you?"

She punched on his shoulder, "Next time don't underestimate me now let's get out of here before they return, we can eat later."

They were packed up in five minutes and back on the road towards the red mountains heading in the same direction as the day before but now they were making their way around the lake and up a small grassy hill. Only the chirping of birds and the horses hoofs on the ground disturbed the silence as they rode most of the morning without speaking to each other while the both of them were replaying the mornings events in their heads. His sister didn't want to run the horses too hard and he didn't feel the need to either so they were on a slow trot forward. There was a nice refreshing breeze blowing through their hair and hitting them in the face and even though the sun was up, the wind betrayed the fact that the weather was going to be changing. They could easily smell the rain in the air and see that many miles ahead grey clouds were starting to form and gain momentum. He stood up in his saddle and stretched his legs while turning back to look at her, "How are you doing?"

"I'm fine, can we stop and rest a bit? I could really use something to eat now."

They would soon be leaving the comforts of riding on green fields and could see some distance ahead of them the terrain would be changing to a more rugged and possibly rocky one. The closer they got to the mountains the bigger and more ominous they began to appear.

"Let's stop right up here," he said, indicating a nice little spot in the open with just a few skinny trees for a backdrop. She tied her horse up to one of the thin trees took out an apple from her saddle bag and with it in her open hand fed the hungry steed.

She began, "You know what? You could have been seriously hurt back there even killed! Why didn't you just change into a tiger or something and really give those idiots back there a good scare?"

I fell asleep when you left and the next thing I knew I was getting yanked up out of my sleep by that smelly guy. I know, I know, he caught me off guard."

"Do you think this is funny?" She snapped.

"Of course I don't, he also had the point of his knife jabbed into my right side here," pointing to his waistline, "I can still feel the point of it, I made a little mistake is all?" Displaying his two fingers indicating a little. "Thanks for your concerns sis, but I'd rather forget about it now."

"Fine," she huffed, "how about this, have you given any thought at all about how we are supposed to find a hidden book let alone tear one page out of it?"

"Nope! I don't know what to tell you," he replied bluntly.

"Think about it like this, two weeks ago we thought Atlantis was a myth and that Poseidon wasn't an actual person who could talk to us. As I see it, we are actually making history so maybe finding a book won't be as difficult as we think."

Closing his eyes he laid flat on his back on the grass and let the sun's rays soak into his face and body while she stood beside him looking at the scenery.

"This is really a pretty area, we have never been to this part of Tundar before and literally from where I'm standing I can see for miles in every direction."

Out of nowhere he asked the strangest question.

"Do you think these weapons will adapt to us?"

"What are you talking about?"

"I mean let's say I change into a wolf or small bird or something what will happen to my sword? I held onto your sword when you looked for the village last time."

With her hands uplifted and shoulders raised, "Honestly, I hadn't given that any thought."

He stood up, his sword still at his side closed his eyes and thought to himself what animal he wanted to change himself into, a moment later he transformed himself into a bluebird, something small he thought would be a good start. He looked up and saw her still standing there looking down at him, but he didn't see his sword at his side, nor did he feel the weight of it next to him. He changed back into his regular human form and checked for the sword at his side.

"That's weird."

"What's weird, what happened?" She asked curiously.

"I didn't see the sword at all that's why I changed back so quickly I thought something was wrong."

"Change into something larger this time," she insisted.

He closed his eyes again and a moment later there was a large black wolf standing next to her, he turned his head and as a joke growled, showing her his vicious teeth.

"Are you kidding me?" She yelled.

She knew it was him, but the fact is wolves were a sore spot for her like spiders or snakes are for other people and he knew that.

"Ok, he wants to play that game again?"

Closing her eyes she changed herself into a huge Bengal tiger and turned the tide on him by letting out a terrifying growl and showing him her teeth for good measure. Her point was made because seconds later he was back to being just her brother again. During their testing they hadn't noticed but the wind had picked up and dark clouds were really starting to move in on them. She changed back herself and scolded him, "What was that about? You know I hate it when you pull that kind of prank on me!"

"Sorry I couldn't resist. I'll have you know I still didn't see my sword by my side but it has to be there magically is all. Did you see or feel your bow?"

"No, but I was too mad at you to remember to look for it."

"So, that answers that, whatever animals we change ourselves into our weapons will still stay with us automatically."

Due to the changing weather the horses started making sounds and nervously moving around a bit, at the same time it started to rain very lightly.

Rayne headed towards her horse untied him from the tree and jumped up, "Great, that's all we need is rain, let's keep on moving it's only sprinkling for now, but it's probably going to start raining harder and we need to find someplace to camp for the night."

They started off again leading their horses down the moist grassy hill heading that much closer towards the mountains. After a few hours of constant riding they came to a small stream that ran horizontally in front of them causing them to halt for the moment.

He felt confident after visually inspecting it's depth, "The stream looks like it's not deep sis so I think we can cross it, just ride slowly."

After they both had crossed it something caught her eye so she motioned to him to look to his left, "Hey, what's that over there?"

The weather had gotten progressively worse, he raised his left hand up to his forehead to try to shield his eyes from the falling rain so he could effectively look in that direction.

"It looks like an old cabin, kind of broken down looking, but a lot of people build near the river not only for water but also for a food source."

"Well, I don't care, let's see if someone lives there because my clothes are soaking wet from riding in this rain for the past two hours."

They couldn't see any signs of activity, but still approached the cabin warily noting the fact that it was old, brown and grey looking and had somewhat blended itself ingeniously into the surroundings trees. Their green grass had long since gone, replaced by dirt, small rocks and a multitude of leafless trees that sprinkled the entire landscape. Their horses were just walking as they neared the front entrance of the cabin.

"Hello, is anyone home?" He announced.

"Try again," she insisted quietly.

"Hello, is anyone home?"

He dismounted and approached the front door while his sister choose to remain seated on her horse and watch his back.

Chapter Ten

The Cabin: Reuniting With An Old Friend...

There was a four foot post mounted in the ground in front of the cabin so they tied their horses to it and started looking around. Raven walked up to the front door and knocked which caused the partially opened door to open up a little further revealing mostly darkness and clutter inside the cabin. It wouldn't normally be dark for several hours, but due to the rain clouds it was decided to stay the night in the small cabin. They opened the door all the way and walked inside, there was an old bed in the corner along with a few small wooden chairs that were laying on their sides, a table and at the far end a fireplace. Raven walked straight towards the back to get a fire started, "I've seen worse," he joked.

After some cleaning up he had a decent fire going and the warmth of it could be felt throughout the tiny cabin. He went outside and removed the saddles from the horses and brought them indoors with the hopes of drying them off.

"Did you feed the horses?" She asked.

"No, well, not yet I mean."

She walked over and reached into her bag and grabbed a few more apples and carrots then walked outside, "Don't worry I'll do it."

While she was out there he changed into some dry clothes and placed his wet ones near the fireplace. When she returned he asked her, "How about stew for tonight?"

"Sounds good, I see you already changed out of your wet clothes so give me a few minutes to do the same."

He walked out front and waited for her to call him back inside, while out front he realized that the cabins roof overhang the front door by a few feet so he could stand out front without getting rained on. Going back indoors he retrieved the pot that was in his bag along with some vegetables, spices and a few pieces of dried meat the old man had given them and got started on the stew. He grabbed a chair to sit comfortably next to the toasty warmth of the fire while tending to their stew, "It's not a bad little place considering the small roof leak in the other corner," he commented. "I think it's been vacant for a while; I wonder who lived here and where they went to?"

"Who knows, sometimes people just pick up and go or they just die quite naturally it's impossible to say which one," she replied. "I was thinking I wish we could talk to Queen Aaneesa again, I'd like to ask her some more questions. By the way how long do you think before we reach the city?"

"I would say less than a week, we'll reach the mountains by tomorrow and then we'll see where we go from there. I wouldn't mind asking her a question or two myself," he added.

It was quiet for a bit until a lightning blast lit up the outside sky and the accompanying thunder shook every inch of their small cabin.

"Wow, good thing we found this place in time Raven, the storm has certainly gotten worse."

He pulled the pot away from the fire and prepared two bowls for them, "The stew looks to be about ready sis."

He handed her a bowl that she immediately placed to her nose to inspect while he sat there, eyes fixated on her for a decision, however, she was pleasantly surprised, "It tastes pretty good and at least it sounds like the rain is slowing down a bit."

With a sigh of relief and a mouth full of food he spoke, "That would be great because I'd like to sit out front for a little while." Once they finished eating he picked up his chair and started to carry it out through the front door.

"Come on it's nice out here, it's a little dark, but we can still see."

She walked out front carrying her own small chair and noticed that the horses looked to be asleep, "Yes, it is nice out but chilly I guess all the rain has dropped the temperature a bit so now I might actually need a jacket."

While they were discussing the next day's plans a small light from high above in the treetops close to their cabin caught their attention.

"What is that up there?" She asked curiously.

"I'm not really sure it almost looks like embers from a burning fire?"

They continued to watch the strange lights dance and flicker in the night sky.

"Raven, I don't think so the lights are actually getting lower," she paused to check her own answer, "oh I see now it's a bunch of fireflies."

The group of fireflies continued their slow decent from the tree tops down until they were hovering only a few feet above their heads.

"Wow, they're so pretty and small," she commented, "there's a lot more of them than I thought."

Several of the little light sources separated from the main group and floated down, almost right in front of their faces. She thought that watching fireflies was a little bit challenging because it always seemed like their flying was a bit erratic, like watching an old man's hands shake. One of the fireflies stopped bouncing and was now hovering perfectly still in front of them both. The tiny object started to get bigger and started to glow a little brighter until they had to put their hands up to shield their eyes from the light. There was a sudden gush of wind in their faces and when they lowered their hands Queen Aaneesa of the Fairies was standing there before them. Rayne jumped out of her chair and sprang forward in an attempt to hug her," That was incredible," but before she could complete her first step she realized she was frozen in place and could not move a muscle.

The queen said in a soothing voice, "You cannot touch me my guardians will not allow that, do you understand?"

"Yes," she managed to say, at least she could answer to her.

"Release her," the queen said softly and at that moment her foot finally touched the ground and she was able to move freely again.

"I'm so sorry, I'm just so happy to see you we were just saying that."

"Yes, I know," the queen answered.

"How do you know that?" Raven asked.

"That's not important now what is important is I'm glad to see you both remembered what I told you earlier about not trying to grab your new weapons and fly to Bytar that would have been a big mistake!"

"Yes, well it would have saved me from almost getting killed a day ago and getting rained on today."

"I never said there wouldn't be any dangers during this adventure and you will face more of them before this is all over, but I believe you both have the abilities and strength to overcome them all. Before you arrive at Bytar you will receive another helpful tool that will allow you both to locate the book, the tunnels below the city are vast and it's easy to get lost if you don't know where to look."

"How will we know what page in the book to tear out and destroy?"

She replied to his question with a smile, "I'm sure by that time you will know what to do. Tomorrow you will reach the mountains and several days after that the desert, I will watch over you as I can, but for now I must go."

"What?" So quickly but you just got here," Rayne insisted sadly.

"You both have power, if you need to you can choose to change into any animal you want or need to, remember the red moon eclipse will be upon us in less than two weeks that's all the time you have."

The queens body started to glow brighter again. They were going to raise their hands up to shield their eyes in anticipation of the brighter light they figured to come but before they could even raise their hands up there was another small gush of wind and the area where the queen was standing was now flooded by all of the fireflies that had been flying closely above. The queens light was now mixed together with thousands of other fireflies lights and in a few minutes the erratic bunch of lights had flown back up and into the tops of the trees and then quickly out of view.

Chapter Eleven

Crossing The Red Mountains: The Tree Spirits...

The wind picked up creating an eerie whistling sound through the nearby trees giving Rayne the chills.

"Did you hear the answers to any of your unasked questions?" She mocked, "I mean for someone who mentioned they wanted answers, I believe I only heard you ask one."

"Clearly she did most of the talking," defending his shyness, "but, to answer your question yes, she did! At least we're on the right track, I just hope I live to make it to Bytar."

"Don't be ignorant!" She snapped, "we'll both be fine and anyways, she's going to look out for us whenever possible so that's a great sign as far as I'm concerned. I'm tired and cold so I'm going to go back inside and set up my bedroll near the fire how about you?"

He turned his eyes and looked out into the darkness, "I'll be there in a few minutes sis I'm going to sit out here for a bit and think."

"Ok," she huffed, "well don't hurt yourself," then got up and walked into the cabin.

He stayed outside in his chair listening to her move items around inside of the cabin while he pictured what she was doing just from the sounds. He closed his eyes and began to drift hopelessly in his own thoughts, "I hope everything will be fine, I'm sure it will be, she's right though, I can't hesitate the next time I get into a fight. We have food for five days so we will be fine going through the mountains, but I might have to catch a few rabbits or fish along the way." The howls of distant wolves prompted him to open his eyes and made him realize that he had almost fallen asleep on the front porch. He stood up, yawned and stretched his hands above his head in a feeble attempt to touch the stars then turned and walked back inside to get his blanket. Raven shut the door quietly behind him and felt the warmth inside of the cabin embrace him like a friend. The bouncing yellow-orange flames of the fireplace were hypnotic and invited him to lay down and close his eyes. A last minute glance at his saddle told him that his bedroll was gone and she had already laid it out for him, but looked to be fast asleep near the fire. He walked over and got under his blanket, "Good night," he managed before the weight of his eyelids overpowered him. For whatever reason he woke up before Rayne this morning so he changed back into his regular clothes put on a heavier jacket and boots then saddled both of their horses.

"Wow, I can't believe you woke up before me? What happened, did you have a bad dream or something?"

"No, I just couldn't sleep any more, I don't know I feel fully rested is all."

After breakfast they were off, it was a sunny day and the weather was cool there were blue skies with assorted white, small pillow-like clouds slowly making their way in front of them. The horses felt strong and rested as they trotted forward over the hard ground. There were hundreds of round patches of high brown grass mixed in with the small rocks and dirt that made up the road before them. They had never passed through the red mountains before so they didn't know exactly what to expect besides cooler weather. The mountain range consisted of five small to medium sized offset mountains with a valley and river flowing between them like a giant snake making its curvy way through. They rode all morning without any problems. On either side of them stood the mountains they are large, rocky topped sentinels of time blocking any and all potential cross winds that would have helped them detect far off sounds. Due to the uneven ground and especially with the rocks being somewhat slippery and the wide river they kept the horses at a slow pace Raven felt it would be safer not to try to run them and break a leg by accident. He gently walked his horse through the shallow water to cool him down a bit and said, "I guess the river we crossed over yesterday comes down from these mountains and just curves down throughout the entire land, it might even end up in the ocean at some point?"

There were thousands of green pine trees running along the river and up the sides of the mountains. The tops of the mountains looked to be much more rugged and rocky, similar to some of the larger rocks they were riding by now that were dark, odd shaped and sharp.

"Do you really think this could run all the way to the ocean?" She said questioningly.

"I don't see why not."

Raven stopped and jumped down from his horse while she trotted hers on by him, "Why are you stopping?" She slowed down and turned back to observe what he was doing.

"I just wanted to jump down for a minute and stretch, besides I think my horse is thirsty."

"I wonder why they call these the red mountains sis? There's nothing red about them that I can see."

She huffed, "I have no idea? People give names to all kinds of stupid things like boats, swords and even their animals. If I ever get a dog or cat in the future I think I'll just call him "dog" to be different than everyone else."

Raven continued to fill his water pouch, "Yeah, that's not stupid."

She was about to respond to his sad excuse for whispering, but heard a branch break from her left side near the tree line. She turned her head to look and scrutinized the approximate area but couldn't see anyone or anything moving.

Raven was crouched down looking into the water while filling his water flask, "We should eat in an hour or so don't you think," With no answer he looked up and saw that she was repositioning herself in her saddle and intently looking at the tree line.

"What's wrong?" He asked.

"Didn't you hear that branch break a few minutes ago?"

"No, I couldn't hear anything with the sounds of the water by my ears. Do you think someone is there?"

She turned her attention back to the trees. He remembered what he had told himself last night about not procrastinating and trying to take the initiative so he walked over and handed her the reins, "Hey, hold onto my horse.

"What do you think you're doing?"

He didn't answer he just winked at her then changed himself into a black wolf and immediately took off towards the trees.

"Raven!" She yelled after him, but it was too late in a matter of seconds he had disappeared into the tree line. Several tense minutes later she saw him exit but from a different spot than he had entered. Raven transformed back to his regular self while he was several hundred feet away from them and then walked the rest of the way.

"What happened? Did you see anything?" She said frantically.

"There was something there I'm sure of it. I found the broken branch on the ground, but I couldn't find any footprints coming or going just one set of prints in a stationary spot.

"Hmm, that's weird."

"I went up the hill a bit and searched but didn't find anything. I don't know who or what it was so we'll just have to pay a little more attention to our surroundings as we move on."

He grabbed the reins from her, climbed back upon his horse and patted his neck saying, "It's ok boy, it's ok, Let's go sis."

They continued walking their horses along the side of the river and over some long sections of green moss and grass. Up ahead on the left the tree line came to a point at the spot where the river had a bend going in the same direction. They could either make another river crossing there or just follow the rivers lead around the trees and straight from there. They decided another river crossing wouldn't be the best idea because the river was over one hundred feet wide at this point and they couldn't judge the depth of the water. Raven dismounted, grabbed the reins of both horses and tied them around a huge rock then looked up at the sun, "It's got to be about two o'clock by now so what do you say, stop here, eat something and rest for a while.

"That's fine," she said.

"I feel like eating some fish for lunch, how about you?"

She stood on the river bank with her hands on her hips, "Are you going to catch them?"

"Of course," he turned and casually walked over to his horse to get a few items from his bag, then inspected a few trees until he found a suitable branch from one then he then cut it off along with the little branches that were attached to it. He made a sharp point at one end of it with his knife then walked over to the river with his new spear and waded into the water to wait for an unsuspecting trout. After several misses and missteps on the slippery rocks he finally had his catch and headed back to the bank; he cleaned them and with a satisfied grin walked up to her to present his prize while she was tending their small fire.

"Yeah ok, don't say it," she said sarcastically taking the fish from him.

Making use of the nice weather he took out his blanket and used it as a pillow to grab a quick nap. The soothing sound of water running over rocks and the minor breeze that he felt was a natural sleeping aid so after eating they were able to rest for over an hour peacefully. Once they were ready, packed up and the fire put out they continued along the path of the river, there was a few hours of daylight left and they wanted to at least make it past the end of the second mountain by nightfall. At this point the trees had started growing a bit closer to the river's edge, the terrain had also changed again which only left them about fifty or sixty feet of a rocky, pebbly beach on either side. Instead of the wide flowing river they had grown accustomed to seeing the last several miles it had also narrowed to a mere fifty feet or so. They continued riding along slowly discussing the earlier events of the broken branch in depth, unfortunately without coming to any real conclusions.

As darkness approached he asked, "Do you think we should camp out in the open close to the river or closer to the tree line?"

"I'd rather be closer to the trees so at least we have some protection in case we get another secret visitor. We are going to have to be more careful in this mountainous forest because if my ears didn't deceive me I thought I heard the howls of wolves last night."

"Oh, you heard that," he stammered.

"Of course I did, I don't fall asleep as soon as my head hits the pillow as you might think. She trotted her horse by him, "By the way you're welcome."

"*What a smart-aleck,*" he thought realizing that she wasn't asleep after all when he laid down and went to bed last night.

"How about over there Raven, that looks like a good spot," but without waiting for his answer rode over towards the left and shortly dismounted from her horse.

"Ok, it looks good," even though he thought there was still enough daylight they could have ridden for a little while longer. It was a decent spot being situated with trees all around them but still having a great view of the river in front. He tied up the horses and gathered a bunch of firewood while she prepared their typical ring of rocks that their fire would burn inside of, but this time they piled the rocks up a little higher than normal to try to hide the fire as much as possible. During the day they had heard and seen plenty of animals including: birds, deer and elk, but nighttime in a dark forest was usually a little different, that could bring quiet sleepy times or keep you up all night with a bunch of spooky, weird unknown noises. More than once they had been elated by the fact that they have the magical gift of being able to change into and talk with other animals, it meant that they could always defend themselves and go anywhere without that fear of the unknown. While eating Raven suggested changing back into a wolf so he could patrol around their campsite after they were finished, she insisted on going with him, "I love the eyesight that wolves have at night, it's so clear and besides it'll give us the chance to cover double the ground in a shorter amount of time."

"That's fine with me I know you can handle yourself." Although he always worried about her this was one battle he would not win.

So as not to spook their horses they walked a little distance away before transforming into wolves; Raven of course, was the black wolf she always favored her grey colors more. With barely a sound they took off at a slow pace, smelling and looking for any signs of people around but they didn't find anything on their side so they decided to cross the river at a shallow point and thoroughly scour the other side. A light rain had started to fall and with that came the accompanying clouds, beautiful intermittent flashes of lightning and distant rumbling of thunder It was going to be an uncomfortable night for the both of them. Over the years they had become very proficient at being certain animals more so than others, but the eagles and wolves were their favorites. Without finding a thing so far Raven asked, "So what do you think?"

"I don't see or smell anyone around," she replied.

"Neither do I."

Suddenly, they heard a wolf's howl from the distant trees.

"That came from up higher in the mountains on this side of the river," she tried looking up the mountain and through the trees but that was impossible with this thick forest and foliage. "We know that call is to locate other wolves of their pack."

Soon a second, third and fourth howl was heard further away up the mountain, they both turned their heads in the direction of where they came from.

"They're hunting something," he said, "let's get back down to the shore and go back across the river to our camp before they get our scent and we end up with a big problem. I do not want to have to worry about you and dealing with a pack of wolves we both know they can be very nasty to deal with sometimes."

They headed back down the slope and crossed back over the river to their own side changing before they got close to the horses so as not to make them whinny. Rayne approached them reassuring them both that everything was going to be ok. They decided to take turns keeping watch during the night in case the wolves crossed over the river and got too close to their camp.

***

The leader of the pack was a white wolf called Rakai. He was a formidable foe with great tracking skills as you might expect from a wolf but with the power of the sorcerers amulet even this proud leader was no match for the evil that was now taking control of his mind. Unbeknownst to the other wolves as they closed in on their prey, which was a massive buck, their leaders mind was already under the control of Nicias.

"Stop!" Rakai said firmly to his pack. "Forget about this paltry meal! There are two humans not far away that will make a more delectable feast."

The other nine wolves were crazy eyed, hungry and their hearts were beating wildly from the chase, they looked at each other for guidance as they came to a stop due to the sudden lapse in decision making from their leader.

"He's getting away," one wolf said, "we are right on top on him why are we stopping?"

Rakai turned his body stiffly towards his lieutenant Akir, the wolf who had spoken out and with his fangs showing and a nasty snarl said to him fervently, "Because, I said so! You will do as I say is that clear," as he took a few steps towards him. Like all wolves in a pack Akir knew his place so he backed up a step, bowed his head in submission and no longer challenged his leader. "They can't be far away so signal when you get their scent, now find them!" Rakai commanded. The pack spread out in all directions as ordered not even questioning the fact of how he even knew there were two humans in the area in the first place.

***

"I'll take the first watch, it's no problem."

"Are you sure?" Rayne asked.

"Yes, I'm sure, I'm not tired at all," he sat on the ground and placed another small piece of wood on the fire then raised his hands up to warm them. Looking up at the sky and amidst the millions of stars he noticed for the first time the crescent moon; the light pitter-patter sounds of rain hitting the ground blended in well with the rhythmic trickling sound of the river.

"Look at her, she already looks to be asleep, but I don't even know any more if she really is or isn't, she could by lying there just watching me," Raven thought.

He heard a howl from across the river but it sounded to him to still be a ways off so he didn't give it too much concern.

She laid there under her own blanket thinking, "Look at him, he's oblivious to the world around him. He probably thinks I'm sleeping. I should just get up and slap him on his head."

***

The wolves immediately gathered around the one who had found the scent.

"What have you found?" Ordered the white wolf.

He answered subserviently, "I found some tracks and the scent of two other wolves not humans, they head down to the river, but these wolves are unknown to us."

"That's them!" Rakai growled, immediately taking off down the hill following this new scent. The others, happy to be back on the trail of something turned and followed their leader without hesitation, finally gathering at the at the bank of the river.

"They crossed over at this point, Let's go."

***

Continuing his command of the wolfs actions Nicias sat in the middle of his dark room cross-legged, his eyes were closed as in a trance while grasping onto his red glowing amulet with one hand. He could see everything that was happening through the eyes of his pawn, Rakai.

***

Rayne was startled out of her brief sleep, "Did you hear that?" She whispered.

"I thought," he started to say.

She slid out from under her blanket and raised her finger to her lips, "Shhh," she mouthed to her brother. At this exact same time the horses started whinnying and lightly digging their hooves around nervously in the soft dirt while turning side to side at some unknown presence.

"They're here!" She said, then quickly transforming into her grey and black wolf just in time to see the imminent danger they were both in. Witnessing his sister transform so quickly startled him so he immediately did the same. He looked around and realized his grave mistake too late, the wolf pack had been slowly and meticulously closing in on their position and had surrounded them. The hypnotic sound of the rain had given them an advantage, cleverly and patiently they disguised themselves well enough to avoid detection. From out of the trees Rakai slowly emerged and walked towards them teeth partially showing, "Who are you two?" He growled. "We do not want any trouble," Rayne answered politely. She was frightened by their current predicament but was also upset by her brother's lack of attention and putting them both in this huge mess. "We are just passing through and mean you no disrespect at all, we are not hunting on your land and we will be gone by tomorrow," she answered.

At this point, they didn't display any signs of aggressiveness towards the pack. The three of them stood there poised looking at each other as a second and third wolf came into view on their sides and two more appeared from behind them.

"I said who are you?" Growled Rakai.

Feeling like the situation was getting a little out of control Raven answered, "We are humans and have the ability to transform into other animals and like she said we are just passing through and mean you no harm." In the background they could hear the other wolves growling and starting to lick their lips in anticipation of fresh meat. Raven saw that the time for diplomacy was almost over and the time to fight was upon them. Rakai's eyes started to glow bright red and stood out among the darkness of night. A massive lightning blast finally set the tone, the temporary light from it showed several other wolves around them eager to pounce. "Did you really think that the both of you would make it to Bytar alive?"

Showing his long fangs he said, "You will never take my book!"

At that the siblings had had enough and in a split second the white wolf was looking up at a huge male lion. Feeling like there was no way to avoid the fight Raven had transformed himself into a huge lion, his protective mode was in high gear now and if he was going to fight he was going to kill as many of them as possible. His sister changed into a Bengal tiger and was ready for the battle. Raven arched his back and let out a terrible roar showing his larger teeth, in shock Rakai took a few steps backward contemplating a retreat but Nicias had other plans without a choice the white wolf leapt forward with everything he had and attacked but before he knew what had hit him Raven gave him a mighty slap knocking Rakai backwards and into a tree. His sister spun to her left and with a roar smacked an incoming wolf with her huge claws, tearing deep scratches across his face and causing him to twist and fall to the ground yelping in pain. A third wolf leapt at Raven but he had anticipated this foolish move and with his massive body hit him so hard he knocked him back several feet, lifeless into the dirt. As more lightning flashed above their heads Raven turned around to see three more wolves coming at him, one jumped on top of his back while another was trying to tear at his back legs. He spun around again quickly forcing the one on top of him to fall then grabbed onto his throat with his fangs and tore the life from him speedily flinging the dead body aside. He felt a nip at his heels so in turning to address it he witnessed his sister tearing away at another wolf with several others around her. The ground was slippery and he wanted to get to her as fast as possible but during the attempt and out of nowhere several of the nearby tree branches came crashing down on them like an anvil causing everyone to become disorientated. While they were trying to figure out what was happening a second barrage of branches thumped the remaining wolves sideways and to the ground. This being too much for what they bargained for the remainder of the pack, with the exception of the white wolf all scattered and ran back across the river. Rakai made a final run at Raven but with his front claws extended he pounced on top of the lone wolf pinning him securely to the ground. Rayne called out to her brother not to kill the wolf but he was so enraged at this point it took all she had to stop him. She focused her attention upon the sad creature laying at his feet watching as the bright red in his eyes disappeared and became a yellowish color, "I think someone else was controlling him."

Raven grabbed him by the throat with his paw and viciously roared into his face, showing him who was actually in charge; he flung him backwards then watched him stagger to his feet, look back at the huge lion, then run away back across the river confused and not knowing how he even got there. They both changed back and Raven ran over to check on how she was, "Are you hurt?"

While catching her breath she held up both hands, "Yes, I'm fine. What the hell was that all about? He knew we were going to Bytar and about the book."

"I can only guess but I'm sure that sorcerer is behind all of this," he muttered.

Suddenly, ghostly apparitions that looked like a blurry type of people materialized from many of the neighboring trees and into their view for the first time. The greenish wispy beings stood there quietly staring at the brother and sister for a few moments while the siblings stood in place completely dumbstruck.

"We are tree spirits," one said.

"Every tree in the world has a spirit of its own."

"We do not feel pain, love or hate."

"We nurture ourselves and other trees around us."

"The fairies asked us to watch over you both."

"Thank you for your help," she said inquisitively.

"We will safeguard you through the mountains so you do not need to worry about any more wolves or beasts while you are here. This will not be the last time you speak to us."

Like wispy plumes of smoke they vanished as quickly as they appeared.

"Where did they go?" Rayne asked.

"You're asking me? I'm not even sure what the hell we just saw! I know one thing for sure, without their help we would of had a longer fight on our hands, they had great timing. I think it's also pretty safe to say if this sorcerer Nicias the queen told us about is behind this attack we can probably expect more. Although, after this defeat it might be a while before he figures out his next move."

He looked over towards the horses and was very happy to see that they had calmed down and were no longer pulling vigorously on their reins.

"We should try to get some sleep now. I don't think we need to waste time keeping a watch for the remainder of the night with these tree spirits doing that for us. Come on now," patting the ground with her hand, "come lay down and rest."

He stood there for a minute and finally dropped his shoulders at not being able to think of anything clever to say. The scene, so violent and action packed minutes earlier had now gone back to being quiet and still except for the same rustling of wind through the trees and sounds of falling rain. After moving the dead wolves from the immediate area they finally tried to get some rest. Raven looked up at the night sky and focused his attention on one of the brighter stars. He was now lying down on his back and thought about what all of the other little white dots up there were until he fell sound asleep.

He awoke to the smell of smoke in the air and opened his eyes to see Rayne sitting a few feet away from him relaxing and eating a red apple. The clouds from the day prior had fortunately given way to the sun and blue skies with hardly a cloud in sight.

"What time is it?" He asked.

"About ten, you were really tired I guess?" She answered with a strange alertness about her. "The horses are ready so after we eat we can go."

Yawning his Ok, "Have you heard any noises at all from the wolves?"

"Nope, not a sound."

After breakfast they cleaned up their area and were kneeling down next to the river bank washing their hands and the pan she had used to cook with when she said, "What's' wrong with the river? It looks like the water here is slowing down."

He quickly yanked his hands out of the cool moving water and noticed the same strange thing. Miraculously, the water just in front of them started to form into something before their eyes. They both stood up and jumped back a bit as the water continued to form and grew into the shape of a man. The strange water man spoke to them, "Come over here please." Raven stumbled backwards on the smaller wet rocks and held out his right hand to grab onto Rayne's left hand then yanked her back behind him. Standing in front of them both was a man completely made out of water, he was about six foot tall and you could clearly see that the river was still coursing throughout his body as well as flowing by him like a normal river does.

"You must be Raven and Rayne," the water man asked.

"Yes," she answered now standing alongside her brother.

"My name is Kishtar, and I have been sent to bring you a gift from the sea God Poseidon himself."

"Really?" She replied.

"Please give me your left hands," the water man asked politely.

They were both a bit hesitant a first to offer up their hands so eagerly to this messenger in front of them thinking maybe it was another attack of some kind from Nicias.

"I will not harm you! Give me your left hands," he asked again.

This time he saw positive results as two shaky hands came forward per his request. His touch on your skin was absolutely no different than putting your own hand under running water.

"I placed onto both of your thumbs a ring with special properties," as he gently released both of their hands he said.

They both examined their hands at length, turning them from side to side but really couldn't see anything special at first.

"I don't see anything," she said slowly.

Rayne twisted her hand around at different angles then held her hand up towards the sky and began to see the faint appearance of a ring at the base of her left thumb especially when the clouds gave way to the sunshine. There it was, unbelievably, the tiny circular colors of a rainbow only visible with the aid of sunlight and at the precise angle.

Curiously she asked the shimmering water shape, "What kind of a special ring is this?"

He quickly replied to her, "This ring will allow each of you to temporarily change into any form of water if choose to do so. During that time you will have total consciousness, you will be able to move effortlessly and can float as a mist or go through cracks in a wall. In a time of emergency you need only think about what type of water form you want to become and it will happen but beware, the magic of these rings is temporary. This magic can only be used until the end of the red moon which gives you less than two weeks from today. After the eclipse the rings will disappear and completely and the spell will be gone for now.

"I don't know what to say," Raven replied.

"Thank you very much and please tell Lord Poseidon the same," she replied.

Kishtar signaled to them with a small bow of respect then started to dwindle down again into the stream and disappear when Raven suddenly remembered something that he desperately wanted to ask their watery friend.

"Excuse me sir. How did you ever find us way up here in these mountains?"

The man's shape became full again so he could answer the question.

"Earlier when you placed your hands in the river to wash them that's how I found you. I was instantly able to sense you. Lord Poseidon also says to tell you that the river does in fact reach all the way to the ocean," as he silently shrank back down to into the river and disappeared from their sight.

"Well, I won't be doubting him anymore," Raven mumbled to himself. "Let's get going."

"Is that all you have to say about what just happened?" She asked.

He turned back around, "What am I supposed to say to that? It seems like every day more and more incredible things are happening to us. I thought the last hundred years or so with our ability to change into different animals was an oddity not to be topped, but look how wrong I was."

The trees at this part of the valley had grown closer to the shore but after several more miles on horseback they started growing again farther away from the river. The ground had changed from rocks to a brown sand so they were able to trot the horses along at a quicker pace. It was turning out to be a cloudier day today than they expected. The sunshine was poking through the clouds periodically now and again and that displayed a range of yellow and orange bushes to the left of them growing between some of the trees. For the next two days they were able to ride along without a single problem. By the end of the second day they had come to the beginning of where the river flowed down into the valley while continuing straight a bit then curving to the right and it looked like it kept on going around the mountain and out of their view. They rode straight for a mile or so past the curve in the river to where the ground had leveled out some giving them the chance to see for miles ahead. Unfortunately, the only thing they could see was the beginning of a vast desert which looked barren and treeless.

Chapter Twelve

Dinner in The Desert: The Nomad...

Raven stood up in his saddle, squinted and peered straight ahead to see if his eyes were playing tricks on him.

"What are you looking for?" Rayne asked him.

"You know what I'm looking for, something anything that we could use to help us through that," pointing his finger into the vastness of the open desert ahead of them.

"We have food for what three days now if we're lucky? Not to mention the fact that we have not only ourselves to feed but our two horses. Just how long will we last with only four leather bottles of water for all of us? Unless of course, we stumble into another flowing river out there," he said sarcastically.

"Wait a minute," he said.

"What is it?"

"Hold on, let me think for a second. I think I have a good plan that'll allow us plenty of time to get through this desert and also have enough water that you'll be fine."

"What do you mean I'll be fine. What about you?"

"I know that I kind of messed up back there with the wolves you don't have to tell me, I had heard something but thought it was nothing."

"You didn't mess anything up Raven! We are not perfect, we can only do what we can that's why mom and dad always talked to us about teamwork and helping each other out. I don't want you to think that way anymore."

"I know, but you could have been seriously injured back there."

"But I wasn't. Now, what's this idea of yours?"

"As much as I don't want to do this I know it will work. I think we should ride back to where the river starts turning and from there we could ask the tree spirits to take care of our horses. What I mean is you could change yourself into a horse, then talk to our horses and tell them to head back the way we just came from and go back to their master on the beach, you know the old man."

"What's that going to do for us?" She asked curiously.

"Here me out. I don't know if my standing there talking to a tree is going to work or not but I'm pretty sure they will hear us. We take our stuff off of the horses and organize it all to fit into two sacks or something then I'll change myself into a camel! I can go to the river and drink enough water to last me a long time in the desert. We also don't have to travel the whole time. We can start early in the morning just before sunrise travel for a few hours then make a camp to get away from the sun then start out again in the late afternoon until sunset."

He heard her voice distinctly mumble the word, "Hmm."

"Think about it, if we both head out there on the horses even loaded down with as much water as we can carry how far will we go before we run out? They need water just as much as we do and they have been great with us so far so it'll be better for all of us if we just send them back and move on like this. What do you think of my idea?"

She sat on her horse thinking for several minutes trying to come up with some better options of her own or at least to discover the usual loop holes in his logic. "Maybe he has a point this time," She thought. "I think it's an excellent idea. Worrying about one person during the day is probably better than worrying about four, the two of us and the horses. Anyways, as I look out there into the desert I see plenty of tall cactus' and thousands of green and white bushes so I'm sure during the heat of the day I'll be able to find some shade to hide under. Let's turn the horses around and we'll make camp tonight back at the river and get everything ready for an early start tomorrow."

"So you think it will work?" He said surprised.

"Yes, I think it will. We have never gone into a desert before, and if you remember the last time we were in Bytar we traveled there by boat up that river. Do you remember?"

"Of course I do," he nodded.

They turned their horses around and rode back to where the river started it's curve around the last mountain arriving at a nice spot close to the bend in the river. He took out his trusty spear for the last time to catch a few fish for dinner while she removed the gear from the horses. Over dinner they discussed their travel plans for the upcoming day and they noticed that they had enough food for only two more days which included several carrots, potatoes, apples and also two pieces of salted meat.

"Raven, if you're ready I'll transform myself into a horse and speak to our horses while you try to speak to the tree spirits, be sure to ask them to keep watch over them so they make it safely back through the valley."

"I will."

He walked away from her and stood in front of a group of trees. "Excuse me," he started to say to the tree, "I feel like such an idiot standing here," he thought. "Tree spirits, if you can hear me I'm asking for your help once more please look after our two horses and make sure they make it back through the valley safely, they are good horses and are just looking to make it back to their master." He approached the closest tree in front of him and placed his hand on it, "If you are listening, thank you for everything."

Rayne was already sitting at the camp by the time he returned from having his one-way conversation with the trees.

"How did everything go with you?" She Inquired.

"Fine, I guess. They didn't make any kind of appearance like the last time and even though I said please I still got nothing from them."

"It doesn't matter. I'm sure they heard you and everything will be fine. Our horses were to say the least, surprised to see another horse but happy about going back instead of forward through the desert. They did have something interesting to say though."

"What's that?

"There are supposed to be some dangerous nomads that live alone out in the desert, they don't believe that they are bad just that they travel by themselves and enjoy the solitude I guess, who knows."

He looked up at the stars and saw what he feared, the moon is almost half now."

She joined him in looking up, "Don't worry we'll make it in time. In the morning you go over and drink as much water as you need from the river then we'll load up at sunrise and be on our way."

Just as promised she was up early had dispatched the horses on their way back and was making a few final touches to their bags. She had four leather pouches full of water and had wrapped her head with a large white cloth to try to reduce the effect of the sun. While she sat there waiting for her brother to return from the river she went over her plans one more time.

"When he returns he'll kneel down, I'll load up our stuff, jump up on top of him and we'll continue walking northwest like we've been doing the whole time. When it's gets too hot I'll tap his side which is our signal to stop and rest then we'll wait for the sun to go down a bit then start again." Seeming satisfied so far she cast her attention on what was taking her brother so long.

Fifteen minutes had passed and she was starting to worry. She could see him in the distance knees on the ground and his head lowered into the water but she figured, how much water could he actually drink? Finally, his head popped up from the river and he was finished. He slowly made his way over kneeled down next to the gear which then allowed her to load their items on top of him and once she had everything ready she jumped up, got comfortable and slapped his side. Raven slowly stood up and headed into the desert. Thankfully, this desert was not a barren wasteland.

The usual lonesome scene of miles and miles of sand hills that the winds have battered on either side seemingly don't exist here. This is a beautiful place full of life; it contains many different kinds of plants, animals and even a few people who make their homes here. While he was making his way further and further into the desert he began to admire the four legged animal he had changed himself into. He had been walking for several hours and even though he tried to avoid stepping on many of the bushes sometimes it was inevitable. He realized that he hadn't really given it a lot of thought this choice of animal other than the fact that they didn't require a lot of water, but it was turning out to be a better decision than he could have hoped for. As he walked along he noticed that he had two large toes but only left a huge single footprint in the hard sand. This place was composed of hard dirt rather than the typical soft beach sand where he figured walking through it was going to be a laborious task with every step. He was able to make decent time while at the same time not feeling the least bit tired with the weight of his sister and their bags on his back. Meanwhile, Rayne was comfortably sitting atop her new perch nestled on a soft spot she found on the one hump of her brothers back. She was observing the landscape from a different perspective than he was. She hoped that this plan of theirs would result in them reaching the end of this desert in only two or three days at the most.

The terrain was not completely flat, there were small dirt hills on her left and right but what she was really paying attention to was the variety of plant life, including several different types of cactus. She was no cactus expert for sure but did recognize the familiar tall, green, rounded cactus' with the typical long finger stretching up with two to four other fingers branching out and up from the main one. Some or most of these cactus' were very tall, maybe eight to ten feet high while others of the same type were only just stubs sticking out of the ground two or three feet at most. The most curious looking cactus had small red bulbs growing out of the top of these flat green prickly pads. This variety of cactus grew as a huge prickly bush with no organization at all but to Rayne these little red, egg shaped bulbs gave it all the character it needed so she made a mental note that if she ever had time she'd investigate them further. It was about ten o'clock because the sun wasn't directly over her head yet and she had only taken a mouthful of water so far. Speaking to her brother was impossible now while he was a camel and she was a human so she'd have to manage the silence. Fortunately, she was still amazed at the amount of color here in this desert. There were loads of small bushes with yellow, purple or white flowers decorating their tops but there were also these fast-flying little red birds that had somehow managed to make nests on top or on the sides of the larger tall cactus'. Occasionally she would hear some movement at their feet like an animal running from bush to bush but she was never able quick enough to see what it actually was. There wasn't any kind of a breeze to speak of and the sun was beginning to take a toll on the top of her head so she decided that it was time to stop and rest. Rayne tapped him on his side with her feet so he stopped and slowly turned his head around to look at her; she pointed to the ground and he got the message to stop. Going to one, then two knees, then all four she hopped off and was finally able to rub her legs and walk around a bit.

Raven did not plan to change back into his human form until night time when they would eat dinner and discuss how the day had gone. Rayne took out an apple, some water and then her blanket so she could tie one end to her brother who was just standing there and carefully tie the other end to a tall cactus, this way it would give her some shade to rest under until the sun went down. She cleared a small area in the dirt under the shade and sat down to rest. It certainly was quiet out here that's for sure. The sun was still making it's slow march across the sky while above the few white clouds that did exist didn't have much of a chance to release any rain on her. Sitting in the shade made a huge difference to her overall wellbeing and it also allowed her some valuable time to think about what they were going to do once they reached the city of Bytar. Several hours had passed and without realizing it she had fallen asleep. After waking up and getting her senses together some movement by her foot peaked her curiosity, puzzled she pulled out a small knife that she carried at her hip and slid her foot over a tad. While traveling in the mountains they had both changed from their sandals to some warmer boots because it was so cold at night but since leaving them they had gone back to wearing their sandals and had to be careful about the sharp thorns on the cactus'. This was no cactus though! It was a small bug of sorts with a tail that curled up and over its back and fostered a nasty, sharp point at the end, it also had two large claws in the front that looked very similar, she thought it resembled a small lobster from the ocean.

"How could a creature like this live so far away from the water," she wondered. She quickly backed her foot away from this strange little creature and then used the point of her knife to gently poke it. With a quick strike of its pointy tail the insect struck at her knife tip giving her a clear message that it was time for them both to leave. Rayne stood up and used the front of her sandals to dig into the sand just in front of it and kicked the insect far away from her. After taking another small sip of water she untied her makeshift shade and packed it away then approached her camel using only her arm motions, "Ok, Raven it's time for us to go."

He couldn't understand a single word that she was saying but did get her point. She climbed back up and into her spot then tapped him again at his side he slowly stood and started to move forward again through the desert. They left a bit earlier than she would have liked to have but more importantly the suns heat wasn't that bad now. She wrestled with her thoughts but was glad to be gone from that particular resting spot because who knows what could have happened if she had been stuck in her foot by that defensive little insect. When nighttime fell she'd make sure to tell him about this close call and give him a warning about that scary looking bug. She enjoyed looking at the many different colored bushes and shrubs by their feet but her mind was constantly drifting to thoughts of if she would feel comfortable at all sleeping on the ground anymore. Maybe due to the sheer boredom of sitting on top of her camel she didn't care but what she did care about was the sun seemed to dart across the sky more quickly now. The ground had changed to a white colored sandy dirt with a lot of almost, orangish colored dried up bushes around. There were larger open areas of sand with large on the ground with no bushes around at all that's the exact area she was looking for to make camp. Rayne had no idea of how many miles they had traveled during the day but she twisted her body back to look behind her and saw that due to the distance they had traveled the mountains had definitely become much smaller. She patted him again on his side, he looked back and saw that she was pointing ahead to a large open area of sand so he headed right for it. She jumped off of his back and removed their gear from on top of him so he could change back into his normal self. With the sunset came a mixture of blue, red, yellow and orange colors on the horizon but she knew that as beautiful as it appeared to be there was also the potential for real danger. The desert at this time of day had a quiet beauty to it. "Who could possibly live out here in this wasteland? Nomads or not they must all be crazy!" She thought.

It wasn't dark yet and they needed some dry sticks to start the fire. "Raven, how do you feel?" She asked excitedly.

"I actually don't feel too bad at all considering, I must have stepped on at least twenty bushes today but neither the sun nor sand bothered me."

He stretched and ran his fingers through his long hair, "To think of it the only thing I can say is that I'm a bit hungry."

"Don't you worry, I'm going to gather some things for our fire and I'll cook something for you so just relax a bit. Oh, wait a minute!" She said.

"What is it?"

"I'll tell you more about it during dinner but if you see a small bug with a curved tail the size that would fit into the palm of your hand don't touch it! I think it might have some type of poison like a snake, either kill it or kick it far away from our camp."

"Ok," he said dryly.

Although Raven was hungry he wasn't thirsty at all so he gathered as many rocks as he could find for their rock circle and watched as she returned with an armful of small twigs and branches. She did a quick pan fry of one of the salted meats they had while cutting up one carrot and potato which they would split between them along with half of the last piece of bread. They didn't want to run out of food here in the desert and they didn't need a tremendous appetite nagging on their minds or especially their stomachs. She relayed to him all of the things that had occurred to her during the day. The temperature had changed and they both agreed that it was colder now so for this reason they made sure to bundle up. They discussed some ideas of what they would do once they reached the city but couldn't come to a definitive answer. The answer would have to wait until they arrived.

" I think we'll be able to start to see the Bytarian mountain range off to our right side tomorrow," he said.

"I had really forgotten all about those. I probably could have seen them today if I had really concentrated but I was preoccupied with the different colored flowers and bushes as we were traveling," she answered.

"I think we were too far away this morning to see them anyways. It will be a great sign though if we can see them in the morning because that means we're not too far away from Bytar."

"How far would you guess then?" She inquired.

"I don't know exactly but if I were to guess I'd say maybe one or two days at the most."

"You said the mountains are going to be on our right side?"

"Yes," he replied.

"What direction would that be, north?"

"Hmm," pausing for a moment, "it's going to be the north east, kind of, why do you ask?"

"Just curious, I'm trying to get better at directions that's all."

"I think today worked out real well sis so let's try to do the same thing for tomorrow and hopefully we'll be out of this desert before we know it."

He put his head down on his makeshift pillow and rolled onto his left side with his back facing her because they figured if it got too cold their backs touching each other would provide a little extra warmth. The night was cold but tolerable as they fell asleep. The morning came all too quickly and after opening her eyes she saw that she was the first one awake again. Their fire was just barely alive so after cleaning up she walked over and with a loving kick to his behind, "Raven, it's time to wake up."

He awoke with a yawn, "You're right, you're right."

"Yes, the sun should be up soon and we can eat a quick something then I'd like to be on our way." She put the fire out and they ate a small breakfast which consisted of their last piece of bread and an apple for each of them.

"Are you ready?" She asked.

"Wow, you seem like you really want to be on your way," he joked," what's your rush anyways?"

"I didn't like the look of that pointy tailed insect that's all, it still gives me the creeps."

He laughed out loud, "It bothered you that much?"

She answered him very slowly and deliberately, "Yes, it did and the sooner you can change back into my camel," stressing the "my camel" part, "the sooner I can be off of this ground."

About fifteen minutes late he asked her, "Are you ready to go then?"

She didn't bother to reply because the look on her face was answer enough for him. With that he closed his eyes and thought about transforming back into the camel, within a moment he stood next to her like the day before, as a camel. She was all too happy to pack the things up on top of him, jump up and get ready for another long boring day. The day started out much like the previous one had. It was very early in the morning and the sun was just rising up announcing itself with a stunning display of colors it shot beams of sunshine from the horizon throughout the desert that seemed to touch every inch of the land. Rayne was happy for two reasons: first, she was finally off the ground and out of reach of those bugs secondly, she felt like their desert travels would soon come to an end. It was still very early in the morning but looking off in the distance she did see the rigid outline of miles of mountains like Raven had mentioned. It was still a little too cool outside for her liking but she knew the sun would soon tip the scales in its own favor. Rayne had settled down into a good position for her sightseeing but after an hour of traveling she spotted a group of vultures in the sky; there were a lot of them gliding in either large or small circles and at different heights. There was a very large oval shaped boulder ahead and to their right near to a large dark tree that was void of all leaves but was populated by a huge gaggle of vultures that were fighting for positions on the bare branches.

"That's a lot of vultures for one dead animal unless it's a large one like a cow or horse but how many of those would have ventured this far into the desert," she thought.

Curious to see what they were so interested in she tapped Raven on his side and pointed him in the direction of the birds, she figured that would have been enough information for him however, instead of heading over to the tree he just stopped walking altogether. He turned again to look at her but this time she used her fingers indicating a walking motion and pointed to the tree again. Reluctantly, he started in that direction and in about five minutes she was close enough so she jumped down and walked towards the noise. As she approached she could see the birds in the tree much better and it seemed that there beady little black eyes were scrutinizing her every step. The problem with these birds were that they are big and ugly. She never liked vultures they are black with long, scrawny necks and were making all types of different sounds at the same time between a loud, mean hissing sound to the loud cawing of stupid birds arguing over where to perch. She felt like changing herself into the eagle that her and her brother favored so much and showing these scavengers what a real bird is. Rayne was able to control her urge by knowing that if they tried anything nasty at all she would reach back and grab her bow and that would be the end of that trouble. She looked back at Raven who was watching her intently but still a short distance away. She turned back to face the vulture filled tree then reached over her shoulder and grabbed her bow with a steady hand.

"I hate these disgusting birds," she mumbled. "I'll shoot an arrow into the tree to scatter them and that will stop their incessant calls. She held the bow tightly in her left hand and while using her right hand pulled and where there was no string a moment ago one quickly appeared. The resistance from the bowstring was sudden as was the beautiful white arrow of Titan's bow. Rayne spoke these words to the arrow, "Hit the tree," and it left like white lightning striking the tree at chest level with such force it created a hole completely through it which caused all of the squawking vultures to abandon their roost and take flight in a mass of flapping of wings and confusion. She felt a lot better about scattering the birds then waved at Raven so he would come a little closer to where she was standing. Rayne knew that vultures are scavengers so something had to be dead or dying very close by but it was odd that she couldn't smell anything. She walked around the giant rock and nestled just to the side of it was a large green bush on a slanted dirt hill but between the boulder and the bush was a man. His skin was pale and he had a red stained white cloth wrapped around his head, sadly he was motionless.

She called out to him, "Hello, are you ok? Do you need some help?"

He didn't respond so she hurried back to Raven while at the same time motioning to him to kneel down. She really wanted to remove their bags from his back and so he could change back to his human form. That done Rayne took out a pouch of water and they both ran back over to try to help the stranger. They approached him slowly while at the same time trying to maintain their footing on the slanted hill but with all of the loose rocks it was challenging. She continued trying to elicit an answer from him with no luck.

"Hey, can you hear me? Hello, we are here to help you!"

They were close enough to him to see that he had several wounds not only did his head scarf have blood on it but so did his stomach and upper left shoulder areas. Raven poured a small amount of water on his face which startled him into slightly opening both of his eyes and seeing that there were people in front of him. He reached out for the water flask but appeared to be too weak to even carry it so he just opened his mouth and Raven poured a little more water into it.

The fresh water had giving him a miniscule spark of life again so he began to speak to his young rescuers, "Thank you," he managed to say weakly.

"What's your name?" She asked.

"My name is not important."

"What happened to you? How did you get out here?" She continued.

Weakly, he replied, "I live in Bytar, recently our city was besieged by an army that arrived by ships. They have killed many of my people! I was trying to escape and avoid the fighting but I was caught and hauled up to the palace in front of their leader."

"Do you remember what his name is?" Raven asked impatiently.

Without answering his question the man continued. "I was tied up and thrown on the floor in front of our King Thais; they were asking him questions about something but I didn't know what it was all about."

"Yes, but his name, do you remember his name?" Raven asked impatiently.

Rayne gently placed her hand on her brothers arm and without any words spoken he realized that he was being a little rash with the poor dying man.

"Nicias was what they called him."

Feeling a bit like a mother bird feeding worms to her babies Raven poured a little more water into the man's open mouth. With a weak voice the man continued, "They told King Thais that they were going to let me go free but as soon as I got back downstairs to the street the soldiers started to beat me up. I guess they figured I was dead because I had stopped moving but as soon as I could manage I escaped through the south gate and headed into the desert. I didn't care where I went I just didn't want to die in the streets of my own city."

"Poor man," she muttered. Look at the destruction this sorcerer has brought to Bytar it was once such a lively city with such a peaceful people."

"We can't do anything about the soldiers right now sis! That's not why we are going there."

"Sir, are they guarding the city gates?" Raven asked.

By now the man had closed his eyes again and shut his mouth. He placed the back of his hand in front of the man's mouth to see if he was still breathing. Feeling the hand by his face the man spoke up, "Yes, during the day all entrances into the city are being guarded but at night the gates are closeeed," the man's last word trailed off in a whisper as his final breath escaped him. She placed her head on Raven's shoulder and wept for the dead man who had struggled to escape his city so badly and died almost alone in the desert. They buried him the best they could with a bunch of stones across his grave sending a message to the vultures that they would have no free meal here today. They decided to continue their travel and make the best use of their morning so he changed back into a camel and they were soon back on their way. She spent the next several hours sitting and thinking about the dead man and about any different ways on how they could try to enter the City of Bytar.

The mountains to the right were much more visible which gave her hope that they would soon be out of this desert. Out of the four pouches of water they had brought along with them she had only used up one of them. Kicking Raven in his side perhaps a little harder than she had intended signaled the time for them to stop and rest. After setting up her makeshift shade tree with her blanket she thoroughly checked her area for any more insects that might try to surprise her. Finding none but seeing one of those cactus' with the small red bulbs on it close by reminded her that she wanted to check them out. She approached the cactus confidently and looked down towards the larger green pads where the red bulbs were attached to and there they were, sharp thorns. She was definitely not planning on touching any of them. Out of the many thorny green pads she looked at one of them clearly stood out because it only had one red bulb left on it. She removed her knife and without holding onto anything tried to cut the bulb off of the pad it was stuck to. Not succeeding, she tried a different method. She found a spot on the red bulb itself to hold onto and a separate spot on the pad then tried to saw at the base of the bulb to remove it.

"Ouch," she uttered to herself then quickly pulled her hand back and placed her knife back into its sheath using her right hand.

"Great," she said out loud, the one thing I didn't want to do, I did." She had gotten a tiny thorn stuck in her thumb. She could feel that there was something stuck in it but try as she might even using her teeth she couldn't manage to find it let alone remove it. After sitting in the shade a while longer and giving it her best shot to rid herself of the mystery fragment of thorn she gave up and figured she'd try living with it for a while. It seemed like an eternity before the sun was low enough in the sky for her to feel comfortable and pack up her blanket. She hopped back up onto her camel and annoyingly hit her thumb which caused it to start throbbing in pain. She spent the next several hours watching the same assorted small birds fly from cactus to tree or from cactus down into the bushes for small insects. At least she was finally able to figure out the mystery of what animal was running from bush to bush, it was a desert rabbit. It had large ears that stood up straight, at least she hoped it was a rabbit. It was nearing the time of day for them to stop for the night but a small wisp of smoke going into the air caught her attention. Surprisingly, popping up from a nearby bush in front of them was a thin looking elderly man who raised both of his hands to slow her camel. She kicked her brother in his side and as he looked back at her she motioned to him to let her down and that everything seemed to be ok. The elderly man fitted the description she had in her mind of what the perfect nomad would look like. He was short, very thin and had a leathery looking dark tan on his face, his smile displayed a few missing teeth and he wore whitish loose fitting clothing somewhat similar to theirs with the exception of the long white cloth that wrapped around his head leaving a small piece of it hanging down by his ears. Speaking in an unknown language he seemed to be very nice and helpful, he aided her in taking down the bags off her camel and then turned and walked away towards his little camp where the fire was. Once the bags were down on the ground Raven changed back to his regular human self.

"Rayne are you feeling a little better about this morning?" Her brother was referring to the poor man who had died earlier that day.

"I'm better now," she replied fidgeting through her bags.

"What's wrong with your left hand?" He asked.

The nomad approached them again and on seeing two people now and no camel he stopped in his tracks with a perplexed look of on his face. He calmly started speaking again while waving his hands to and fro but they could only guess at what he was saying. Raven tried to explain what had happened but not knowing his language just gave up. Unbeknownst to the nomad, of course their camel had disappeared and was now miraculously replaced with a teenage boy. He was sure that the nomad wasn't buying the excuse because he simply waved them over to his camp and walked away muttering something to himself. She tried to walk past Raven without answering any of his questions about her hand, "I guess he wants us to eat with him?" She said. Raven grabbed her by the right elbow as she tried to hurry past him, "Wait a minute."

"What's the matter with your other hand? I watched you digging through your bag but you were only using your right hand and clearly protecting your left."

At this point Rayne started to nonchalantly wave her hand around but made sure she didn't hit it on anything, "It's nothing really."

"Come on stop playing around."

"I really think it's nothing, earlier today when we stopped for lunch I was messing around with one of the cactus' and happened to get stuck by one of the thorns ."

"You haven't been able to pull the thorn out all day?"

"No, I can feel something in there but I can't get it out."

"Well, let me take a look it."

"Wow, it's getting red and definitely swollen but in the morning when the sun is up we'll have a better look at it.

"That's fine with me," she replied.

They walked over to where their host was because he had been motioning to them to sit down in front of him. The nomads fire was emanating from a clever little clay pot that he had placed on the ground in front of him. It had several little holes in it located around the base of the pot which provided a little extra light around their camp.

"Jahe, Jahe," the nomad said after repeatedly placing his hand on his chest.

"That must be his name." Rayne motioned to herself in the same fashion, "My name is Rayne! This is my brother Raven, Raven," she repeated slowly.

Jahe acknowledged her response with a polite nod but continued to tend to the food he was cooking in the pot. They observed that there were three long sticks in the pot with some type of meat attached to the end of each them. He would periodically twist the sticks around which would move the meat into different positions around the small fire then he pulled them out and placed them on top of a flat stone in front of them. Raven tilted his nose upwards, inhaled deeply and enjoyed the aroma, "Mmm, it smells pretty good."

She ignored the comment and took a sip of water from her leather pouch and said to Jahe, "I have water if you would like some." She held the pouch above her head and poured a little of it into her mouth to demonstrate to him that it was just water. She tried to hand it to him but with a smile and raised hands he refused then pulled out his own little pouch with water in it. He handed Raven one of the sticks with the food on it while telling him a few more things that they still didn't understand. He examined the small chunks of meat with a perplexed look on his face but didn't immediately start eating because he didn't know what type of meat it was. Jahe started laughing in a weird way and grabbed the last stick; he ate a piece of the meat in front of them to show them that it was safe to eat. Raven raised the stick up to his nose again and smelled the food cautiously, "It smells pretty good like I said." He then tore a small piece off and ate it.

"Wow, it is good," looking over at his sister excitedly, "he uses spices."

She tried her piece next and was just as satisfied. She reached for her water but unfortunately in doing so hit her thumb again which caused her to drop the pouch back to the ground and almost drop the food in her other hand.

"You hit your thumb didn't you?"

"How could you tell," she replied.

Jahe, noticed that something had bothered her and tried his best to find out what it was.

"My thumb hurts," showing him her thumb and mumbling to herself about what a stupid mistake it was to even try messing with that cactus. He opened his hand and motioned for her to let him see her injury.

"It's alright sis, let him at least take a look at it," he insisted.

Cautiously, she showed him her swollen left thumb. Jahe moved closer to her and positioned her hand closer to the fire light to get a better look at the injury. He reached into his cloak and produced a small clay jar with a little red stopper at the end of it. He looked at both of the siblings and started speaking apparently trying to tell them what he was going to do next. Jahe pulled the stopper out with his mouth he then very gently poured a few drops of a yellowish goo onto the entire end of her thumb then placed the stopper back on the end of the small jar. He continued to give them instructions while at the same time moving her thumb a little closer to the fire, not to burn her but to dry the material on her thumb. Several minutes had passed and the goo had dried into a type of candlewax material, he then gingerly moved her hand away from the heat and using his fingernail was able to pry under the dried stuff and started to slowly peel it off of her thumb. He smiled then made an obvious display of opening and closing his fist so she would check her wound. Rayne looked at her thumb in the firelight and immediately noticed the pain was gone and so too was any trace of a thorn.

"Unbelievable," she stammered looking over at Raven, "I can't believe that disgusting yellow goop actually removed the thorn."

With a huge smile she thanked the nomad for his help. He sat back where he was and placed the dried material with the thorn still inside of it into the fire to discard it.

"I wish I had something to give him," she said disappointedly.

Jahe was quiet for a little while then suddenly, like he remembered something turned and reached into a bag by his side and showed them a red bulb exactly like the one she had been trying to free from the cactus earlier in the day. Seeing what he had in his hand started her on a two minute speech ending with, "I'm not even going close to that thing again."

He figured out what her problem was and very calmly held his hand up to quiet her then placed the bulb on the flat stone in front of him and proceeded to carefully clean the outside of it with his knife. After that he sliced it in half and placed his small finger into some of the juice that had leaked out then licked his finger with a grin. He then Pulled out a small spoon and removed the inside seeds, then spooned out a small portion of the bulb.

"I think it's some type of fruit," Raven said.

The nomad handed the small piece to Raven and motioned for him to eat it.

"What if it's a trick by Nicias!" She argued, "you eat that piece of fruit and die a horrible death Raven."

"I think if he really wanted to hurt us sis he would have left that thorn stuck in your finger."

He slipped the small piece of food in his mouth and closed his eyes, momentarily savoring the flavor. "It has a nice taste to it, I don't even know what type of fruit to compare it to try it!" He insisted.

When a small piece was dug out for her she didn't even hesitate to try it. Raven could guess by her facial expressions that she was trying to decipher the taste of the strange fruit herself.

"I understand what you're saying now Raven," glancing over at Jahe with a grin.

"You know sis for loners he is a very friendly person."

Jahe spooned out a little portion for himself then put the rest into the fire, he then turned to face them and politely said a few more words then rolled over in his own blanket and went to sleep.

"I guess that was his goodnight speech," she said. "Do you think we might arrive at Bytar tomorrow?"

"I think we might be closer than we think. Listen, there is no way we'll be able to just walk right through the front door."

"I agree with you," she said.

"Good, so when we see any part of the city I'm going to stop so we can figure out what we're going to do. We might have to walk around the entire city wall to find a way in."

"Maybe we'll get lucky and figure some other way in," she replied.

"I hope you are right, let's try to get some sleep so we are rested for the morning."

Chapter Thirteen

Bytar...

Rayne was surprised how cold it actually got during the nights in the desert considering how hot it got in the afternoons. She rubbed her eyes and saw that the sun was just barely pushing up the low clouds on the horizon and knew that the pleasant colors of sunrise would soon pleasantly fill her vision. She sat up and looked over at her brother who was moving around under his blanket getting ready to wake up. She held her blanket close to her body and stood up walked the five or six steps over to where Jahe had laid down, but found his area to be completely empty, there was no sign of him anywhere around their camp, he had gone…

"Raven!" She whispered, "I think Jahe is gone?"

"What?"

"Our nomad has left, I guess he really does wake up early?

The bags are still on the ground over there so at least he didn't rob us," half chuckling to herself, she knew that he would not have done that anyways.

Raven started to gather his things together, "I can't say that I'm too surprised, I mean he is a nomad after all, don't they prefer to be by themselves?"

He could tell by the look on her face that she was a little sad though.

"I——I would have liked to have thanked him once more for removing the thorn from my thumb is all. By the way, you were correct in saying the mountains were on our right side, look at them now they must run at an angle because it looks like we're much closer to them now than we were yesterday."

Raven turned his head to look at the large mountain range, "I suppose you're right, those mountains stretch for hundreds of miles, it would have taken us weeks to travel through them instead of the ones we went through."

They were both a little nervous and excited about heading out today because they knew one journey was ending and a much more dangerous one was about to begin. She secured the two bags on top of her brother, jumped up and their last day in the desert began. Atop her perch she recalled the last time they visited the city of Bytar. She remembered the hustle and bustle of merchants in the streets and watching them trying to pawn their wares off on every passersby. This is what stuck out the most in her mind. Not only was it was a city of opportunity it was a place where some families were just trying to get by and make something for themselves and their children. The older and more experience folks teaching and mentoring the younger generation in some of the many trades like: fishing, metal works, stone masons and even carpentry. Of course, one of the city's biggest problems like many in these ancient times were the pickpockets. The sounds people of speaking different languages combined with smells of different types of food being cooked was a stark reminder of the contrast to their own small village. Hythor, their hometown, was also located near the ocean, but was much smaller compared to this city. Bytar is a major place for trade and the home to thousands of people. She turned and looked to her left knowing that somewhere in the distance was a large river that flowed from the ocean through much of Tundar. She was so engrossed in her own thoughts that she didn't notice that her brothers pace had slowed down considerably and that was because his eyes had been drawn to the large city in front of him that was apparently rising out of the sand in the distance. Raven looked back and at her and made a moaning sound which Rayne figured was his way of saying it's time to stop. He got down on his knees because he was all too ready to drop his passenger off and start to explore their surroundings.

"Look at that Rayne! Another hour of walking and we will be at the south gate of the city. I've been thinking all morning of ways to get in there, it'll be easy for us."

"Really?" She replied, "How's that?"

"We can change ourselves into any animal we want to so when we get a little closer to the city we can find ourselves a nice little hiding spot, then I'll change into something simple like a small bird. It will give us a great chance to look for an opening in their defenses."

At this point, the ground was very flat and hard the soft sand had almost completely disappeared. There were very few trees of any kind towards the left side where the river was located so they knew they would have to start walking to their right. This side would bring them closer to the mountains and provide them with what looked like some suitable areas to hide. As they walked closer they started to see groups of men who were tending to their flocks like goats and sheep. Raven still had his sword by his side with the golden hilt covered so as not to attract any attention. They stopped only once for water and a brief snack because he wanted to find a good spot where they would be able to keep a low profile while he was away. He remembered that Bytar had three main gates, one north and south and another facing the river on the west side. He wasn't sure if there was one on the east side facing the mountains so that's the side he wanted to check out first. The mountains on the right were only a few miles away so if they needed a place to disappear to quickly that is where they would go. It was relatively peaceful as they walked past the groups of animals tended to by their masters who were keeping them in line with quick slaps to their backsides with thin sticks. Rayne pointed to a quiet spot near several large rocks that seemed to be guarded by a few large palm trees and would afford them a comfortable and concealed position while Raven was checking out the perimeter wall. It was much warmer now and she wanted to be able to not only be hidden from any soldiers but also from the sun. They had never seen the outside of the eastern walls the last time they were in Bytar they had been so amazed at how the ships would travel up and down the river bringing all sorts of things for people to buy that the majority of their time was spent on the western and northern gates. She was all too happy to drop her bag on the ground and sit there taking a larger than normal drink of water. With a sigh of relief she said, "I needed that, I don't know how these nomads can ration their water so well while being out in the desert for so long."

Raven stood and sipped a small amount of water, "I don't know, maybe they're all camels too?" He said sarcastically. "I'm going to change into one of those small birds that we saw in the desert because they are small and fast. I'm also going to fly into the city for a while and really see how bad things are on the inside."

"You'll have to be very careful, don't do anything stupider than usual," she begged him.

"What do you mean stupid?"

"Just be careful! I only have one brother."

He looked over at her again and gave her that stupid wink of his then changed before her eyes into a little red bird, then he was on his way flying in quick, jerky up and down movements headed straight towards the wall to find an entrance for them. Once he flew off he didn't even bother to look back at her. They had less than a week before the eclipse and the appearance of the red moon. They didn't know what would happen if they couldn't find the book and destroy the page.? The fairy queen had entrusted them with this this task and he didn't want to think about what if they failed. Since giving them their magical gifts of being able to change into any animal they wanted to she had never once asked them for anything.

He reminded himself, "We will not fail, we can't!"

Raven didn't see a single person anywhere on his way to the wall. He did however see a multitude of short, stocky trees though and landing on one of the branches he recognized it to be an olive tree, there was a small grove of them. He took a moment to investigate his surroundings. Raven could see and hear plenty of other birds flying from tree to tree but they didn't try to speak with him at all because they were so engrossed in their own daily tasks. He wanted to start his search from the corner of the cities wall closest to the desert and then fly the length of it to the other corner which would have put him near to the ocean. While perched in the tree he noticed that the wall's construction looked to be made up of all types and sizes of stones. He recognized the square, rectangular and even the odd triangular shaped stones that were keeping this old wall together but so far couldn't see a way in. While flying from tree to tree like all of the other birds were doing he found what he was hoping to find, an entrance! Located almost directly in the center of the old wall was an open door, he didn't see any guards watching it so he decided to fly over the wall and find a safe spot on the inside to check. Finding a good little rooftop to land on was easy enough, he was more surprised to find that the door he was interested in was located below a set of wooden stairs. These stairs led to a wooden walkway where soldiers could walk on and very easily look out onto the olive trees where he just came from.

"What a ridiculous spot for a door," he thought.

It seemed to him like this door might have been installed as more of an afterthought rather than being original whatever the reason he didn't care, he just knew that there were hardly any guards watching it. There were a few guards quite a ways a way talking on the walkway but seemingly without a care to the open door. Situated just below him was a rectangular shaped pool of water, it was a small non-working fountain where a few men had gathered and were seated talking and laughing. They didn't appear to be in distress so maybe the people here have learned to live with the soldiers presence. He had seen enough though so he flew back over the wall and continued his checking of the perimeter. The northern gate was much larger and had a superior number of soldiers who monitored every aspect of movement in and out of it, probably due to the fact that their ships were still anchored right off shore. He didn't attempt to count the number of ships he saw believing it to be over fifty. Bored, he watched as a couple of small boats paddled into shore from one of the larger ships. It was noisy, the laughter and yelling reminded him of the city it used to be. When he was able to get to the western entrance he saw several small ships tied to the large dock by the river, they were still engaging in trade with the city. That would make sense because the city had a lot of people in it all with their own needs including feeding the extra mouths of this army. This looked to be the busiest of the entrances so far. There was a lot of activity at this gate, not only people and soldiers but merchants leading their oxen who were pulling carts of food, weapons and supplies. Raven made several stops as he flew, sometimes stopping on boxes, rooftops and once he even landed on top of one of the boats masts close to several pelicans. Finally, he made his way around the corner to the last gate. This would be the southern gate where he witnessed some disturbing behavior. Although, most of the day he was able to watch people come and go into the city now he had to helplessly watch as a group of soldiers bullied a few people. They appeared to be merchants of a sort trying to sell their fruits and vegetables. He witnessed a soldier punch one of the men in the face while at the same time a few of the other soldiers unloaded two of the boxes from the man's cart for themselves. There were two oxen pulling the cart each ox had a man standing alongside it along with a mother and child seated in the cart. He lowered his head in shame unable to help the poor family. There was a line of people trying to get in through this gate. Once the soldiers took what they wanted from a particular cart the line would start to move again through the doorway. He flew back to where he had left his sister and was pleased to find her safe and waiting for him to return. Changing back to his regular self she immediately started in with the questions. After catching her up with all that he had seen they agreed to wait until nightfall to attempt to enter the city through that single doorway.

"Do you think that the door will be open at night?" Rayne asked.

"I have no idea? We'll have to wait for nightfall to get a better look. There's still a lot of people within the city and once we get in we'll be able to blend in with everyone else. Did anyone see you out here?"

"No, no one came anywhere near to me, the closest were those goat herders, and they are way over there," pointing to her left.

"Good, I was a little worried about you."

"Well, now what?" She asked.

"Now we wait."

Once it got dark they would be ready to go. Rayne pointed towards the moon.

"Yes, I know don't remind me," he replied dryly. "We'll make it on time, I just hope we can find the entrance to these tunnels to get to the book."

The moon was three quarters full now and they were starting to feel that time was no longer on their side, it was slipping through their fingers. It was around one o'clock in the morning when they made their last move. For the past few hours they had slowly made their way from the safety of their hidden spot closer and closer to the wall simply by going from tree to tree, inching their way nearer to their objective. Finally, they were within several feet of the door, they had taken particular care to avoid stepping on any dead tree branches which could have given them away.

"Ok, the door is just up ahead," he whispered, "just follow me and I'll look to see if anyone is there. Once we get in we'll need to quickly disappear into the city streets at least until the morning, then we'll figure out what to do."

With a simple nod of her head she silently agreed with his statement. They tiptoed up to the door he then placed his hands on the door frame to check if the door was unlocked, it was! Raven leaned in and saw the light from an oil lamp near the far wall opposite the wooden stairwell he then turned and waved for her to follow him in and they proceeded to walk past it. He looked up above to check if there was someone there but not seeing anyone he waved her forward again; they kept on going but just as they passed the rectangular water fountain they heard a loud shout, "Archers!"

In an instant the footfalls of many soldiers were heard running in front and above them. A whole row of hidden archers, arrows at the ready appeared behind them on the walkway ready to shoot them both. The clamoring of men with swords being drawn and shiny pointed spears filled their immediate view.

"Keep your arrows at the ready!" A voice in front of them commanded.

Emerging from the shadows in front of them was a stocky man, he walked forward closely followed by another man, he was a tall, thin older man. This man had a long black cape but what was most visible was the small red glowing object hanging from his necklace. With his hands behind his back he looked over his two new young captives with a self-satisfying grin on his face, similar to how a cat would look at a mouse that she finally has cornered.

"Did you actually think you could enter my city and I wouldn't notice?" Nicias said with a sneer. "Captain Asal," he said, "I believe you know what to do with these prisoners."

Chapter Fourteen

Interrogation: While Time Dwindles...

"Don't worry they're not going to kill us!"

"Shut your mouth boy!" Captain Asal said abruptly. "Tie the prisoners up and follow me and if they even look like they're trying to escape you have my permission to kill them."

Rayne looked over towards her brother but was so scared she didn't attempt to speak. They were led through several streets and finally into from what Raven could only tell in the darkness, a two-story building. Fortunately, their hands were tied up in front of them instead of behind where it would have been much more uncomfortable to sit down in. They didn't see the tall man the rest of the night whom they both knew must have been the sorcerer Nicias. They were escorted through what he felt must certainly have been the palace due to the amount of guards present and from the size of the hallways they were both taken up some stairs to the second floor. Without arguing with them Raven was pushed into a room just ahead of her on the right side by three of the guards. Rayne quickly glanced inside of his room while passing the doorway but a second guard had opened another door on the opposite side of the hallway and shoved her inside. It was a decent sized room having one regular bed, nothing fancy and a small oil lamp burning on the wall. Most of her guards stayed in the hallway talking amongst themselves but two of them sat in chairs inside of the room with her.

"Go to sleep!" One of the guards inside of her room told her.

"How am I supposed to go to sleep with my hands tied up in front of me?" She thought. Instead of saying that out loud she figured it would be safer to just lay down and keep quiet. Raven's luck wasn't any better. All of these guards were wearing red and black striped capes but none of them seemed to have ever learned the meaning of common courtesy as he was forcefully pushed onto his bed. He laid there quietly and wondered what he had done wrong. He believed that they had taken all of the necessary precautions so they wouldn't have been caught, yet here they both sat, tied up and unable to do anything. He fell asleep unable to unravel the mystery of how they were caught so easily.

***

King Thais woke up as he had done for the past week or so, with the smell of food and his friend and cook Simo attentively standing by.

"I heard a lot of sounds in the hallway last night Simo what has happened?"

Replying quietly, "Sir, they were finally caught trying to enter the city by Nicias and his men. They're being held in two rooms down the hallway, I have to take them some food now if you don't need anything else?"

"No, I'm fine."

The cook bowed and exited the kings chamber. He had already brought up their food and drink on a table, now he prepared himself to enter the boys room first.

"Excuse me," he said to the guard at Ravens door. "I was instructed to bring the prisoners food and water this morning."

"Go ahead," one of them answered.

He entered the room and was surprised to find two more guards sitting and talking with each other quietly, he turned and faced the boy who was laying in the bed staring at him.

"Good morning young sir I've brought you some food."

"To be honest I'm not really hungry."

"It's good hot food young sir, I believe you'll need your strength today?"

Raven sat up and saw that the cook had brought a dish of hot eggs, bread and several slices of apples with figs.

"Thank you," he managed to reply.

Simo exited the room and walked over to the girls room next informing her guards of his task. As he entered her room he saw that she was already sitting up in her bed and was intently watching his every move.

"Can she speak freely?" Simo asked one guard.

"That's fine I see no problem with that," meanwhile they continued to quietly talk to each other with no particular interest in their prisoner.

"Good morning young miss."

"Good morning."

Simo couldn't get over the fact that they both appeared to be so young, like teenagers.

"Are you hungry?" He asked.

"Yes, I could eat."

"That's good, I had to convince your young friend over there to eat something."

"He's my brother."

"I didn't know that, but I do see the resemblance now that you mention it."

"How is he doing?"

"He's fine young miss." Simo pulled the small table that was in the room over in front of her and placed the food on top of it.

Rayne looked down at the plate and inhaled, "It smells really good!"

Inadvertently, he was blocking her vision of the two guards behind him so she started a small conversation with him, "You look a bit familiar."

He raised his eyes to look at her but didn't respond.

Rayne took a bite of her bread, "We ran into a nice man in the desert recently, a nomad, his name was Jahe, you remind me a little of him."

"Thank you young miss," he replied, but inside he was stunned to hear that his longtime friend was so dangerously close to the city. Simo turned from her gaze, "I will be around all day young miss, I hope we have another chance to talk."

Simo nodded to her guards then casually walked out of the room and headed downstairs to the kitchen. A short time later the prisoners were taken from their individual rooms and corralled down the rest of the hallway to the end where a huge double door opened up into a large room.

"Well, good morning my two young mischievous intruders," Nicias started. "Sit down," he instructed them pointing to the two chairs that were placed side by side in front of him. They could see much better with the light of day that he looked ancient, beyond old Rayne thought. He sat at a table in front of them with his boney fingers tapping on the top of it as he scrutinized the both of them. Several of the guards who had entered the room stood behind them quietly. There was an older, heavier set man wearing a type of a thin gold crown across his forehead who was also seated at the same table. Standing next to the boney sorcerer was a solid looking soldier with thick arms, a burly beard and a very unpleasant looking face.

"Captain Asal," the large man looked down at Nicias, "what do you think of our two young captives?"

"They look like kids."

"Oh, my dear captain," he said condescendingly, "that's not very nice."

"You see Thais, I've brought you some company, at least for a few days."

At the sound of his name Rayne immediately recalled that the king of Bytars name was King Thais.

"What are your names?" Nicias asked them.

His sister started to answer first but he cut her off quickly, "My name is Raven, this is my sister Rayne."

"Well, how cute is that," he replied sarcastically. "Raven and Rayne is it? I have a feeling that we're going to have a very productive day today." Nicias pretended to use some kind of magic power by pressing both of his hands to his temples and closing his eyes. Changing his posture the sorcerer placed his elbows on the table and his hands together and started to drum a beat with his fingers as if he was praying. "I've been waiting for this day since the last time I saw you both by the river. I had honestly only intended my wolves to scare the two of you away, in a word discourage you from continuing your foolish movements towards my city. He looked down at the table for a moment then continued, "I must admit it though, somewhat sadly at that, I truly underestimated your youth and fortitude."

Without warning he slapped his hand down on the table which caused their eyes to widen. "Although, I believe that this is a very fortunate turn of events that will in no short order benefit me a little more than it does the two of you. I've learned that the both of you are also looking for my magical book, but what I don't know is why. So let me start with you young lady," standing up and walking around the table. "Rayne is it? Why are you looking for my book? It's ok, you can speak freely, we are all friends here. I don't think friends should keep secrets from each other, do you?" He was slowly walking around them, inspecting them and even though he was speaking to her nicely, she clearly felt it was in a condescending cold sort of way, it was making her nauseous.

She was desperately thinking of a quick excuse, "I don't really know why sir?"

"Sir?" He said with a surprised look, "you don't have to call me sir, you can call me Nicias. How did you even know the book was here in Bytar?"

"It was more of a dream I had, I guess," she started.

"Really, a dream, that's interesting to learn."

He stopped walking and stood behind her, placed both of his boney hands on her shoulders and spoke, "Did you know Captain Asal that for some reason I very rarely ever remember my dreams, I must be getting old," he joked, as his captain cracked a smile.

"Did you know Rayne," slightly tightening his grip on her shoulders, "that another favorite way of getting information out of people is by the use of pain."

He released his grip on her and continued to walk slowly around them.

"Yes, sadly it's true. Captain Asal here," looking back at his man, "is a master of getting information out of people." Nicias raised his hands and shrugged his shoulders, " Now, I don't condone that type of behavior in any way, but unfortunately it is sometimes a necessity."

She was trying to maintain her strong position and not wanting to let on how scared she actually was she tried to answer him without stuttering. The prospect of being tortured in any way hadn't really occurred to her.

"Like I said, it just came to me in a dream, all I knew was we had to come here and look for this stupid book. My brother didn't want me to go alone so he came with me."

"I have over one hundred men in the tunnels that run below this city searching tirelessly for this book and we've only seen it once. Can you believe that? Supposedly, one of my soldiers walked by a room and saw it just lying there on a table in the center of the room. By the time I got the message and arrived at the room the book was gone. He told me that he never entered the room, that the book had just disappeared into thin air. Do you know how frustrating it is to hear something so ridiculous. I mean after a week of searching and with only a few days left I still don't have it. It certainly hasn't made its way back to that room. He snapped his fingers, "Unfortunately, that particular guard is no longer with us, I think the drink got the better of him."

He looked over at Raven, "How about you? Any dreams populate that empty head of yours. No I didn't think so you look like you might be a bit vacant up there," the sorcerer rudely commented while making his way back over towards his sister.

"No, she's the one who was blessed with those dreams or as I always tell her cursed with them."

Raven was thinking of any and all scenarios to try to figure a way out of this mess. King Thais, who had been sitting by silently watching this showy display by the sorcerer with a kind of bad taste in his mouth finally spoke up.

"Nicias, it's possible that these two kids had a dream and just took off on a blind quest not fully knowing what to look for or what to expect in the end."

He responded to the king so violently that a little spit came out of his mouth, "No, I don't believe that! He yelled. "It's not a coincidence that she had a dream about my book and that they can both change their bodies into wolves or lions or whatever, those are not ordinary gifts."

"I'm so sorry for that rude outburst kids, please forgive me, but I do have another way to get the truth out of you and it's not really that painful."

He placed his right hand on top of her head, closed his eyes and while holding onto the amulet around his neck started mumbling something quietly to himself. She couldn't speak, her body immediately tensed up and her back arched in the chair.

"What are you doing to her?" Raven asked, alarmed at what he was seeing.

The king knew what was going to happen having had Nicias probe his mind for answers previously, but Raven had no clue of what was going on and he started getting very mad, very quickly.

"Leave her alone!" He yelled at the sorcerer.

Captain Asal placed his hand on his sword and went to stand in front of the boy before he could do anything really stupid that probably would have gotten him killed. Fortunately, the sound of several plates, bowls and other items landed on the floor next to the king startling the sorcerer and causing him to release his grip on the young girl and take a step back from her chair.

"I'm very sorry sir," Simo said, he immediately bent down and started to pick up the huge mess he had made.

Raven looked over at his sister, "Rayne, are you hurt?"

"Hurry up! Pick up that mess fool," the captain yelled.

"Yes sir, I am."

Rayne, not quite recovered from whatever Nicias had started to do to her hadn't spoken yet.

"Hythor is it?" Nicias spurted out of his mouth.

"What?" Raven said with a stunned expression on his face.

Nicias continued in his relaxed demeanor, "I told you there are many ways to get the truth out of people."

Raven took the opportunity to turn his head away from the glare of the sorcerer while he was making his way back to sit down next to the king

"Hythor, what is that? Is that where you live?"

"Yes, that is the village we were born in but it's very small," he was stalling now, just trying to keep the attention off of his sister.

"Maybe later when we have a little more time I'll pay it a visit; if your parents are still alive I can have Captain Asal here make their acquaintance."

Raven looked at him with a blank expression. He was clearly getting the sorcerers message. "What do you want from us? I told you, she had a dream and we have no idea where this book is or how to find it."

"Yes, I know what you told me but I'm having a difficult time believing you, that's all."

By now Simo had finished cleaning up the mess and was leaving to get some more food. With no one to cruelly interrogate, the captain took his leave from the room to go and check on the progress of his men who were still searching the tunnels. He left several of his elite guards in the room with the sorcerer and gave them explicit instructions that the captives were not to be left alone under any circumstances.

Even though there was a good breeze blowing into his chambers the king felt the room to be a little stuffy. Having to sit next to the sorcerer most of the time was bad enough but with the addition of two young prisoners and four guards standing behind them and all in the same room he felt the need for fresh air. In the meantime, Simo had come up with a plan of his own while he was in the kitchen. While mixing the poisonous powder into the cups of the four guards he was at the same time mentally organizing the order of events that had to take place for his rescue plan to work.

"These kids have to be here for a reason and I will not allow this sorcerer to destroy their lives as well."

He knew that what he was doing would result in a death sentence but he would rather save them and go back to being a nomad in the desert before seeing his friend the king, broken down any further. The king would have to understand the sacrifice he was willing to make for him and the city. He would return one day to explain his actions and gladly accept any consequences that was demanded of him once the sorcerer and his men were either dead or gone. The king was still outside on the balcony when his cook re-entered the room and started pouring the prepared cups of wine for the guards. He started walking with his head down towards the table but was intently listening to what Nicias was saying to the siblings.

"What I am interested in now young man is how your sister came by this strange bow," which a guard had placed on the table in front of him earlier. "Stranger still is the magnificent golden sword that none of my guards, including Captain Asal, has been able to properly lift by himself but somehow a teenager like you have carried without a problem. I will certainly enjoy this next part of getting into your sisters mind and discovering these little secrets." The gleam in his eyes accompanied by his sinister grin really worried Raven.

Simo had very calmly walked behind the sorcerer because he knew that it would only be a few minutes before his poison would take effect on the soldiers then he would show this sorcerer what he was made of.

Chapter Fifteen

A Narrow Escape: Grandson of a Thief...

A few minutes after drinking the poison two of the four guards believing they had headaches grabbed their foreheads but then collapsed to the floor unconscious. The other two guards felt a bit dizzy so they leaned on the large shelf next to them and soon dropped to the floor as well, dead. By the time Nicias knew what was happening the cook had struck him on the back of the head with his dagger knocking him out cold.

"Don't say a word!" The cook quietly told them. The siblings remained in their chairs stunned by what had just happened while at the same moment King Thais was walking back into the room from the balcony. Simo didn't know when Captain Asal would be coming back into the room so he quickly hustled over and untied the brother and sister. "Go young sir, get your sword and hurry back here. Is there anything you need from your room young miss?"

"No, my bow is here on the table." Like a nervous habit Rayne checked to see if the necklace her parents had given her with the small rings on it was still around her neck, it was. She tried to block the sorcerer from entering her mind by thinking about what her parents had said the rings represented. She had done all she could do to concentrate on that one thing.

"What's going on here Simo? You're going to get yourself killed!" The king said.

Simo quickly looked down the hallway and saw that Raven was already returning from his room so he started adjusting the sword by his own side.

"Sir, I've given this great thought, I have to do all that I can to help you and these kids find the book so they can destroy it or take it away from the city."

Surprised at hearing these words Rayne said, "We're not here to destroy the book."

Out of breath Raven ran back into the room and up to the cook, and said, "What are we doing? We have to get out of here! I am not going to be tied up again."

Simo looked over to the King, "Sir, please forgive me for this but it's for your own good." With a heavy heart Simo hit the king on the head knocking him out.

"What are you doing? Are you crazy?" Raven shouted.

Simo dragged the kings unconscious body closer to the table and replied, "No, I'm not crazy young sir. Listen to me carefully you two we don't have much time. He pointed down the small passageway in their room that led to the kings dressing area, "There is a secret hatch hidden under the chair in that room down there." The cook had his left hand on Ravens right shoulder and was watching for anyone to come down the hallway. He was in the middle of explaining things to them when over Ravens shoulder he saw Captain Asal reach the top of the stairs and start walking down the hallway. He was beginning to look more like a protector and less of a cook as the minutes passed. Simo's eyes met the captains at the same time. Seeing the sorcerers body lying on the floor behind the cook the captain yelled, "What the hell is going on here?" He ran towards the entrance of the chamber. Simo instinctively pushed the kids back behind him then reached into his shirt and pulled out a small orange rock and forcefully threw it at the ground in front of the doorway before the captain reached it. The weird little rock hit the ground with a white flash which then created a burst of orangish smoke causing the captain to almost freeze in his steps. His eyes had gone wide open and his face looked to have turned pale, even if it was for just a second, Rayne did notice it. He drew his sword and started slashing in the air madly at nothing in front of him while yelling for reinforcements to come and help him. She had already grabbed her bow and was about ready to release an arrow at the captain when Simo turned and yelled at her, "No!"

She released her fingers without giving the arrow its target.

"I could have shot him," she replied.

"You will have time for that later," he said. "There is a chair at the end of the passageway like I mentioned before under it is a secret passageway that will lead you to the kitchen. Once there turn right, open the wooden door and head immediately into the streets and disguise yourselves.

"Why is the captain swinging his sword like that and not entering the room?"

"He believes he's fighting a dragon young miss. Don't stop until you find the large street market it's about twenty minutes away, I'll meet you there in thirty minutes or so."

"What are you going to do?" She asked.

"I'm going to try to hold them off so you have some extra time to escape."

"What! You are crazy like my brother said, you can't hold them off."

He turned to face them both pulled a sword from his side and said, "Jahe is a good friend of mine, now go I can take care of myself," He said firmly.

They ran to the end of the small passageway and found the chair with some clothes on top of it. They slide the chair away exposing a small trap door beneath. After lifting the trap door they could make out a narrow stone staircase that wound itself down for several feet. They did the best they could to shut the door place the chair back on top of it. They couldn't find the exit when they reached the bottom of the stairs so, frustrated and with the pressure of trying to get out quickly she decided to push on the wall in front of them. It gave way just enough for them to squeeze out of what they realized was a false brick wall. They closed it headed out of the door they found to the right, thanks to the sunlight coming through the cracks in it and walked outside of the palace for the first time. She hid the bow under her cloak and lowering their hoods to conceal their faces walked as fast as they could without running into the crowd of people that were just ahead of them in the street.

***

Captain Asal was fighting his heart out trying to slash at the terrible clawed beast in front of him. He thought he had already slashed one of its arms off but it didn't seem to slow this beast down at all. Several of his elite soldiers ran up behind him with their hands on their swords as well but they never unsheathed them.

"Help me kill this beast!" He ordered them. "Get over here! What are you men doing standing there?" He was tired and full of sweat at this point but was more surprised by the blank faces on his men.

Perplexed, one of his guards answered, "There's nothing there sir."

"Sir, there is no beast, unless you're talking about the cook," another guard said.

The captain looked back at the doorway and could still see the ferocious dragon waiting to claw at his face. He watched while one of his soldiers casually walked past him and into the kings chamber, at that precise moment the imaginary dragon disappeared. His vision cleared and coming into view was the kings cook who was holding a sword with two unconscious bodies lying behind him on the floor. Captain Asal walked through the doorway with a renewed sense of hate for the cook who was now standing in his way. Without saying a word Simo had already struck one of the guards down and as the other two scrambled to pull out their swords in time he was able to, with a few moves have these elite guards on the ground lifeless. The captain walked to his right preparing his attack, "I see that you are not just a cook, you move like a younger person instead of the old man that I know you are. I will enjoy ending your life."

He wanted to buy a little more time for the siblings, "I move like someone who is not going to allow you to boss me around anymore." He knew that the sorcerer was going to be waking up any minute now and he needed to get out of there to make it to their rendezvous.

150

"If I'm such an old man then you should be able to beat me easily."

The captain charged forward using a downward slicing move that Simo blocked easily. They exchanged several more blows and with it came the resounding sound of steel on steel which reverberated throughout the chamber. He could tell that the captain was tired after slicing him on his upper arm which made him drop his sword. Before Simo could deliver the final blow he saw several more of the guards running down the hallway to join the fight. He looked down at the captain, who by this time had gone to one knee and backhanded him letting him know that he had been beaten. He ran to the balcony then climbed over the small wall and holding on by his fingers, dropped to the street below and disappeared into the crowd.

***

"Rayne was unable to contain her excitement any longer, "Can you believe that crazy cook? I don't know how he got us out of there alive?"

"He was certainly full of surprises. I'm just happy it didn't take us longer than twenty minutes to find this place."

The sounds and smells of the crowded fruit and vegetable market were all around them now. Initially after leaving the palace they had gotten a bit lost and having to ask for directions twice didn't help them at all. Rayne marveled at the multitude of people walking past her. Some of the people were merchants that came from all over Tundar trying to sell not just food, but live animals, clothing, herbs, potions and even jars of wine. There were also the odd drifters, thieves, disgruntled old soldiers from past conflicts as well as some regular people trying their luck at a new life. Well, that's certainly not all that was for sale around here. Tundar had a small reputation where you could find not just regular people but some crooked ones, the ones that looked for work on boats or could be hired for much darker purposes.

"Keep your eyes and ears open, this cook, nomad or whatever the hell he is should be here soon. You know I thought we were so prepared and careful about things, but I'm starting to think that we didn't know nearly enough when we started out." He reached into his pocket felt around and pulled out five measly silver and one copper coin, granted it was more than some people had but he was still unable to suppress his feeling of disappointment. His sister, who knew is entire facial library only consisted of about five expressions knew something was brewing in his head. She would have to find out what is was later because the cook had already spotted them. Simo saw them talking several feet away and silently approached them, he gently placed a hand on each of their shoulders and was about to speak when Rayne gave out a startled scream.

"Be quiet!" Simo told her quickly covering her mouth with one of his hands.

"Well, I'm sorry," she replied with a surprised tone, "you startled me."

"I'm glad you found this place, now I need to tell you both something, you have to get out of the city today. There is a secret entrance to the palaces underground tunnels located about one mile away on the western side of the nearest mountain."

"It will be easy enough for us to get out of here," Raven assured him. "Where exactly is this entrance located?"

Simo pointed to the mountain nearest to them. "The lower portion of it is made up of mostly loose dirt and rocks. The entrance is on the west side of it but due to some of our past rainfalls water tends to trickle down the mountain in an odd way so you will see what looks like a small valley cut into the side of the slope. There are several very large flat rocks laying on their sides along the slope, once there you will see an opening that you will have to crawl down into. After you crawl inside you will enter a small cave that progressively gets larger. I haven't been there in over a year but I'm sure it still exists. There is an old iron gate inside, pry it open and follow it down until the floor levels out that is the secret entrance to the palace tunnels."

There was a lot of shouting in the background causing them to turn their heads towards the direction of the palace where unknown to them, hundreds of soldiers were starting to aggressively search for them.

"Will you two be ok?" He asked.

She answered without a pause, "One of the many great things about being able to change into any animal is the one about changing into a bird. We can simply fly out of here."

"That is truly a remarkable gift you both have."

"What about you?" She stammered.

"Don't you worry about me young miss if I choose not to be found they will not find me, I could almost hide in the open without being found." He smiled at them and give her a wink, turned and casually walked into the crowd of people disappearing before their eyes.

"What is it with that wink before taking off and doing something stupid?" She said.

"I have no idea what you're talking about." He placed his hand on her head and spun her around, "Come on, let's find an area where no one is around so we can change and head towards the mountain."

There was a lot of chaos around them now and people were hastily trying to pack up their small areas or just protect their wares from being broken or stolen. Because they were walking within a crowd of people she almost didn't feel the smoothness of the crime, they had only taken a few steps from the time they left the cook so their pickpocket almost got away with it.

Feeling his prize Findle was about ready to pull the small change pouch loose and walk in the other direction when a tight grip on his wrist made him realize he was caught. Turning around quickly with one hand grasping onto his wrist and the other holding a knife at his abdomen Rayne confronted him, "What do you think you're doing thief?"

"Are you kidding me? Of all the worst times for this to happen. Let him go, we don't have time for this right now we have to go," Raven insisted.

Heeding her brothers advice she reluctantly put her blade away but with a disgusted tone in her voice said, "Get out of here thief before I cut you," then followed Raven.

The thief ran to catch up to them, "Wait, wait, you're not going to kill me?"

They kept walking, she didn't bother to look back at the short kid talking to her now being more annoyed than anything. "I will if you keep following me."

"I owe you now."

"What! You don't owe me anything, more importantly I don't want anything from you so leave me alone before I change my mind."

He hustled to keep up with their pace, "My name is Findle, I'm at your service."

She halted and grabbed onto the back of Raven's cloak stopping him midstride. "What did you say your name was?"

After being jerked backwards Raven tried to compose himself by standing motionless alongside her. Even though he was listening to them speak an irritated look began to take shape on his face because he had been stopped in the first place.

"You said your name is Findle? Is that a popular name here?"

"No, I was named after my father who was named after his father, why do you ask?"

"We knew someone by that name a long time ago who owned an antique shop."

"My grandfather owned an antique shop many years ago but he died when it burnt down. Besides, you're both way too young to have known him."

She made an obvious show of saying her words slowly to her brother, "Did you hear that, his grandfather owned an antique shop."

Raven didn't answer her, but did look at the young thief a bit differently to see if he could find any resemblance from the Findle they used to know. He asked the thief a question of his own. "Did he have a large carved elephant at the entrance of his shop?"

The young thief put his head down and quietly said, "Yes, that was his shop."

Findle noticed the fact that they began to get very nervous at hearing the sounds of the soldiers in the background getting closer.

"You can hide in my home for a little while if you like."

"What makes you think we need to hide from anything?" Raven snapped.

"I didn't mean to offend you with my offer."

They stood for a minute weighing their options. Findle began to walk away from them but turned back and waved his arm for them to follow, "Come on I'll show you."

"He sure does speak fast," she joked.

The three of them walked for about ten minutes. The trip took them by a bunch of small run down shanty type stone shacks until they found his home and went inside. Immediately upon entering the doorway they realized his home wasn't as small on the inside as they thought it would be. They also walked right past a charred carved elephant that had been placed on the inside of the front door.

"You'll be safe here. There are so many little homes in the city it's impossible for the soldiers to check all of them besides, they have never come to our home."

Rayne took it upon herself now to say something to this thief. "Findle, we really appreciate you taking us in like this but I would like you to know that we really did know your grandfather we just look young." She knew that this Findle looked to be about their own age and she could only hope he would believe her. Hearing strange voices coming from the front of her house Findles grandmother walked into the room to see what all the commotion was about.

"What's going on in here Fin?"

The sibling's eyes were still adjusting to the darkness in the room so Raven took the opportunity to make sure that Rayne knew that they shouldn't stay for too long.

"As soon as we can we're going to have to be going so we can make it to the mountain before it gets dark," he said.

"Who are your new friends Fin?" His grandmother asked.

"No one Pia, they just needed a place to stay for a while." Pia was the nickname Findle had given his grandmother ever since he was a small child. Rayne examined the older woman's face to see if she could recognize a hint of the younger woman she once knew but being unsure she looked over at her brother reassurance. "Yes, I agree, as soon as it quiets down outside we'll have to leave," she answered.

"You have a nice home ma'am," she commented.

With a child's enthusiasm for getting new gifts regularly Findles eight year old little brother walked into the room. He came from out behind the grandmothers dress and hugged his older brother, "Hi Fin, did you bring me anything today?"

Fin reached into his shirt and pulled out a small wooden carved bird. "As a matter of fact I did." The younger boy hugged his brother again and took the gift from his hand and quickly ran into the back room. She was always a softy for the big brother taking care of the younger sibling, "He's cute, what's his name?"

"Findle."

"You're kidding me?" Raven said in astonishment.

"My parents will probably be here soon so if you'd like some soup you're more than welcome to it. They like the name a lot! Anyways, I'm a third generation and my little brother is the fourth generation Findle."

They were invited into the back room and were both invited to sit on a large faded red carpet of sorts. Rayne sat next to the little brother while the grandmother served them a simple soup. The soup had the aroma of meat, although they didn't see any and it also contained one small potato and several pieces of carrots. There was only one bedroom in his small home and his parents shared it with his little brother, he and his grandmother slept where they now sat, the floor. Raven reached into his pouch and removed three of his silver coins and placed them into the hand of the older Findle.

"What's this for?" He asked with a surprised but happy look on his face.

He exchanged looks with his sister, "Buy your family some food when we're gone. We made a promise a long time ago to a good friend we knew named Findle," referring to his grandfather, "that when we returned here we would look after his family."

"Thank you. Since my grandfather, Tata passed we've been able to survive as pickpockets and "minor thieves," he emphasized with a pointed finger. "Why were you two hiding from the soldiers?"

Without wanting to disclose too much information and with a mouthful of bread Raven replied, "It's got a little to do with finding an entrance into some tunnels below the city."

"I know how to get into the tunnels! Even my little brother here knows that I take him down there all of the time. Of course, now the tunnels are filled with soldiers but they are stupid and have no idea where to go."

Rayne's spoon fell onto her lap, "What are you talking about, there's another entrance into the tunnels, here in the city?" She asked.

"I don't know how many secret entrances there might be but my grandfather made his own. He heard a story one day from a man who had had too much to drink saying that he'd seen tons of gold down there so for more than two years he dug his own entrance down into the tunnels."

"If you would like I can show you where it is."

He waved them into the small bedroom and while they stood in the doorway watching he slid his parents entire bed away from the wall exposing a large wooden trap door partially covered by sand.

Chapter Sixteen

To Kill A King: The Unturned Stone...

"Can you stand Your Excellency?" The Captain asked.

With the aid of one of his loyal elite guards and with the help of a nearby table Nicias managed to stand up, his eyes slowly opened and he could hear the sounds of shuffling feet and the unmistakable voice of captain Asal barking orders at people. His vision was a bit blurry and he had a headache which was confirmed by the small lump on the back of his head. He nodded his answer at being no so they placed him into the chair so he could regain his faculties. The captain was beside himself with anger, "I want all of the palace gates shut, now! Did you hear me?"

The captain noticed a small trickle of blood running down from the temple area of King Thais as another guard was assisting him into a chair of his own. The king was groggy himself.

"Captain Asal, if you would be so kind to stop yelling," Nicias said.

He looked over at the sorcerer whose elbows were now resting on top of the table while his hands were cradling the weight of his sore head. A guard attempted to clean the cut on the captains shoulder but he was harshly pushed aside. He started to yell at the younger soldier but caught himself, "Attend to the king," with a dismissive wave towards King Thais. Another soldier promptly ran into the chamber, "We lost him sir."

"What do you mean you lost him?"

"By the time we heard who we were looking for sir he had disappeared into the crowd."

He slammed his fist through a nearby wall, "Is anything going to go right for me today!" He faced the soldier and planted his finger into his chest, "I want no less than four of you to stay with Our Excellency at all times is that clear?"

"Yes sir!" Came the response.

"He'll need some time to clear his head but in the meantime I will see to it that the cities gates are all closed." He spun around and quickly marched down the hallway. A short time later as Nicias was beginning to regain some more of his composure he turned to ask the king a few critical questions. The kings head was wrapped up with a white cloth but the little red spot where he had absorbed his blow was clearly visible.

"I asked you this question before Thais, where did you find this cook of yours and you told me that he just walked into the palace about five years ago asking to cook for you."

Due to the extreme pain pulsating on the side of his head he honestly didn't want to have a conversation with Nicias right now but he did manage a weak answer. "Yes, as I have already told you, that is exactly how he came to cook for me. I don't know where he came from, I just liked how he prepared my food. That is honestly his only duty."

Nicias stood up slowly but still felt a little wobbly in the knees. "You will pay for his insubordinate actions, do you hear me?"

With the assistance of one of his guards and not wanting to wait for the king's response he walked out of the chamber and down the hallway towards his room. Captain Asal was more than mad he was fuming, if he could have produced fire out of his hands he would have burnt the first several people he saw in the streets. He knew the palace gates were probably already closed so he jumped on his horse and headed straight for the north gates that faced the ocean. After fifteen minutes of hard riding he and two of his elite guards arrived at the gates. He climbed down and saw that the gates were indeed shut. He had ridden down the middle of the streets like a madman making people dodge his horse for fearing being trampled. The red and black striped capes that he and his elite guards wore always brought the regular soldiers to attention. Now, similar in construction to the other two entrances into the city this gate was very wide and required two large doors to be closed, one swinging from the left and the other the right. There were over a hundred men who were stationed at this gate and they did an assortment of jobs.

The captain yelled at the Lieutenant who was in charge of the gate, his name is Rezie. "I need five of your best men."

Without knowing the purpose of the request, "Yes sir," came the reply.

Five names were called out and soon the five men approached and lined themselves up in front of the inspecting captain. Regular soldiers never wore the red and black capes because it was a privilege for the elite guard only.

"Do you vouch for each of these men?" He asked Lieutenant Rezie.

To be in charge of the gates was also a special duty in itself, but not as special as being chosen to be part of the sorcerers elite guard.

"Yes sir I do, these are five of my best men."

He reached into a large pouch on the back of his saddle and pulled out five red and black striped capes and threw one in each of the five awaiting soldiers chests. This was the best thing that could be awarded to a regular guard, the pinnacle of what they worked so hard for, to be in the inner circle.

"You five are now part of my elite guard! You answer directly to me or Our Excellency. If you fail in your duty to protect him you will pay with your lives is that understood."

With the excitement of having their new found freedom they all yelled at the same time, "Yes sir!" The newly minted elite guards assisted each other donning their new decoration and proudly faced Captain Asal. He pointed to the three on his left, "I want you three to ride to the south gate and make sure it is closed, no one gets in or out, you are elite guards now and I want you all to act like it; you other two will proceed to the west gate by the river and do the same thing."

Five horses were immediately brought up and the newly promoted soldiers took off like the wind to make their captains wishes become a reality. Captain Asal made sure a full description of his lost prisoners were known to all of his soldiers he then headed back to the palace. The captain's thoughts drifted towards the book, "This book has to be found today..."

When they first arrived in Bytar they had no idea that the tunnels stretched for miles under the city and in different directions with hundreds of small rooms. He was going to have to provide his soldiers with a new form of motivation if they were going to find the book before tomorrow night.

***

Nicias was assisted into his room by one of the elite guards, "I need to be left alone for a little while," then closed the door behind him.

He could heal himself in privacy and also use his power to search for the troublesome siblings and cook. He sat in the center of the room, closed his eyes and grasped his amulet with both hands and started mumbling a healing chant that he had been taught many years ago. His hands started to glow bright red and he began to float just a few inches off the ground. He spoke to the evil spirit inside of the amulet telling him of the pain he felt in his body and no sooner had he finished his sentence than he felt a cooling sensation at the back of his head. He reached back to feel for the bump on his head but amazingly it was no longer there. Nicias had a clear mind now and with his eyes still closed focused his attention on any small rodent or dog so that he could take over their minds to see what they could see. With only two days left until the eclipse and the red moon he was more than willing to get rid of the king for good for what he felt was his lying. It was getting late in the day as his magical amulet started the search for a set of new eyes for him. By simply using his mind he felt like he was floating through the crowded city streets full of people, like being carried on the back of someone's shoulders. He was effortlessly moving from street to street like an invisible intruder until he spotted a mangy sleeping dog in a corner. The dogs head popped up, but not seeing anyone in front of him he thought to go back to sleep but that was not his choice anymore, Nicias had taken control of his mind and body. With the aid of his temporary body he ran through the back areas of streets looking for the siblings and that treacherous cook.

***

Captain Asal arrived back at the palace doors having gone over in his mind his, "fear of death speech" he was going to give to his men. One of his elite soldiers ran up to him as he was dismounting from his horse but he was in such a hurry he tripped and fell in front of him.

"What in the hell is wrong with you soldier?"

The soldier jumped to his feet with excitement, "We've found the book sir! I've posted several men in the tunnel and instructed them not to enter the room."

"Where was it found?"

"The soldier said he found it by accident sir. He was adjusting a torch on a wall when it gave way and he ended up pulling it downward like a lever, that's when a secret door opened up in the wall."

"Great job! I'll tell Our Excellency.."

Captain Asal ran into the palace and bounded up the stairs like a man on a mission heading directly for King Thais' chambers closely followed by the soldier.

He asked the guards posted by the King Thais, "Where is Our Excellency?"

"Sir, he was taken to his quarters over an hour ago."

He immediately turned around and headed back down the hallway, passed the staircase he had just run up and continued on a short distance until seeing the same two guards he had assigned to Nicias. Both of the guards could see his lowered brow and stern look as he approached them. The first guard asked nervously, "Is everything alright sir?"

"Yes, of course it is." The door to the sorcerers room was shut. "Is Our Excellency inside his room?"

"Yes sir, but he specifically asked not to be disturbed."

The captain knocked on the door, "He'll want to be disturbed for the news I have."

"Your Excellency, it's Captain Asal. I have great news."

The soldiers were all looking at each other wondering what news could be this important. He knocked on the door several more times with the same message, "Has anyone entered the room since he went in it?"

"No sir, no one has entered his room."

There was no response from the inside and he was starting to get a little concerned. He drew his sword and was about to kick the door in when it suddenly opened, "I thought I told you I wanted to be left alone," addressing his comment more at the guards rather than at the captain. Re-sheathing his sword, "I'm sorry Your Excellency, but I have great news, we've found the book! I have not seen it yet myself but this soldier has." All the attention was now shifted towards the guard standing next to him.

The guard bowed, "Yes, Your Excellency, I have seen the book and I placed several men to guard it with strict instructions not to touch it. It is about a mile away from here through some winding tunnels, but I can assure you it is there!"

"Very good Captain it seems our luck has changed for the positive. If you would be so kind as to assemble Thais for me we will be escorting him to his new quarters in one of the rooms below."

"Of course Your Excellency."

The sorcerer gathered a few things while Captain Asal walked back into the kings chambers with the good news. Although King Thais had been able to rest he hadn't eaten very much today and still needed some rest for his headache.

"You two," referring to his guards, "grab the king and follow me he will be residing in different quarters tonight."

"What's going on here?" King Thais stammered.

"Get your things and follow us sir," the soldier said.

While gathering his things he couldn't help but think that today might be his last day alive. He felt the weight of regret, things not finished in his life and the emptiness he had about not having a wife or children, depression and a bit of fear started to take hold of him. After being pushed down the hallway like a criminal he saw Nicias waiting at the top of the stairs, but before he arrived the sorcerer started to walk down them.

"Where are these idiots taking me now?" The king thought.

He hadn't even had the freedom to walk around his own palace for almost two weeks. Once down the stairs they made their last turn and he knew where he was being corralled to, the tunnels. They walked through the large iron gate and down into the tunnels. Once they reached the bottom of the stairs the king looked around and what used to be a constant darkness was now somewhat pleasantly lit up with an assortment of torches running the length of the tunnel.

"I told you Thais that you would pay for the actions of that cowardly cook of yours."

Without a care in the world as to what was going to happen to him anymore he answered, "So you did Nicias. So this is your plan? Lock me in a room and throw away the key. I must tell you I'm a bit disappointed I figured you to be the torturing type of sorcerer."

"Well, we can always come back to that if necessary Thais."

"Take me to my book soldier."

These tunnels were not mere dirt passageways. The one they walked through now was elaborately dug it had a squared column in the center and another one every fifty feet. It was also very wide, more than twelve feet from end to end with the ceiling being about eight feet tall. There were torches placed alternately on the walls, one left side then about fifty feet away there was another one on the right side. The entire system was made up of tunnels throughout and chiseled into the side walls either to the left or the right were different sized rooms that had small wooden doors with iron bars in the front of them so a person could peer into the room. The floors were dirt but due to the years of foot traffic it was a compacted dirt and the walls were in some areas rock. The one constant was the presence of the soldiers standing at intervals throughout most of the tunnels. King Thais had only been down here a few times himself and the last time was over a year ago. At this point he had no idea where he was, it would take absolutely no effort at all to get completely lost in these maze of tunnels. After what felt like an hour of walking the one soldier broke the silence, "We are almost there Your Excellency."

They had already taken several right turns and a few left turns when Nicias suddenly stopped them in front of a room.

The king was forcefully pushed inside, "Enjoy your new quarters Thais."

He fell on the dirt floor and heard the loud clanging sound as the door was shut behind him leaving him in near total darkness. Nicias peered into the dark room through the iron bars, "Now, this suits you Thais." He turned and continued walking through the tunnel. He was pleased with himself in confining the king to that little cell. after thirty minutes he was beginning to lose his patience, "How much farther?" He asked.

The guard pointed ahead, "At the next tunnel to our left Your Excellency."

There was a noticeable presence of extra guards standing around as they made the last turn; within a few steps they were standing at the open doorway on their right. Normally this would have barely been considered a doorway, it was a very narrow opening with a lit torch just in front of the door. For fear of not wanting the door to close Nicias ordered another torch be brought to him. He lifted the torch up and cautiously took a step inside the room; his eyes beheld a large closed golden book which sat atop a stone podium in the center of the room.

Chapter Seventeen

The Burning Torch: Just Empty Rooms...

Raven ran over and went to his knees next to the Findle and started to brush the dirt off the wooden door with his hands. "Is this what I think it is?"

"If you think it's a secret passageway then yes."

"How in the world did this get to be under your parents bed?"

"It was the only place my grandfather could think of that would allow him to dig in complete privacy."

"Why that clever little," Rayne started to say.

"Clever little what?" Findle asked.

Changing the subject she replied, "Your grandfather was always one to think ahead of other people, I mean look at this ingenious plan he devised. So, you've never found gold down there?"

"No, but it's possible that we simply just missed it. The tunnels run for miles and it's dark down there so we always have to carry a torch back and forth."

Findle grasped a rope handle and lifted the cover straight up and leaned it against the wall in front of him. "There are a lot of soldiers patrolling down here lately and they have placed torches all over the place so we'll have to be very careful."

Raven peered into the hole where a makeshift wooden ladder went down about eight feet to the bottom. Findle stood up and got into position to crawl down the ladder when unexpectedly his little brother entered the room.

Excitedly, he asked, "Can I go with you Fin?"

"No, not this time, we'll go later I promise, I have to show our guests around a little bit."

The grandmother listened nearby to the younger boys complaints but after a few minutes of negotiations she came in and snatched the younger boy up in her arms and whisked him into the other room.

Findle took two steps down the ladder then popped his head back up, "I don't even know your names?"

"Oh, I'm sorry." She looked behind her to make sure the grandmother wasn't listening and said, "My name is Rayne and this is my brother Raven."

Satisfied, he continued his decent down the ladder and once on the bottom he instructed them to follow him down. Rayne was a little concerned about getting a splinter stuck in her finger while descending the ladder since she had already had a bad experience with the thorn but her fear was for nothing when she realized that the rungs of the ladder were so smooth from the years of use.

"Let me ask you a question Findle, how long has this entrance been here?"

He looked at her and thought for a moment, "Wow, good question, I would say more than thirty years. Now, I'd like to give you two some advice, these tunnels might all look the same but they are very different ."

When Findle started his explanation she took the time to briefly examine the space they were currently in his voice began to trail off silently in the background of her ears until it was barely audible. The tunnel was just over six feet tall and very narrow, she could stretch her arms out and touch both sides but it was still big and wide enough to comfortably walk in. It was a small miracle that his grandfather had dug the whole thing by hand because it must have taken quite a while to make. The small tunnel made a left turn up ahead but just before the turn was a squared hole that had been cut into the wall that contained some type of object inside of it. She was too far away to see what it was, but there was something definitely there.

With a doubtful expression and raised eyebrows Findle asked her, "Did you understand all of my instructions Rayne?"

"Yes, sorry, well some of it," she admitted. "I think you said don't get lost," shrugging her shoulders.

"The tunnels seem to be have been dug in different sizes so some are very narrow like this one while others are wide so we will have to be very quiet because the sound will travel." He walked towards the end of the passageway and while making his left turn casually reached his hand into the squared opening and touched a small carving.

Before continuing Rayne asked him, "Hold on a minute, what was that you just did?"

"It's a wooden carving my grandfather made of a small elephant. It's a habit, I touch it for good luck before I go ahead. You should try it."

She was the first to act in giving the small statue a quick rub, "It can't hurt, besides we can use all of the luck we can get."

They walked a little further until seemingly they couldn't walk anymore. "Ok, once we pass this part we'll be in one of the main tunnels, it's very large and lit up so remember to be very quiet because our voices will carry."

He took one step made a quick right then another quick left which was a weird little design that his grandfather had made. He purposely created a clever little zig zag type of entrance, it was a bit narrow, but it was also near impossible to spot. They waited for Findle to give them the ok and then they both followed his lead until they exited the small space and were standing in a massive hallway. Looking to the right and then straight ahead she was amazed to find out that they were in a corner and couldn't imagine how his grandfather had dug this thing so precise, talk about luck. Compared to what they just had walked through this was huge. They could see at least fifteen columns that dotted down the center of both tunnels.

He gathered them together and whispered, "Just follow me, I'll take you to some places that there shouldn't be any guards."

With as much care as they could the three of them walked through the huge tunnel making sure to stay in the middle using the columns as shields to hide behind. Rayne thought it was very pleasant down here not at all what she had imagined it to be like. They whispered to each other the whole time until Findle pointed out a small room on the right side that had an old door that opened to the inside.

"What's that?" She asked."

"My dad thinks they used to keep criminals or anyone they wanted to have disappear in these rooms but honestly if you're locked up down here your never getting out."

The more she listened to Findle speak the more he reminded her of his grandfather, especially the quirkiness of them both being fast talkers.

"How many of these types of rooms are there down here?" Raven asked.

"I have no idea, hundreds maybe thousands I don't know why there are so many though."

Raven walked inside of one of the rooms. He was overwhelmed with a sense of loneliness and despair and said in a low voice, "I can see what you mean it's cold and dark in here without the light from the torches in the hallway it would have been horrible to have been locked up down here." When he exited the room he made a dramatic gesture of wiping his whole body down with his hands like he had walked through a wall of cobwebs.

"Shh," Findle said, "Do you hear that?"

They tilted their heads to aim their ears down the hallway for better reception.

"No," he replied, "wait, I do hear something it sounds like footsteps and people talking."

They had already walked away from the room but quickly hustled their way back so all three of them could duck back inside of it. Moments later, two guards walked past the doorway but on the other side of the columns. They overheard them talking about how the book was found a few hours ago and that their Excellency was in the tunnels somewhere right now doing some type of magic. She also heard the kings name mentioned at the end but the soldiers were now too far away to clearly make out what they were saying.

"They've already found the book so we've failed her," Raven said. He leaned on the wall while his back slowly slide down until his butt hit the dirt floor. With his head in his hands he now felt the weight of failure pressing him down onto the floor. Rayne started to pace back and forth repeating in her head the whole conversation the guards had been having.

"Is that what he was looking for the whole time, a book?" Findle asked.

"I don't know what his plans were when he entered the city but I do know one of them was finding this magical book!"

Raven didn't answer, he was despondent. To him it felt like the whole world had just crashed down on top of him and all of his hopes.

"Raven, pull yourself together it's not over yet. We still have two days until the eclipse and if we have to steal the entire book from that old sorcerer then we're going to do it."

He lifted his head up for the first time in five minutes, "You're right, you're absolutely right. Findle can you show us some more of these tunnels?"

"Sure, but it's going to be dark soon, I think it might be better if we come back later when it's really late because most of the guards will be on the ground asleep."

Findle peeked his head out of the doorway to make sure the coast was clear then they followed their guide back to the corner zig zag entrance and headed back up the ladder and securely closed the lid. Hearing noises his little brother returned to the room and stood in the doorway displaying his little grumpy face, "Mom and dad want to talk to you Fin."

"Ok, don't be angry with me, I told you we'll go later," but the little boy had already turned and gone.

"I see he's a little upset," she commented.

He wiped his sleeve across his forehead to dry some sweat, "Ah, he'll get over it, I'll be back in a few minutes." He then walked out of the room to see what his parents wanted.

"Raven what do you think of these tunnels?"

"What do you mean what do I think?"

"I was thinking, we'll be able to cover more ground if we change into a smaller and faster animal. I don't want to have to rely on Findle to take us everywhere. We barely scratched the surface on the length of tunnels down there and as humans we'll get lost in five minutes without a guide. Dogs are too big so I was thinking more along the lines of a cat. Listen to me, I'm definitely not talking about splitting up because the place is way too large, but cats are fast and have a great sense of smell which we can use to our advantage to find our way back to the entrance, which as you just saw is almost invisible. Lastly, they are incredibly quiet I mean we could almost run through the tunnels and sneak by any soldier we see." She finished her appeal and waited for his answer while he sat on the ground and pondered her words.

"That sounds like a good idea he said, we'll test it tonight."

Just then Findle re-entered the room, "My parents would like to meet you both."

Standing up Rayne saw that Raven had unknowingly developed a habit of reaching for and reassuring himself that his sword was still by his side by touching the hilt. As far as he was concerned he was not about to leave it behind under any circumstance. They walked back into the main room of the house where everyone was already seated on the red carpet. There was some prepared food as well as a nice a colorful bowl of green grapes adorning the center of the rug.

"In case you were wondering I gave your coins to my grandmother when we were leaving and my father went out and bought the grapes and some food."

"No, that's great, that's why I gave them to you in the first place," Raven said happily.

For the moment there was no rush to get back down there without a plan so they would have to use this time to formulate one. They sat down with the rest of the family but Raven could tell that Findles parents were watching them closely. The father was breaking a small piece of bread for the youngest boy, "We are very pleased to meet you both. Our son has only been able to tell us a little bit about you both, can you tell us why you're here?"

He had asked them in a very calm and pleasant manner but Raven wasn't sure how much he should really tell them. The grandmother wasn't really paying attention to them she was more interested in how her grandson played with his bread. He started his explanation of the events that brought them to the city but kept a close eye on the older woman to see if at any point she recognized them.

"This is not our first time in Bytar, we were here some years ago but recently we received word that the city was under attack so we came to try to help in whatever way we could."

With an air of skepticism the father asked, "Don't take this the wrong way young man," looking to his wife, "but how do you think two teenagers could make a difference? We have soldiers everywhere and an sorcerer who has made our kings palace his own."

He lowered his head and thought if he should take the chance and tell them everything, well, maybe not everything just an edited version of it. Getting the "ok" nod from his sister he reached out and plucked a few of the grapes and began his story like this, "Although we look to be very young we are not ordinary teenagers."

"Really?"

"Yes sir. I mentioned that we were here in this city before and that much is true." He clearly had the families attention now even the grandmothers wary eye waned from the young boy. He looked directly at the grandmother and began his questions, "Ma'am, do you remember many years ago the two kids who and I stress stupidly tried to "Borrow" a camel that had been tied up in the front of your husband's antique shop. He had only just opened the store a few weeks earlier. My sister and I had been in the city for only a few days but we had been pick pocketed of all of our money. He caught us and took pity on us. Thankfully, hearing our story he invited us into his home for a few weeks until we could get back on our feet."

They could tell by her facial expressions that she was trying to mentally rewind and remember that specific event. Her eyes slowly widened like a haze had been lifted, she finally recognized the two kids in front of her as a single tear lazily ran down the old woman's face. It was an emotional moment for them all.

"That is impossible!" The old woman managed to repeatedly say.

"No, it's not," Rayne replied, looking at the older woman.

"I am the same girl from back then we just age slower than you do."

The grandmother caressed her face with both hands only letting go to give her a big hug. Unable to come up with any words to express his shock at learning the news that the two teenagers were actually older than he was the father sat quietly in his place. Even though they had only lived with them a few weeks she had become quite close with the older woman all those years ago. Rayne had looked at her almost as a second mother.

Raven continued, "You see, we are not your ordinary kids we came here looking to find a magic book that was supposed to be hidden in the tunnels below the city. We recently found out that it has already been located by the soldiers, now we have to find out where they have it."

While Raven spoke to the father of their plans his sister spoke to the grandmother in hushed tones, "Later tonight we are going to go back and continue our search for the book, once we get what we came for we want to figure out a way to get rid of the soldiers, permanently. This city needs to heal and get back to the city that it used to be."

"I can go with you and show you around," the father said steadfastly.

"I don't think that's going to be a great idea sir. We can travel much quicker without a third person," not wanting to disclose the fact too soon that they can also magically change shapes into different animals. Over the next hour they exchanged ideas on where and how to look around without getting caught or lost. The sounds of their voices bored the younger boy which put him to sleep next to the warmth of his mother. Finally, the time had come. They gathered in the parents room again, the father lifted the door and securely placed it against the wall.

"Please do not follow us," Raven asked the family.

Even though there are miles of tunnels I doubt we'll have to go through the entire labyrinth of them in order to find what we're looking for. He started down the ladder and looked up at his sister, "Are you ready?"

"I'll be right behind you."

Hand over hand he finally touched the bottom and whispered, "Ok, it's your turn."

She lifted her leg onto the top of the ladder and made her way down until she felt Ravens helpful hand aiding her off.

"Let's go," he whispered.

They didn't talk until after they made the first left turn and of course the quick touch of their new good luck piece, the small elephant.

Raven looked over, "I think that went very well, better than I thought it was going to go. We have to really make up some time tonight considering we only have two days until the eclipse."

"I know, I told you if I have to steal the whole book I will."

He simply closed his eyes and thought of himself becoming a black cat and as quickly as that he shrank and changed into the animal. Following her brother she did the same but as a grey and black cat she then followed him as he nimbly made the right, then left zig zag turns and stuck his little head out of the corner and checked for any patrolling guards. Nobody was there so they continued forward, "I don't see or hear anyone around," he told her.

As long as they were the same type of animals they could always speak to each other. After taking a few steps into the passageway he looked back at where they had just exited from to see if he would be able to find his way back and was pleased to see and smell a clear path back, now they could continue without a worry.

"How are you,?" He asked.

She ran past him with an enthusiastic response, "I'm great, now let's go and get my book!"

Last time they went right but this time she figured they'd go straight. They made several turns going further and further away from their starting point. It was true, going by the presence of lit torches on the wall most of the tunnels had been visited by soldiers however, they did find a few that were narrow and very dark these usually opened up into larger ones with one or more torches inside. Another constant was that there were quite a lot of rooms with open doors Rayne wondered at who could have built this elaborate place and for what purpose had they been made for. Most of the ceilings were all the same height, she estimated at roughly about eight foot but as they exited this last tunnel they entered into a huge room at least three times the width of the largest one they had seen all night, it was also much taller than all of the rest but was a dead end to the left and right.

"What is this room?" She asked.

"How would I know? Why do you think those stones are there."

There were two stone columns off to their left about six feet from each other, they both went up half the length of the ceiling and there was a larger piece of stone placed right on top of both pieces. There was an eerie atmosphere in this room.

"It looks like a type of doorway or someone's weird sense of artwork."

"I don't care what it is Raven; we've been looking for hours and besides the sleeping guards I've seen we've got nothing to show for all of our work tonight. If it wasn't for that lit torch on the wall I'd of thought no one had ever been here; at least we actually reached the end of one of the tunnels." She was getting a little irritated at not being more productive in their searching and was eager to find something, anything so they headed back the way they had come.

"Hey do you hear that light tapping sound?" He asked.

"It's echoing off of all the walls." She continued to walk down the immense hallway pausing periodically to gauge which way to go. "Yes, it's definitely coming from this direction. A person could get lost for weeks down here," she thought.

They followed the tapping sound for quite a ways until they finally stood in front of a closed door, the first one they had encountered. Rayne approached the door slowly and listened, there was someone just on the inside who was making the tapping sound and when the person coughed that fact was proven.

"I think there's someone actually trapped inside of this room Raven!"

After checking their surroundings for a second time they felt it was safe and changed themselves back to their human forms.

She whispered through the two little iron bars on the doorway, "Hello, is anyone there?"

There was some movement on the inside so she asked her question a second time. In the meantime, Raven had been keeping a watchful eye on the passageways while also inspecting the old latch on the door. It was too dark inside of the room to see anyone and she was wary about putting her face too close to the bars to take a proper peek inside. Finally, as she was about to give up a man's face slowly came into view, "Can you help me?" He asked.

"Yes, of course," with a sense of urgency in her voice. "Who are you?"

"I am King Thais!" Came the reply. He had been leaning on the door while using his small crown to tap on the bars for help because he was still a bit wobbly from the cooks blow to his head. After fiddling with the latch for a few minutes Raven was able to open the door. He slid the latch over and pushed the door in then the older man they had seen from the sorcerers table earlier came stumbling forward.

"Grab him," she said.

"Can you stand up by yourself your Highness?" Raven asked.

"Yes, I can stand, I was thrown in here earlier by Nicias and his guards."

"What are you doing locked in a room down here.?"

"They left me here to die young lady."

"Yes, but why here of all places?"

"I don't know why here, his twisted sense of punishment I guess. I know that they found the book and were on their way to look at it."

Raven pointed in the direction of the right tunnel, "Did they go this way?"

"No, they walked off that way," but he pointed to the opposite direction.

"Well, that figures," Raven huffed.

"When they left me I remember them mentioning they were not too far away from it.

"We have to take him back to," but Raven cut her off with his uplifted hand.

"Don't say names out loud I know what you mean."

They decided that Rayne would change into a tiger and use her sense of smell to find their way back to Findles while Raven would do the same while explaining to the weary king what he was doing. Unfortunately, before they got started voices were heard fast approaching from their left and suddenly two guards emerged from the tunnel. Instantly their eyes met and only one solution entered her mind; quick as lightning she pulled the bow from behind her back and had an arrow at the ready. The two guards reached for their swords when the flash of a white arrow pierced the first guards chest. The second guard, seeing the quick demise of his buddy decided to turn and run back down the tunnel to get help but he only made it a few steps before ending up with the same fate.

"You know that I had no choice in that?"

Raven placed a hand on her shoulder to comfort her, "I know, you did the right thing."

"What are we going to do with their bodies?"

"I have an idea hold onto the king." He said.

He grabbed the first guards body and carried him back into the kings old room and did the same with the second he then shut the door and closed the latch, "Maybe they won't notice, now let's get out of here."

She changed back into the shape of her cat but did so in front of the king which almost gave him a heart attack and caused his eyes and mouth to open wide in disbelief.

"We have to get out of here now," Raven told him. "I'm sorry we don't have the time to fully explain things to you right now your Highness. You will need to trust us. I know this is going to be difficult to understand but I am going to change my body into a lion. Please do not be afraid because I will need you to climb on top of me and hold on so we can get back to safety. A moment later he had changed into the lion and the king, ever so hesitantly grabbed a hold of his mane and managed to pull himself onto Raven's back. Fortunately the knock he received to his head was still somewhat affecting him. Raven followed her lead and they eventually made it back to the narrow zig zag entrance which was what they were looking for.

"Ok, sir, you have to make it through there?"

The king inspected the narrow entrance, "Are you crazy? I will never make it through there, I'm too fat!" He said half-jokingly.

"We've been very lucky so far sir to not have run into more guards, if you can't squeeze yourself through there they will definitely kill you the next time, not just put you in a dark room."

With no other alternatives the king sucked in his gut the best he could and with the extra help of two hands pushing him from behind was able to squeeze his chubby self all the way through to the other side. Raven himself now exited the narrow entrance and saw that his sister was anxiously awaiting him on the other side. They helped the king the last few feet until they made it back to the wooden ladder. She climbed up first figuring that the whole family would be asleep but seeing a small light appear above her head she knew that the father had waited up for them. One by one they exited the tunnel. The father lowered the trap door back down over the hole and noticed for the first time the thin golden crown worn around the forehead of his new guest, for once he was left speechless.

Chapter Eighteen

King Thais: A Key by Any Other Name...

Even the dim light of his candle couldn't hide the face of the person Findles father had only seen twice before, and far away at that. A bit embarrassed by the less than kingly surroundings for his new guest the father started stammering for words.

After a quick glance at the siblings he started, "your Highness, it's a great honor to have you in our home."

"I'm very glad to be here, but I must admit that I'm in need of rest."

His wife and younger son were already asleep in their bed and so with nowhere else other than the living area for people to sleep the siblings, while helping the king along followed him to the back area of the home. They made up a comfortable little spot nearby where his older son and grandmother already slept and within minutes the king had followed suit.

"Where did he come from?" Mr. Findle asked.

Rayne answered, "We found him locked in one of those rooms down there. Believe me we were in as much shock as you are at finding him down there. He told us that the sorcerer had left him there to die."

"It's lucky for him that you two found him now try to get some rest and we'll talk in the morning." He headed back towards his room mumbling under his breath about how he couldn't believe the king was sleeping in his home.

"It'll be a miracle if I get an hour's worth of sleep tonight," Raven said. "Do you think you can find your way back to the room where we rescued him?"

"You're thinking the same thing I am aren't you? It won't be a problem finding my way back there then we can head in the direction he said Nicias went off to."

With a yawn she said, "I don't know about you but I won't have a problem at all sleeping here tonight."

Rayne was awoken by a sad attempt at shutting the squeaky front door which was then followed by hushed whispering in the fathers room, that confirmed that something was going on that was supposed to be a secret. Some minutes later the front door reopened and closed and she saw the father quietly pass by and back into his room. Obviously, she knew they were just being courteous enough to let the king sleep without interruptions. Unbeknownst to her sleeping brother she had been roused out of her sleep two more times during the night by the moaning sounds of the king who was having some kind of restless dream. With the sounds of a bustling city just on the outside of their door, eventually, the whole household was awake, including our king. He sat up and touched the back of his head tenderly, "So, where am I this fine morning?"

The father heard his new guest speaking and walked into the room, "You are in our humble home your Highness. I apologize it's not much, but it is our home."

King Thais was humbled by the honesty of his new host, "Let me tell you something sir, this is as good of a palace as any. What is your name?"

"My name is Findle your Highness."

"Do you have breakfast planned for us Mr. Findle?"

"Yes I do, again, it's not much but," the king raised his hand and stopped him from speaking further.

"Come over here Mr. Findle." He reached into his coat pocket and pulled out three gold coins and placed them into the palm of the fathers hand. By now the rest of the family had come into the room to get a look at the kings face. The fathers eyes were as large as saucers as he looked at the golden coins he looked to his wife for something to say but instead saw happy tears rolling down her cheeks. They were not rich people but the grandfather had raised his daughter to be kind to others especially those in need and she imparted that knowledge to her sons.

"Your highness, I can't accept this it's too much money for us."

"You will accept it Mr. Findle. Do you know that sometimes the greatest good a person can do is simply helping another person in need. Whether it's with a coin, a small piece of bread, a drink it doesn't matter it's the thought that goes behind such an act that fuels the truly great people in our would."

Their home had become totally silent after hearing the kings words.

"Do you have any coins for me?" A small voice from the back said.

"Quiet now," the grandmother told the young boy as the rest of the household erupted into laughter. They ate a very nice but modest breakfast while listening to the kings account of what happened after waking up from the cooks blow to the side of his head. Both sides were now caught up with the latest information so Rayne informed them of their plans to go back and try to retrieve the book.

"He will never be able to get any information out of that magic book!" The king said.

His bandage had been redressed and even though he knew he couldn't go outside he also knew he was perfectly safe right where he was.

"Why do you say that Your Highness?"

"Young lady that book has been in those tunnels for hundreds of years, finding it does not mean you can read it eclipse or not. He needs the key! Without the key he can only move the book out of the room he cannot even take it out of the tunnels which he will soon find out for himself. He will also never be able to decipher a single word."

"Just because he doesn't have a key?"

"That is correct young lady."

"I need to find out where that key is. I'm sure if Nicias' little mind trick couldn't forcefully extract the information from him then maybe the way to get it is to tell him the whole truth."

"Your Highness, we have a confession to make," Rayne started.

"Great, I was waiting for this. I'd be most interested to know how you transformed yourself into that cat in front of my eyes."

"Oh, well, that's another secret entirely your Highness. I don't know how this book came to be in this place but my brother," waving at Raven, "and I have been on a journey for weeks in an attempt to get our hands on this book. We were sent here by a fairy queen."

She recounted the majority of their adventures, including the fight with the wolves, also mentioning the finding of the Bytarian man who they found in the desert and how they tried to help him, his dying and the burial they gave him all the way up until they were captured entering the city by the soldiers. He sat across from them and without interrupting listened to the account of their troubles then he stood up, paced back and forth in deep thought for several minutes and sat back down.

He started off by saying, "I remember that poor man being brought into my chambers; they told me they were going to let him go, they lied to me! I have allowed these creatures to destroy my city and assault my people without lifting a hand of my own."

"Your Highness, I'm sure there was nothing you could do to stop the initial attack. You are alive! There are thousands of people within the city who still need you and just want their king to take command again."

She was hoping that these words would motivate him and that would compel him to want to give up the key to her.

"The main problem is that even if we were to get our hands on the book we still can't read the book or destroy the page within it without having this key you speak of."

That was the last stick she could think of to throw on the fire, if that didn't do it she'd never get the key from him. King Thais sat there, apparently weighing a similar idea of his own then reached up and removed the plain golden band that sat wrapped around his forehead.

"The key is not a key at all," He uttered.

"What?" Raven replied, "maybe the cook hit him harder than we all thought?"

"A key is not always what it sounds like in this case it's right here in my hands," displaying his crown. "For this key to work you have to place the crown on top of the book while it is closed and before the end of the red moon. The book will absorb the key! Then and only then will you be able to read every page within its covers. You must keep the book open, that is very important. Even after the light of the red moon passes you will be able to read from it. If the book is closed after the light of the moon has passed you will not be able to reopen it again for another one hundred years. The key will then be returned to you and the only choice left is to wait. To be clear the moons light does not have to touch the book but it has to be opened during the time of the eclipse."

He handed his crown over to her and smiled, "I expect to get this back from you very shortly then and as casually as that added, "Who wants goose for dinner tonight?"

Rayne didn't have the words to thank him for what he had just done she gave him a hug and whispered in his ear that she would definitely return his crown to him.

***

Nicias had become more obsessed lately in finding this book than that of thinking about the troublesome teenagers lately so the search for the siblings had gone somewhat cold.

***

Raven and Rayne organized their plans for tonight. The eclipse and red moon was tomorrow night and they wanted to make sure they were on the same page. The king had devised his own plan that relied heavily on the remaining Bytarian people. Although the soldiers were more armed than they were he wanted to use the soldiers own tactics against them. There were a lot of ships that were still anchored out in the water and if he could secretly assemble enough people he could coordinate his own attack

183

against them. The plan was to sink several ships while at the same time having his people attack the soldiers with swords and arrows which would create enough panic that maybe they would drop their arms and give up. These soldiers were probably used to constant fighting but during the last several weeks some of them have become very lax, drinking and sleeping their days away.

"Mr. Findle, I wonder if you could help your king?"

"What is it that you need me to do your Highness?"

"A lot of our soldiers have been killed as you know," simultaneously there was a knock at the front door.

"Are you expecting any guests?" The king inquired.

"No, not at all."

The father, not having a sword of his own in the house grabbed a knife from his kitchen and with it hidden behind his back went to answer the door. Rayne stood by with an arrow at the ready to let it fly if soldiers burst through the doorway and Raven had a firm grip on his Atlantean sword ready to do his own damage.

"Who is it?" Mr. Findle asked the stranger.

A muffled response was heard from the doorway.

"Hold on a minute," the father said, then turned to face King Thais.

"I believe the person whispered his name as being Simo. Do you know someone by that name?"

Rayne immediately lowered her bow and went to the door to open it.

"What are you doing? It could be a trap!" Raven said.

"It's Simo, if he wanted to kill us we would already be dead."

She cracked the door open and even though his head and face was partially covered with a white sash she clearly made out the face of the cook, who with another wink asked, "Well young miss, are you going to let me in?"

She quickly opened the door and he slipped inside and removed the cloth from around his face to show her that it was in fact him. The door was shut and the entire household beheld another visitor in an already crowded home.

"What are you doing here Simo?" She asked, "I thought you were leaving the city?"

"That was my intention but when I was leaving I spotted several soldiers nearby searching for the both of you so I had to dispatch them and hide their bodies. I've stayed close by keeping a watchful eye on this place so no one else would discover your hideaway."

Rayne waved him into the back room, "Come in and get comfortable she insisted."

The king stood up to face his friend, "Well, look who it is?"

Poor Simo dropped to the ground at seeing his king standing there and started apologizing for his actions prior to his leaving the kings chambers. After hearing his cooks story told to him from the ground the king knew that he had acted appropriately and done the only possible thing he could do to save the three of them. In a firm voice the king ordered him to stand up. Simo stood there waiting for any punishment that the king was going to disperse unto him, thinking at the very least it would be something that was going to be painful. Instead the king pulled his cook close and thanked him, acknowledging the sacrifice he had performed although, still not entirely happy with the blow to the head he had suffered.

The king pointed to the father who still held the knife in his hand, "All is forgiven my friend, now Simo I need you to help Mr. Findle here organize a fight."

"I will do all in my power to help you sir." Curiously he asked, "How in the world did you enter this home without my seeing you sir?"

Without disclosing any information about the tunnel entrance in the other room King Thais simply stated, "Magic my dear friend, magic."

After a long discussion and several revisions made after that they both agreed to recruit as many of the Bytarian's as they could for an attack on the soldiers tomorrow night. The front door was opened and the two organizers left, entrusted with a mission that they could not fail in completing. The siblings had already discussed what they were going to do so with the sons help he removed the cover from the tunnel entrance and they went back down to find their prize. Moving quickly through the large tunnel they were able to retrace their steps back in the direction to where the king had been held. They crept silently along the tunnel as it opened up to a larger one up ahead when a handful of the elite guards wearing their red and black striped capes unknowingly passed by the front of them. They relished the fact that they were so small and at how easy it was to conceal themselves. They were not able to understand the guards speaking so Raven decided to quickly change back to his human form and lay flat on the ground to conceal himself but eavesdrop on their conversation. After they passed he changed back and told her what they said, "I could only make out the fact that the book has been moved."

"Do you think we should follow them?"

"What choice do we have. We can't risk searching for this thing any longer if it has been moved."

He crept up to the opening of the tunnel and looked to his right he could clearly see the soldiers carrying their torches and continuing on their way. They followed the men for twenty minutes or so taking care to watch out for adjoining passageways so no other soldiers would surprise them like the last time. Finally, they stopped some way up, it looked like a few of the soldiers actually walked up a stairwell on their right. While they were following the men they were aware of the fact that a lot of the passageways that were previously lit up with torches were all dark now, like the soldiers were concentrating all of their attention on this one section. He left her by one of the middle columns while he ran behind them and quickly changed to his human form again with Rayne on the lookout he eavesdropped on their conversation again for as long as he could, then he waved to her that it was time to go. They made it all the way back safely and after climbing up the wooden ladder Rayne asked him what he had learned.

"They were talking about a lot of useless stuff at first, but one of them mentioned the fact that he hated being responsible for such a huge job guarding the sorcerers book. The palace is right above the stairwell right next to them and the book is in a room right behind where the guards were. I guess the king was right because one of them said Nicias was furious about not being able to take the book upstairs. Something about an invisible wall, I think they tried to get different people to try to carry the book upstairs or past a certain point."

"So why didn't we just attack and grab the book from them?" She asked.

"You have the nerve to ask other people if they're crazy and yet you ask me that question. We can't open the book until tomorrow night anyways so we can rest a bit now, then we'll go back and wait until the time is right. Secondly, if you didn't notice, there are quite a few of them and we'll need some type of plan before we go bursting in and waving a sword and bow around."

"We haven't used the magic rings the water man gave us."

"We can use them but I think it's best to save them for an extreme emergency."

Simo and Findles father were not planning on returning to the home until tomorrow and that was only to retrieve the king and begin their attack against the soldiers. That's the precise time the siblings would make their move on the guards and the only chance they would have at getting to that book.

Chapter Nineteen

The Golden Book: And The Taking Back of Their City...

Nicias had grown angry at the whole world since returning to the kings chambers yesterday. His discovery and complete failure in not being able to even take the book out of the tunnels infuriated him. His initial tantrum of throwing things all over the room had passed and now he sat in a chair contemplating what his next move would be. In his quest for power and gold he hadn't given any thought to the idea of failing. He was not going to allow the seeds of fear to take root and grow just because those damn teenagers escaped him. The thought of them beating him to the book was too much, he would destroy the whole city and everyone in it before that happened. Up to now he had not been able to locate them and because he was running dangerously low on time the majority of his attention was being spent on finding the book. He sat there in silence, but thoughts of his own soldiers scheming behind his back had recently started to fill his head more and more. They would pay for such treacherous thoughts.

"Captain Asal!" He yelled.

"Yes, your Excellency."

"Have we any progress with my book?"

"Any progress? I don't understand what you mean your Excellency?" The captain had noticed that as of late the sorcerers mind was not altogether.

"You heard me go and check it!"

Captain Asal angrily exited the room but looked back over his shoulder and saw the sorcerer talking to himself. Nicias stood up, pushed his chair back and proceeded to sit on the ground with his legs crossed over one another in an attempt to consult with the evil inside his amulet. He closed his eyes and grasped the amulet with both hands; he appeared to be in a trance but really he was concentrating on making contact with the evil spirit that lurked inside his fiery little prize.

"I'm asking for your guidance, things seem to be falling apart all around me." The response was heard in his head immediately while his hands glowed bright red like fire. With a deep and methodical voice, "You are a fool for allowing those two young ones to escape! I picked you because I thought you could accomplish this simple task. I provided you the command of a small army and yet you still give me excuses. I will not tolerate any more failures from you. Set a trap for the young ones; they will come for the book very soon."

After hearing that last word he felt a hand violently slap him out of his trance. He sat there on the ground fully alert, sweating and shaking.

***

Raven and Rayne had been pacing around the room visibly nervous for many hours as their new friend Findle watched them from a seated position on the floor.

"You've found the book haven't you? I can tell just by the way you both looked at each other that I'm right. Let me go with you the next time you go down there."

"Listen Findle, it's true," she said. "We have located the area where it's being held but there are a lot of guards watching it and the passageways. It will be much too dangerous to bring you along with us. Try to be content with the fact that because of your trust in us and in showing us your grandfathers entrance all of this was possible. Besides, who is going to look after your little brother if something happens to you?"

They looked over towards where the young boy was laying on the ground playing with some toys. Findle crawled away from them and headed towards where his little brother was playing, he was disappointed at their decision to not let him accompany them but didn't want them to see it on his face.

"Good job laying the guilt trip on him, that was potentially a huge problem avoided."

"Shut up Raven. I meant it. I don't want him to get hurt following us around down there," as she plopped a grape into her mouth. "Do you think that we'll be alright?" She asked.

"Listen, you take the key and follow the instructions that the king gave us. We sneak into the room, locate the page concerning Atlantis and tear the thing out, rip it up and we'll burn it later for good measure to make sure no one can ever read it. We're only going to have one chance at getting this right so we will play it by ear as the night progresses."

The king was in the same room as the siblings but he was sound asleep. The cut on his head was healing just fine and with the money he provided the father they had had a good meal last night. He was going to need all of his strength for tomorrow. While the evening passed the whole house felt the immense pressure of the upcoming events. They had also spent the night trying to get as much peace of mind as they could not daring to reenter the passageways until the precise time had come. This last morning they woke up a little later than they would have liked to have considering what was at stake. They were going to spend most of the day hiding in the tunnels waiting until the exact moment that they felt the fighting would start. Simo and Findles father had not returned yet so they prepared to leave for the final time.

She pleaded with the young thief, "Please Findle, do not follow us because we can't protect you and also do what we need to do."

"I know don't worry, I have my little brother in mind but please be careful down there."

They climbed down the ladder and disappeared from his view.

"Can I go with you Fin?"

"No, I told you the next time I go! I'm not going right now so go back with Pia."

He had answered the young boy in an irritated tone because it had reminded him of his own limitations in not going. The older brother meandered his way back into the front of the house and couldn't help but overhear his mom and Pia speaking about their concerns for his father's health. King Thais entered the room and his mom actually stood up for him, "Are you feeling better your Highness?"

He carefully removed the bandage around his own head that revealed a very small scar near his temple, "Yes, I am. Thank you."

"How are you young man?"

"I'm ok," Findle replied.

"I'm ok, your Highness," his mother also said.

There was a series of knocks on the door and Simo's voice was heard again. Findles mom opened the door a little bit to double check who was there, seeing the same man as before she opened it further to allow him to enter.

"Good morning your Highness."

"Good morning Simo. I'm very interested to find out how things have been going since yesterday." They proceeded into the main room where they could talk with a little more privacy.

"So tell me my friend, how has the recruiting been going?"

"I think it's been going very well sir. As word spread more and more people were willing to join with us and fight for the chance to regain their city back. Everyone I spoke with is fed up by the demeaning treatment of the soldiers and they want vengeance for their friends or loved ones who have died. I'm afraid I was only able to recruit a handful of small ships to help us in burning some of the sorcerers ships. There's also the idea that if we can't burn them maybe we can cut their anchors loose and let the ships float out to sea unmanned."

"That's a great idea. I know we can't destroy them all that is simply impossible because there are too many, we just need to create some confusion out there in the water as well as here in the city. Where is Mr. Findle?"

"I don't know sir, we spoke briefly when we walked outside yesterday but we headed in two separate directions. He should be here soon because we agreed to meet back here before nightfall."

"Is everyone clear on the time to start the attack against the soldiers?"

"We don't have a loud bell or horn to start the attack so there isn't a specific time but people will start getting into whatever positions they are going to take right after dinner. It will definitely be after dinner because most of the soldiers will have started their drinking."

"Then my friend, we will be ready at the same time."

Simo looked around for the brother and sister, not seeing them he asked the king of their whereabouts. He made a show of looking for them by over exaggerating his head movements to the left and right, "I guess they have gone to try to accomplish their task. They told me yesterday that they had located the book in one of the tunnels but that it was also heavily guarded."

"How did they get access to the tunnels? I told them about the secret entrance at the base of the mountain but that's pretty far from here."

"There's another entrance my friend."

A second knock on the door came which was followed by Mr. Findle entering his home, he hugged his wife and joined the king and cook in the back room.

"Hello, your Highness."

"How did things go for you Mr. Findle?"

He looked at Simo and gave him a respectful nod. "It was a bit slow going at first your Highness. We've lived in the city for so many years I think people thought I was joking around at first. Once they saw I was not kidding and my plans were serious the word started to spread quicker than I even thought it would. There are a lot of angry people out there that want the strangers out of our city. Even the women who heard our plans were more than ready to join in for tonight's attack and help in any way that they could. Some of the bartenders want to take large cups and smash the heads of the drunken men. He exhaled slowly, well that story was actually told to me by Guinda, she's a very large and angry bartender."

"Excellent Mr. Findle, you both have done an excellent job. I hope that we can not only get rid of these troublesome soldiers but also distract the ones who are guarding the book long enough so that our young friends can steal it."

"If you'll excuse me your Highness I need to speak with my wife."

They watched him walk into the other room before rekindling their talk.

"I did not forget your question my friend," smiling at the cook. Standing up he waved him into the bedroom, "Come over here."

"What is that?"

"That my friend is another secret entrance into the tunnels."

He knelt and looked down into the opening amazed at how such an entrance could have been constructed.

"This is absolutely amazing!" He laughed a little to himself and echoed the kings thoughts on how ingenious the grandfather had been in concealing his little secret. Findle at seeing the two men laugh, had been sitting on the edge of his parents bed watching them, "My grandfather thought there was gold in the tunnels."

Simo replied, "Really young man, the only thing I see down there is a small wooden bird on the ground."

"What!"

He leapt out of the bed and ran to look down into the entrance. He realized the small bird he was looking at was the same one he had given his little brother just the other day so he ran into the other room to alert his parents. His startled mother ran into the room shadowed by the crying grandmother who was holding her hands up to her mouth to prevent herself from yelling down into the hole after the boy.

"I'm going to kill that child when I get my hands on him," the father was saying.

"You'll do no such thing," his wife said vehemently.

"Dad, let me go and get him, I know where he usually goes and you'll have to be leaving soon anyways."

Out of nowhere Simo announced, "I'll go with the boy!"

He produced a smaller sword from his left side and handed it to his king. "Sir, I can protect the boy better than anyone else here, we'll find him. Besides, there are other armed guards down there and if two unarmed children are found down there wandering alone I think you know what will happen to them."

"Yes, you're right my friend, of course."

Mr. Findle was still consoling his wife, "Your Highness, where are you planning on making your stand?" Simo asked.

"If Mr. Findle is still up to the task and would accompany me I would like to go to the place where our nightmares began, the north gate."

"Then, if at all possible I will meet you there."

Simo still had a hidden dagger in his belt and his regular sword was on his right side as he grabbed the arm of the elder son. With a serious look on his face he told him, "Listen to me, you will lead me to where ever you think your little brother is, once we have him we will immediately come back here and deliver him safely into your mother's arms. If we run into soldiers down there you are to get behind me and let me deal with them, is that clear?"

"Yes, it's clear."

Everyone else stood by making sure not to interrupt his instructions, meanwhile the king was very impressed by how his cook had handled his emotions and given clear directions to the boy. At the bottom of the ladder Simo reached down and picked up the small carved toy, he looked up, saw everyone looking down at him, then walked out of their view. The grandmother whispered in her daughters ear that he'd be ok but she started to cry nonetheless into the shoulder of her comforting husband. The king walked out of the room to give the three family members some more time to console each other. Shortly thereafter the father walked into the room and sat down next to the king, "She'll be alright, she just wants to wait in there for when they return."

"Do you have a sword Mr. Findle because we will be leaving soon."

"No, but they are easily obtained from someone in the streets."

***

The siblings had made their way through the passageways and were keeping their distance from the talking soldiers ahead. They were still cats, crouched low to the ground and very silent so they could maximize the use of shadows. Periodically, they would take turns walking a distance behind them to make sure no guards were approaching from the back. There were still several guards that for whatever reason still patrolled the short passageways around them. Being that they were so small it was very easy to remain unseen and by timing their walking around the stone columns as that of the guards they were never spotted. They might not be able to hear the start of the actual fighting from here, but they figured that the confusion up above would drift down here and alert these guards. The combination of boredom and the exhilaration of knowing that the fighting was going to soon begin was almost too much for them to bear. Rayne's ears pricked up suddenly at hearing some crying in the distance. A bad feeling started to grow in her stomach so she asked her brother, "Do you hear that?"

From her obstructed view she peeked her head out from around the stone column and double checked to see if the guards had heard the crying sound. Not believing so, they hustled back down several long passageways trying to pinpoint where the sound was coming from. It was echoing off of all the walls but they knew they were much closer to the source. It was definitely the sound of a person who was scared. Crouched in a dark corner they witnessed two of the elite guards half pushing, half dragging the crying form of Findles little brother towards their direction.

"How the hell did they find him?" Raven asked in shock.

Watching these two brutes laughing and pushing this terrified little boy along the tunnel made her blood boil. She didn't hesitate to transform herself back into her human form right in front of the two soldiers. The surprised look in the first guards eyes was only matched by the surprised look in his partners face as a mysterious dagger struck him solid in the back knocking him to the ground. With a burning white arrow already in her hand the last guard didn't have a chance to yell out before he also fell lifeless on the dirt floor. Raven had since changed back to his human form and watched the tunnel behind them to make sure no one was coming but Rayne immediately ran forward to comfort the crying boy. As she grabbed him two dark figures came running from the other end of the tunnel one shorter than the next. The older brother got to the small boy a moment later and with his hands over his mouth to quiet his crying carried him from Rayne. He let his little brother know that it was him then gave him a big reassuring hug to let the smaller boy know everything was alright.

"I had a gut feeling it was you Simo with the dagger."

With a bit of difficulty Simo removed his dagger from the dead guards back, tucked it away then turned to face the traumatized young boy, reaching into his pocket he handed him his favorite wooden bird.

"We didn't know that the boy had snuck into tunnels, but by the looks of it I think he'll be just fine," reassuring the older brother.

"Do you remember how to get us back?" Simo asked the older brother.

With a nod the older brother gave his approval. Simo was more than ready to escort the two of them back but first he dragged the two bodies of the guards to a darker section to hide them better.

"Thank you for your good shot with that arrow young miss."

Rayne pointed in the direction that her and her brother had come from, "I think we could hear his crying better than the soldiers could."

"Young miss, if there is a set of stairs near to the soldiers then you are below the palaces entrance to the tunnels."

"Yes, Raven did see a few of the guards going up some stairs."

"I know exactly where you are then I must return our two young men back to their parents who are worried sick about them. I will see you both again I'm sure."

Simo placed his hand on the shoulder of the older brother turning him around in the direction he wanted him to go. As they walked out of view Raven and Rayne returned to their cat forms and ran back down the passageway to continue their wait, hopefully without any more disruptions.

The attack was going to be beginning very shortly and he needed to get these two boys back to their home. He recognized the last turn when the older brother waved at him and started pointing his finger towards the corner of the last passageway where their secret entrance was located. While they were heading back Simos mind and body was on high alert because the last thing he needed was more fighting and killing. He didn't enjoy killing the soldiers or anyone for that matter so thankfully they made it back safely. Simo lifted the small boy up as high as he could to make his climb up the ladder that much shorter. Having already said his goodbye to his wife, Findles father and the king were about to leave but he heard a ruckus coming from his room so he ran back in. His wife was hugging their youngest boy while his mother-in-law stood nearby with tears of happiness on her face from the mere sight of him safely returned.

"We were just leaving son," the father told his older boy.

Simos head and then body finally exited the tunnel. After hugging the small boy Mr. Findle looked over towards Simo for answers, "Where was he hiding?"

"I told you we would find him dad."

"Yes, he had been captured by two of the sorcerers elite guards they were dragging him through the tunnels."

After hearing that news Mr. Findle pulled back from his wife and started to meticulously look the boy over for any hidden injury.

"Sir, I believe they were taking him back to the palace for some reason. The palace's entrance to the tunnels are less than a thirty minute walk from here."

Although, the father was ready to head out and fight before this incident, now knowing that his smallest boy could have been killed fueled an anger within him that he had never felt before. It was not a blind, reckless fury but more of the protective instinct that all parents share towards their children. He extended his hand to shake the cook's, "Thank you for bringing our son back to us."

With a completely different attitude Mr. Findle walked out of the room and headed for the front door saying to King Thais, "Now, I am ready to go and retake our city!"

"Your Highness, there is something else I need to do," Simo said.

"Can't it wait," he replied.

"No, but don't worry I will not fail in meeting you at the gate."

He climbed back onto the ladder, "If I don't help them all will be lost!"

The king looked down into the opening but he was being called from behind by Mr. Findle, "your Highness, it is time for us to go."

With his royal manner King Thais put both hands squarely on the older brothers shoulders and gave him this advice, "Lock the door when we leave and don't let anyone in!"

They exited the front door and walked down the mostly vacant dirt road towards their destination. Yes, it was true, even though the soldiers had a firm grip over the city during the daytime, the nights were usually filled with the sounds of laughter and merrymaking. It was always associated with drinking men and the people who served them, but tonight was going to be clearly different. King Thais followed his guide and was very aware of the ominous feeling growing in his chest. They walked past a bar and a small group of soldiers, some were huddled together talking while others looked to be half asleep at tables. On their way to the gates they could see that the sun was almost completely gone which meant that the time for their battle would be beginning soon. People had been approaching Mr. Findle during their walk saying quick fleeting words of confidence or telling him they were ready for whatever was to happen tonight. Because the king didn't have his gold crown around his head he was viewed as just another Bytarian citizen who wanted the despised soldiers out. They stopped within ten minutes of the north gate which the king felt was close enough for now and took refuge near a large group of people. Mr. Findle found out that this was an armed group of men, all having bows, arrows and swords who were just awaiting some type of signal to start their attack. For the first time tonight King Thais stepped forward and addressed the people quietly. "Listen to me all of you," his words were silently repeated and handed off to the others who were farther back so they could understand what was being said. He explained to these people who he was and getting a confirmation nod from Mr. Findle, reinstated the importance of tonight's mission and what was at stake for all of them. He stressed the fact that the killing of all of the soldiers was not what he wanted nor why they were there he just wanted them out of their city! The word of their revolt had spread like wildfire since yesterday and they were told of hundreds maybe thousands of people who were ready for tonight. The group split up with several of the men vowing to help protect them both till death. Moving like a well-oiled machine who had done this many times before the group spread out and quietly made their way closer to the solders at the gate. They got close enough to literally hit a soldier in the head with a rock if they wanted to.

"Are you ready for action Mr. Findle?" King Thais asked.

"Yes, I am your Highness, more than ready."

He looked at his guide a bit nervously, "I don't know how long we should wait considering it's already dark?"

Full of confidence Mr. Findle answered, "I'm done waiting your Highness." He made eye contact with several of the others around him then borrowed a bow and arrow from the man next to him. He notched the arrow in the string and fired it at the guard who was standing nearest to the gate. With the collective yells of their entire group the taking back of their city had begun. The soldiers were monumentally unprepared for the coordinated assault that was being dealt to them from the majority of people within the city. The sounds of war echoed throughout the city but it was the soldiers this time who were caught sleeping. The drinking men were clobbered over their heads with everything from glasses of wine to the sticks that were usually reserved for the swatting of the goats behinds. Swords in hand and arrows flying King Thais' men charged forward with enthusiasm and courage. Many of the soldiers bodies began falling fall from different areas of the wooden walkway that surrounded the gates. They wanted and got the gates opened so any of the fleeing soldiers could make their way back out to their ships and leave. Immense fires broke out on some of the soldiers ships because King Thais' small fleet was sending their own flaming arrows onto their wooden hulls. While no parts of the city were left untouched the frustrated Bytarians took revenge against the soldiers. Even the palace guards, hearing the familiar sounds of metal against metal were caught off guard because they were usually the ones causing the trouble. The eclipse and red moon would be full soon and Nicias was barely any closer to solving his puzzle with the book than he was two days ago. The sorcerer walked to the balcony with a face of uncontrolled fury and the feeling of déjà vu at how things had completely changed. He was now the one standing on the balcony when an attack took place. Nicias barely escaped an arrow that hit the wall behind him he walked back inside and called for his captain. Not getting an immediate answer he ran down the hallway to get downstairs and see to his book before those troublesome teenagers could ruin everything.

***

They laid in wait in the tunnels for hours waiting for the precise moment to strike. Seeing and hearing the confusion of the guards they knew that the city was in revolt, their time was now. The guards were tougher when they had the upper hand, but now a few of them whined about how they didn't want to die. There were still too many of them to risk trying to sneak into the doorway so they decided to use the magic in their rings and change themselves into mist to easily enter the room. They were running out of time and had absolutely no choice. Changing back into humans they sat in the darkened tunnel.

Raven started, "Listen, follow the plan that we talked about, once we're inside that room I'll stay by the doorway and protect you. Now, we're supposed to be able to close our eyes and just think of changing into this watery mist so here goes nothing."

Raven looked at his hand and the invisible clear ring around his thumb that he knew was there and thought of what he wanted to change his body into. Quickly, his body began to get very thin, almost transparent until before her eyes her brother transformed into a hazy mist. He glided down the passageway towards the room where the guards were. She closed her eyes and tried to think of something easy, but the only thing that she could imagine was a morning fog. Her vision started to get blurry and her hands suddenly disappeared her thoughts were still the same but her vision was shaky, like in a weird dream. Without knowing it, just willing herself forward she passed the stone column and made her way down the hallway towards the room. Passing by a group of guards who only had the cognizance to wave their hands by their eyes quickly like they were swatting at a fly she entered the room where the book was. The urge to change herself back to human form was strong but she made the willful decision to look at all of the corners in the room to make sure no one was in there with her. There were several torches in the room that provided sufficient lighting to display the huge golden squared book that sat atop the sturdy wooden pedestal. She saw some movement out of the corner of her eye but realized it was her brother who had already changed himself back to human form and was waving his Atlantean sword at her like a madman. She willed herself to be back in her own body and suddenly she opened her eyes and realized that she was human again. She ducked down low behind the pedestal where the book was and tried to control her breathing.

"Rayne, Rayne," her brother was whispering in an excited tone, she looked at him from the side of the pedestal and gave him a quick wave of her hand indicating that she was alright and knew what he wanted. She took the crown out from under her cloak and slowly stood up so that her head was just barely above the height of the book. Raven stood right inside of the doorway sword at the ready in case anyone entered the room. She lifted her eyes up to look at the door, Raven's face was almost white, probably at thinking what was taking her so long. She was so nervous she felt like her heart would explode, "This had better work!" She thought.

She gently placed King Thais' thin golden crown on top of the book and waited to see if anything happened, unbelievably, the crown slowly sank into it and a soft, golden yellow color soon enveloped the entire book.

Finally, she stood up and admired the beautiful cover of the ancient book. She opened it to the midway point and looked down, not trying to read the words but certainly noticing the strangeness of them, the letters were not recognizable to her. Even more peculiar was the fact that the letters didn't stay the same, the words and letters constantly changed so that even if she could understand them they didn't stop moving. Simply watching the words dance around on the pages was mesmerizing in itself to her.

One of the elite guards burst into the room, "What the hell are you doing there!"

Raven took a few steps forward and intercepted him, "Get out of here I don't want to hurt you."

The guard immediately pulled his sword out and charged. Raven knew that there was going to be no bargaining here but he was determined not to allow the him to pass and get anywhere near his sister. They exchanged a few blows until Raven got the advantage over him and was able to hit the man on the back of the head knocking him out and kicking his weapon away. Unfortunately, after making contact with the other sword the crisp sound of the Atlantean blade rang throughout the tunnels, this in turn called more of the guards to the room. One more entered, but before the third could a throwing knife hit it's mark which caused him to fall sideways on the floor outside of the room, dead. The sounds of fighting was heard in the hallway and the screams of pain were echoed throughout the entire city as Raven fought off yet another guard.

Simo walked into the room with his sword out, "Are you alright young sir?"

"I'm so happy to see you," hugging the cook.

The book had over one thousand pages in it and Rayne wasn't making very good progress in trying to figure out the one page she needed to find.

"How much longer?" Raven exclaimed.

She huffed with her arms extended, "I don't know!"

"We can't stay here for long," Simo whispered, "there will be more guards coming."

"I know, we have to give her a little more time is all."

Simo went back into the hallway but turned back to face Raven, "You stay in here young sir, I'll take care of things out here."

Rayne was letting the frustration of the moment get to her and cloud her mind so she closed her eyes and placed both of her hands on the book. She thought of something peaceful. Remembering Queen Aaneesa and how beautiful the fireflies looked that night at the cabin she tried to fill her head with images of the beautiful City of Atlantis and nothing else. She had unknowingly gone into a daydream of sorts, her hands, without her control, flipped through the many pages until stopping on the one page she needed. Her eyes popped open and she looked down upon a beautifully drawn picture of the domed city with letters written in gold and words that she could clearly read, they no longer changed or moved around on the pages. In the background she heard the unmistakable nasty voice of the sorcerer commanding his captain.

"So old man," Captain Asal said, "you have the nerve to return and help these two? I will make you pay for our last meeting."

The cook was trying to give the siblings as much time as possible by delaying his rematch with the captain for as long as he could.

"The last time we met I easily bested you." With a grin he added salt to this insult, "Where is your owner? Has he finally let his dog off his leash." Referring to the sorcerer.

Captain Asal removed his sword in an instant. "I will show you old man who needs to be on a leash. I'm glad this happened, I've thought about the day you ran away from me and into the crowd. You were scared to fight me."

"I'm not afraid of any man and I didn't want to have to fight you and several of your pathetic so called elite guards at the same time. But now I have all night!"

"Rip the page out and let's go!" Raven yelled.

She used her left hand to steady the book and tore the whole right page out, then ripped the page into several little pieces afterwards and put them into her pocket. She walked away from the book and almost forgot what the king had told her. Returning, she slammed the book shut and waited for the kings crown to reappear before snatching it back and running to where her brother was.

They couldn't see the wild look on the sorcerers face as he stood alone at the top of the stairs waiting for his captain to strike the cook down so he could get to his book. The siblings watched helplessly as Captain Asal continued his rage fueled attack on their friend. They couldn't help but feel like he was just acting more on the fact that he had already been beaten once by this man. Simo received a small cut across his stomach from the wild slashing sword of the captain but soon had himself received several damaging cuts across his shoulders, back, cheek and finally his arm which forced him to drop his weapon to the ground, again. With his pride shattered he told the cook to end his life. Simo felt it a better punishment to leave him alive with the knowledge that he'd been beaten by a supposed old cook once more.

"Go run upstairs to your master and have him put you back on your little leash."

The siblings exited the room with a new respect for Simo.

"What are you doing?" Nicias yelled down at the broken captain.

Walking up the stairs until he stood face to face with the old sorcerer, the one person he had believed in and thought could accomplish the simple task of getting a book, but in reality caused him to lose an unknown number of his men tonight. He reached out and forcefully yanked the amulet off of the sorcerers neck. He shoved the now frail looking old man to the ground. He told his next in command to ready their horses because they needed to make it back to the ships. Their hold over this city was over!

"What about Our Excellency sir?"

Captain Asal looked down at the old man lying on the ground and told the soldier, "I am your Excellency now! Grab that old man and bring him along."

Chapter Twenty

Under Watchful Eyes: A Gift Safely Returned...

The Bytarians used similar war tactics against the soldiers and it yielded them great results. Their surprise attack also greatly diminished the injuries sustained to the population because thousands of people had filled the streets, they were yelling and pushing the remaining soldiers forward towards the northern gates of the city. Using small skiffs that were on the beach many of the soldiers were able to paddle back to their large ships and seek refuge. Unfortunately for them several of the larger ships were still tied up to their anchors but completely on fire while a few of the others had had their anchor lines cut which made them drift silently out to sea.

***

Along with many last minute directions to be carried out the newly self-appointed "Excellancy," Captain Asal, stayed long enough to witness the locking of the iron gate that led down into the tunnels. He was going to at least make it as difficult as he could for the siblings and the cook to get out of those tunnels. He admired his new trinket glowing in the palm of his hand while standing in the hallway but he relished the sound of the heavy creaking door being shut and the lock being fastened to it a bit more. Once the door was closed he walked forward for the last time and looked through the bars and down the steps only to see that they had vanished.

"*Damnit,*" he thought, "this is not over, I will have my revenge on those three!"

***

"That was an incredible show of swordsmanship Simo, how did you get so to be good?"

He bowed, "I've had a little practice young miss now did you get what you came for?"

"Yes, we did."

"Come on, we have to get back to Findles home," Raven said.

He turned and faced Simo, "I need you to trust us now."

"What are you talking about young sir?"

"I'm sure by now you know we can change our bodies into animals. I'm going to change myself into a lion now so we can get back to Findles house much faster but I will need for you to climb onto my back so I can carry you."

Simo stood still for a moment with a blank look on his face.

"You don't need to be afraid of what you're going to see."

"Young sir, what if we run into guards down here?"

Sharing a smile with his sister, "Don't worry, it will be their turn to worry about us."

He closed his eyes and in a flash a beautiful lion was standing before them. The startled cook stumbled backwards into the wall trying to put space between himself and the huge cat. Rayne went over to him and comforted him, telling him that it was indeed her brother and that everything was ok. The lion roared at the cook, but in reality he was just trying to tell him to hurry up and get on. With Rayne's help he mustered the courage and slowly climbed onto the back of the huge muscled cat, he then gently grabbed some of the hair from his mane and Raven took off down the passageway. That done Rayne transformed herself into the Bengal tiger and sprinted after them. They were making tremendous time on their return with his sister closely following him. Simo had never done anything even remotely like this in the past which is why he almost fell off of the lions back on several occasions. They arrived back at their entrance quicker than they all had expected to so as both of the large cats came to a stop they realized that they were too large to fit through the narrow zig zag entrance. They changed back into their regular selves and Simo found himself walking back and forth on shaky legs for the next several minutes. "That really was quite an experience for me."

"Are you ok?" Raven asked.

"I'll be fine, I just need to sturdy my legs and maybe my teeth a bit."

They hustled through the small tunnel and back to the wooden ladder taking turns climbing up and into Findles parents' bedroom. Quickly they closed the entrance and slid the bed atop it to conceal the opening. They were just finishing when Findles mom walked up and stood in the doorway.

"I'm so happy all three of you are safe."

The older son walked past his mom and into the room, "Did you get what you came for?"

Rayne could tell that he was still a little upset at not being able to follow them.

She gave him a big hug and said, "Thank you for keeping your word Findle."

With that his little anger barrier had been broken and he was no longer upset at them, "I told you I'd keep my little brother in mind and not follow you."

With a concerned look Simo asked, "Has the king returned?"

"No, not yet. But, we've been hearing people yelling and screaming for hours now. They are probably still by the gates."

"I must go," he announced.

"I want to go with you!" The older boy said giving his knife to his mom. "I don't want to stay here and babysit anymore."

Rayne grabbed her bow, "We'll all go."

Raven took the Atlantean blade out for what he thought quite possibly could be the last time. They passed several chaotic scenes while travelling to the gate. With many of the once organized soldiers now on the run, fleeing and trying to make it back to the safety of their ships the people were quickly feeling their freedom return. It had been a long night and the sunlight was beginning to slowly emerge over the mountains. Even though there were dead bodies of soldiers here and there at this point a lot of people seemed to be doing random jobs like: picking up carts that had been flipped over or trying to recapture loose livestock that seemed to be running everywhere. They turned the last corner and found several hundred people chanting, "It's our city, it's our city." They weren't chanting to anyone specifically they just wanted their voices to be heard by the fleeing soldiers in their tiny boats. The two large gates were open allowing the cool sea breeze to blow into the faces and hair of everyone. They were no longer manned by the guards that everyone had come accustomed to seeing. King Thais' voice was heard up ahead near the beach so they followed the sound of it through the crowd until they emerged and laid their eyes on him and Mr. Findle. They were hastily helping people put some of the remaining soldiers into the small boats. The scene out in the ocean was pure chaos. Many of the sorcerers ships were fleeing and already near the horizon while others were burning freely.

His son ran to the beach to greet him, "Father!"

"Our work here is almost done my friend," the king said.

"Yes, I see that sir. You didn't have need for my sword here after all," Simo said.

"I've already received some positive news from other parts of the city that most of the soldiers are gone but apparently, some of them weren't able to make it back to their ships so they ran into the desert to avoid the fighting."

As King Thais addressed the group Simo took notice that his face showed some signs of weariness, after all, he certainly was not used to this much physical exertion.

Simo asked, "Have you seen that Captain Asal come through here yet?"

"Yes, they rode up on horses trying to run people down but we quickly overpowered them, suddenly their attitudes changed and they begged for their lives. Believe me many of the people around here wanted their heads, but I wanted to demonstrate to them that we are better than they are and certainly beyond their acts of violence." We put them into a small boat and sent them out to sea. The king pointed to a small boat that was rowing out to one of the larger ones, "As a matter of fact, there he goes!"

With a perplexed look on his face Raven asked, "Why did you let them go unharmed?"

"Sometimes young man," the king said, "it's better to let the snake crawl away and keep the knowledge that he has been defeated."

Raven fumbled with the hilt of his sword but mumbled to himself so as not to upset the king, "If it were me I would have let him keep a different knowledge."

Watching the small boat paddle away was frustrating, "I hope that decision doesn't come back to haunt you sir," Simo replied.

Unbeknownst to the cook, at that same moment he was watching the boat leave Captain Asal was watching him and the siblings on the beach. A burning hate had developed within him and with it grew the thought of a new plan that would someday be realized and that would give him the vengeance he now craved, he just needed time.

"Father, can we head back home mother is very worried about you?"

"Go home to your family Mr. Findle, we will talk later," the king advised.

"Your Highness," Rayne started.

The king turned to look at the young girl.

"I have something for you, a promise." She took the golden crown out from under her cloak and very politely handed it back to him.

"Thank you your Highness for trusting us with your treasured crown and key."

There were a lot of people that were watching them and to their delight and cheers King Thais placed his crown back on top of his head. Simo decided to stay with his king to help in any way he could while Raven and Rayne along with Mr. Findle and his son would head back to their home. They started walking down the street very happy with all that they had accomplished during the night and he couldn't wait to get back home to see his wife. On the wooden walkway of the bridge behind them, where the soldiers used to stand to look out at the ocean, a soldier had remained hidden under a dead body. He stood up, took aim and shot an arrow hitting Findle in his upper back near his shoulder, knocking him to the ground. The thud sound that the arrow made as it hit the boy would be a sound his dad would never forget. He fell to his knees and held onto his son who was yelling in pain. Instinctively, everyone turned around and scanned the perimeter to determine where the shot came from. The soldier wasn't finished and fired another arrow this time narrowly missing Rayne. She pulled her bow from behind her back as she had so often done and definitely wasn't planning on missing her target. With her bow in hand, she whispered slowly to her arrow her intended target and let the blazing white arrow take care of its business. In an instant she had dispatched one of the last remaining remnants of the dark time when the City of Bytar had been in the grip of an evil sorcerer.

"I don't think mom is going to be very happy with me now father?" The boy whispered.

Hearing the commotion King Thais and Simo rushed over to try to help. Mr. Findle sat on the ground holding his son trying to reassure him that everything was going to be ok even though he knew that he had received a fatal blow.

"Don't move my son, don't move," but he was unable to control the welling of tears in his eyes from rolling down his cheeks. Someone ran up and handed Raven a large wool blanket to place over the boy so he wouldn't feel cold.

The father pleaded with the people around him, "What can I do, can anyone help him?"

"Can we pull it out?" Raven asked Simo, who in the past had always seemed to know everything about everything now only showed sadness in his eyes, Raven realized all was not ok. Raven started asking, no pleading in his mind for the fairy queen to make herself known and tell them what needed to be done to save the young boy. The father was sitting on the ground with his son right next to him re-assuring him that everything was going to be alright and that he wasn't mad at him for anything, even though he knew his son was dying. He kept him on his stomach for fear of moving the arrow tip even one inch.

Without warning Rayne spoke up, "I can help him."

She hadn't said a word since dispatching that soldier on the walkway because she had been frantically pacing around but her brother thought it was from not wanting to watch what was happening to the young man. She pushed everyone out of her way and sat on the ground next to the them both, "I can help him Mr. Findle."

"How can you possibly help him,?" Raven exclaimed. "You are not a sorcerer or wizard what can you possible do?"

She looked at him square in his eyes, "Give me your sword Raven." She calmly told him with that take control attitude similar to what he had seen when he had been beaten up and she came to his rescue. She flipped his sword over to examine the brilliant blue stone that was fastened securely to the hilt with the Atlantean combination of gold and luxore. She started speaking, he figured for his behalf but it wasn't directed at him it was to them all.

"When the book was open I quickly read something about your sword, there was a picture of it inside the book and I couldn't help but notice the writing next to it.

"Hold onto him," she instructed the father.

She placed her left hand flat onto the boys back and with her right she held onto the blue pearl. Her brother was watching every move she made with all the hope in the world that she could actually help their young friend. She started to speak and when she did her brother recognized the strange language immediately as that of Atlantean. She had only spoken a few sentences when the hand that was holding onto the blue stone started to glow a brilliant bright blue color which was quickly followed by the same on her other hand. Slowly, and by itself, the arrow started to back its way out of the boy's body and fell to the ground next to him. She moved her hand over to cover his wound and kept speaking in this Atlantean language. She lifted her hand from his back only to find the wound had closed up and was healed. Findle finally started to speak, "What's going on here, why am I on the ground?"

The boy, who had been laying on his stomach near death a minute ago rolled over and with the help of his dad sat up for the first time. She handed her brother his sword back and Mr. Findle thanked her repeatedly, gave her a big hug that lifted her off the ground.

"How did you do that,?" He said.

"I'm not sure exactly how I did it sir, I just knew that I could somehow."

They all examined the young boy's back and were all amazed that there was absolutely no evidence of the arrow or any injury.

"You have to show me how you did that Rayne, and since when did you learn to speak Atlantean?"

"I didn't know that I spoke in that language?"

"We'll talk later."

The king with his cook decided to head back to the palace to see what kind of a mess there was, but in the meantime the siblings with Mr. Findle finally made it back to their home. Several days had passed since the taking back of the city and not that everything was back to normal yet, but it was getting there. Last night there had been a city-wide celebration topped off by a stunning speech by King Thais in the front of his palace. He thanked everyone for their help because this job required teamwork, and he promised them that he would instill better security measures for the safety of the entire city. Raven and Rayne said their pleasant goodbyes to all and promised to return very soon because fifty years was certainly not going to be an acceptable time to come back and see how everyone was doing. They walked through the doors that made up the southern gate and looked out into the expanse of the open desert again.

"Do you remember the last time we looked at this gate? Raven asked. We spent many days riding horses through the mountains, I even let you ride atop me as I walked through this desert as a camel. Well, not today! We made a promise to return some items and I'm certainly not walking anymore." With that, he winked at her and changed back into an eagle then spread his huge wings and lifted up off the ground. She couldn't help but smirk at seeing him look over at her again and give her that stupid wink of his. She looked back through the gates of the city with a tiny feeling of sorrow at leaving, but she also had a smile on her face because the people were free again. She could see people walking around and children playing in the streets. She spun her body around to follow her brother but caught a glimpse of a shiny object way off to her right. It was well past the river and high up in the trees so she didn't give it a second thought especially once she heard her brother call out to her with his eagles cry.

"Yes, I know I'm coming!" She mumbled.

She closed her eyes and changed herself into her eagle form and lifted off of the ground. She couldn't wait to drift on the high wind currents for the return trip to Atlantis. High up in the hundred foot oak tree the snow elf asked his friend, "Do you think they'll help us?"

"I don't know, only time will tell."

Until the next adventure…